The Finest Challenge

The Finest Challenge

JEAN RABE

A Tom Doherty Associates Book   TOR®   New York

THE FINEST CHALLENGE

Copyright © 2006 by Jean Rabe

A Tor Book
Published by Tom Doherty Associates, LLC
175 Fifth Avenue
New York, NY 10010

www.tor.com

Tor® is a registered trademark of Tom Doherty Associates, LLC.

Library of Congress Cataloging-in-Publication Data

Rabe, Jean.
    The finest challenge / Jean Rabe.—1st ed.
        p.   cm.
"A Tom Doherty Associates book."
ISBN-13: 978-0-765-30822-1
ISBN-10: 0-765-30822-3 (acid-free paper)
    1. Horses—Fiction.   2. Telepathy—Fiction.   3. Human-animal
relationships—Fiction.   I. Title.
PS3568.A232F55   2006
813'.54—dc22

                                                        2006005928

First Edition: September 2006

Printed in the United States of America

0   9   8   7   6   5   4   3   2   1

Acknowledgments

As always, thanks to my editor, Brian Thomsen, who inevitably manages to make whatever tale I'm working on a much better one.

And to my husband, Bruce, who somehow found time to proof this manuscript during the height of football season . . . and missed submitting his fantasy football picks one Sunday morning because he was busy reading these pages.

The Finest Challenge

Prologue

In the company of cobs, trotters, and warmbloods I discovered that joy is gained not from wanting something, but from treasuring something already possessed. If only all of my Finest sisters and brothers— and all of the Fallen Favorites—could learn such wisdom at a wise horse's hooves.

~*The Old Mare*

The sparrow had a black spot in the middle of its breast and a red-brown crown, with not a single dark feather on its head. No bigger than a man's palm, it had a loud, clear voice, chirping merrily on a beam above the prized norikers as it built a nest. Its sweet song ended in a low warble when it paused to gather straw and strands of horsehair. It wove quietly for a few minutes, then it began to sing again.

Gallant-Stallion would have enjoyed the sparrow's presence were he not in so much pain. He was severely lame, two days past striking a hoof on a sharp rock while fleeing a pack of wolves with his charge, Kalantha. Reaching the royal stables and walking into this stall were quite possibly the most onerous feats he'd attempted since coming to Paard-Peran.

He tried to think about Kalantha, safe with her brother somewhere on the palace grounds. That notion pleased him, but not enough to keep his mind away from the ache that pulsed up his leg and settled in his chest. His hoof had become so sore he could no longer put any weight on it. The groom's ministrations weren't helping—yet—though he appreciated the care and the time the man spent.

Gallant-Stallion watched the sparrow while the groom gently applied a poultice. The smell of the herbs was overly pungent and wholly unidentifiable. It chased away the comforting musty scents of the stable and made his nostrils flare in protest.

"This will draw the soreness out. I took some dried devil's claw from the cabinet. Not enough so the stable master'd miss it—he'd be furious if he discovered I'd used it on a big punch like you. Ground some white willow bark and mixed in ginseng and some other things. Put some ginseng in your feed, though not so much it'll turn your stomach. Should make you feel better."

Gallant-Stallion listened to the explanation, suspecting that the man was simply talking to himself and did not believe that any of the horses in this stable were capable of understanding. The groom was certainly oblivious that the punch only had the form of a horse, and was another creature entirely.

"And this will take down some of the fever."

The groom dipped a cloth in salted water and wrapped it around Gallant-Stallion's leg, just above the poultice that covered the hoof. "The gods know why I'm going to all of this trouble. You'll probably go lame again. Happens once, a horse is prone to it, I say. Sell you for meat then the next time. Break that girl's heart, I 'spect. But maybe it won't happen for a while."

Finished, the groom washed his hands in the salted water, then stroked Gallant-Stallion's muzzle. "A pretty horse you definitely are not," he pronounced. "But at least you've pretty eyes." He stretched a rope across the end of the stall, then stepped back and studied his handiwork. "I'll come back before the noon meal to see how you're faring."

The groom trundled toward the front of the stable, chattering to the King of Galmier's prized norikers as he went. The sparrow continued singing, and Gallant-Stallion was disappointed that other noises now intruded on the tune. The Finest heard the creak of hinges as the groom closed the wide door behind him and set a latch. There was the muted scratching of mice in the farthest corner, the wind suddenly picking up and whistling outside. He heard the clacking of small branches from the trees just beyond the wall behind him. A shrill whinny of a horse on the palace grounds was followed by the staccato orders a soldier shouted. Softest of all came the baying of a hound, probably down by the stream. The persistent nickerings of a pair of jutlands in the stalls directly across from Gallant-Stallion was the most annoying. They were heavy-bodied draft horses the color of honey, used for pulling large wagons. They'd been quiet with the groom present. But now one of them pawed at something it had found interesting in the hay, the scraping finally drawing the sparrow's curiosity and ending its song.

The jutlands and Gallant-Stallion were relegated to the rear of the royal stables and couldn't easily be seen by someone looking in the door. The Finest knew that was on purpose, as the norikers that took up the rest of the stalls were among the most magnificent horses in this part of Paard-Peran. No doubt the grooms and King Meven wanted them to be seen.

Gallant-Stallion wanted a stall near the door—not so he would be put on display, but so he could better hear what went on outside and could better listen for Kalantha. He also wanted the terrible pain in his hoof to ease and the smell from the poultice to go away. He wanted the sparrow to start singing again, even louder this time, and the jutlands to stop nickering, the big one to stop pawing. He wanted . . .

My friend.

Steadfast! Gallant-Stallion had been so engrossed in his misery he hadn't immediately registered the air turning chill or the feathering of his breath. The arrival of his mentor's spirit startled him.

It is good your charge is safe. The misty outline of an impressive steed hovered in the space between Gallant-Stallion and the jutlands. The image was so faint, the Finest wondered if he was imagining it.

Steadfast, so much has happened! The wolves . . .

There will be time to speak of that later.

And Bishop DeNogaret.

The ghost-image pricked up its ears.

Bishop DeNogaret meant to kill Kalantha! Just yesterday at the entrance to this very stable! But I stopped him. I hurt him, maybe killed him.

And saved your charge. Admirable, Gallant-Stallion.

The norikers and jutlands could not hear the mental conversation Gallant-Stallion shared with Steadfast's spirit.

The Finest were using what they called hidden speak.

The sparrow was unmindful, too. It gave up on watching the pawing jutland and wove a long strand from a noriker's mane into the side of its nest. Pleased with its handiwork, it chirped piercingly.

Kalantha is safe, yes, Steadfast. She is with her brother, the King of Galmier.

The one called Meven Montoll.

A nod.

That is good. But it is not good that you are hurt.

Gallant-Stallion snorted. *Lame, the groom called it. I would not call this pain such a simple, pleasant-sounding word. That the horses of this world suffer such a condition! And worse that I complain about it. Some are killed because of it, Steadfast. I heard the grooms talk of such. Butchered for meat.*

Steadfast wuffled sympathetically. *You should return to the Finest Court, Gallant-Stallion. In the lands of the Court you will heal quickly. Whole, you can better serve your Fallen Favorite.*

Gallant-Stallion brightened, but he remained cautious. *I hurt, yes, terribly, but I do not want to leave Kalantha just yet. There is so much to do and . . .*

You suffer needlessly, Gallant-Stallion.

Perhaps you are right. I am overdue reporting to the Finest Court. I should tell them about the Bishop, that Kalantha is safe. I should take time to heal and seek the advice of Patience and . . .

The air grew slightly warmer, and Gallant-Stallion knew that Steadfast's spirit was gone.

1 · War Torn

A proper king's feet should be deeply rooted in his country. His heart should beat with concern for his people. His head should be filled with plans for a better future. And his eyes should always observe the rest of the world.

~Sorrel Wintermane, shepherd to Bernd Sameter,
first king of Nasim-Guri

The large tent had been intended for summer festivals, when long tables spread with desserts and fruits would be arrayed inside for the dining pleasure of noble guests. But the dirt and bloodstains marked the tent's new and grim purpose this early spring.

A guard bowed and held the flap open. "Sire."

"Are you sure you want to see this, Kal?" Meven squared his shoulders and looked down into his sister's wide green eyes. "It's cold out here. It smells pretty awful in there and . . ."

"You know I've seen wounded men before, Meven." A pause: "And plenty of dead ones." She pulled her cloak tight around her. "Besides, I'd rather be with you than in that old palace of yours. I don't like the looks some of your servants give me. Your palace is . . ."

"Our palace."

"Is too big. I could get lost in it." She brushed past him, then threw her hand over her mouth and gagged. Kalantha instantly felt weak.

The cloying odor of diseased and rotting flesh was the strongest, and under that the coppery scent of blood. Cots stretched end to end in rows from the front to the back of the tent, and not a single one sat empty. The most grievously injured rested the farthest away, which was where Kalantha headed. The people tending the wounded huddled back there, clustered near a single cot and talking so their words sounded like the buzz of an insect swarm.

She passed men with bandaged arms, some splinted with what looked like chair legs. A few had woolen strips wrapped around their heads. One man's eyes were thickly bandaged; his cheeks were pink with a fever, and his hands alternately clenched and released the blanket. She stopped and stared, wondering if she should say something to comfort him.

"Why don't you go back to the palace? I'll see you there in a bit." Meven moved up next to her.

She drew her chin against her neck. "No."

"Kal . . ."

"I want to see this."

Meven put a hand on her shoulder, the gesture somehow giving her strength. She straightened and stepped back from the feverish man, nearly backing into the cot behind her.

"I want to see what the war has done."

"What I have done, you mean." Meven sucked in a breath. "This is all my fault. By the gods, all of this is because of me."

She spun and looked up. Though only two years older, he was more than a head taller. "It's not your fault, Meven. It's not your war. Bishop DeNogaret . . ."

"Wanted the war with Nasim-Guri, sure. But I was weak enough to let him talk me into it. I think a part of me wanted Nasim-Guri, and maybe a part of me still does. More land.

More subjects and more power. But I don't want this." He gestured at the cots. "I honestly never wanted any of this."

He dug the ball of his foot into the ground and opened his mouth to say something else. Kalantha took a last look at the feverish man with the bandaged eyes, then went to the back of the tent.

"They're all so young, Meven. Why did you want to come out here this morning to look at them?"

He followed her without answering, then lengthened his stride and passed her by. He nodded to a young knight he'd sparred with once, but the man was unconscious.

"Theron, are these the men brought in late last night?" Meven directed this to the tallest officer in the huddle.

The man separated from the group and stopped at attention in front of Meven. "Aye, Sire. These men fought just across the border, against fifty Nasim-Guri soldiers. They drove the enemy back beyond the river, and killed more than a few of them. About a dozen of our men were wounded in the process. The worst we brought here, the rest were patched up and sent back out to fight. The villages farther south already were full with wounded, no room for these men. Not sure if any of them will make it, after us carrying them so far. Should have stayed with them in the field until the end, then buried them."

Steeling himself, Meven took a deep breath and edged forward.

The men who were gathered around the cot parted.

Theron whispered: "His name is Weldon Smithson, Sire. His father is a prominent wheelwright in Nadir and head of the guild. That's the reason we brought him, his father being in the city. Else we would have left him somewhere along the road and buried him in a field. We're all surprised he's still with us."

Meven knelt next to the cot and took Weldon's hand. The young man offered the King a weak smile.

"Has his father been summoned?"

"Not yet, Sire. We . . ."

Meven's eyes narrowed as he looked up at Theron and the others. "He should have been summoned last night when you arrived. Doesn't matter how late the time."

"We were tending to everyone, sorting things out, Sire, and . . ."

"Summon the elder Smithson now. Right now. His wife . . ."

"She died some years ago, Weldon told us."

"Brothers? Sisters?"

"One brother, Sire, and he's fighting north of Duriam."

"Summon the elder Smithson now," Meven repeated. "Now. Have it done, Theron. Do it yourself."

The tall man gave a nod and whirled on his booted feet, nearly bumping into Kalantha, who'd crept nearer.

Meven returned his attention to Weldon. "Your father will be here soon."

Weldon shook his head, and a line of blood spilled out of his mouth. "Don't want him to see me like this, Sire. I . . ."

"He'll see you now, and later when you're well. I'll have you and him brought to the palace for dinner. Next week, in fact."

Weldon's eyes were fixed, and his hand went limp in the King's grip. His breathing grew shallow.

"Weldon?"

The young man coughed, pinkish bubbles trailing down his chin. Meven raised Weldon's head.

"It will be a fine dinner," Meven continued. "Roast goose, I think. Brushed with butter and stuffed with rice and some of those tiny onions from the fall harvest that the cooks saved in the pantry. They say onions are the food of poor people, but I like them well enough. We'll have soup, of course. The cooks make soup every night. I get tired of it. Dessert. They always make dessert, too. I never tire of that. Have you a favorite cake?"

Sweat beads covered Weldon's face, and his skin had gone

paler in the few moments Meven held him. The young man was practically as white as parchment.

"Spice cake is my favorite, I think. My sister, Kalantha, she's right here behind me . . . she likes any kind of cake. The cooks put the frosting on thick for special occasions. And if we've raisins imported from the south, they use some of those, too. Do you think you'd like spice cake, Weldon?"

"He's dead, Sire."

One of the soldiers pulled the blanket up and waited for Meven to move.

"A dagger to the stomach, they said. Truly surprised he lived as long as he did, considering it took days to get here. We were certain he wouldn't make it through the night. I think he held on just because we told him you were coming by to visit everyone this morning. Said he'd never seen the King up close."

Meven pulled his arm free and released the dead man's hand. He stood shakily, his eyes locked on the corpse's fixed gaze.

The soldier tugged the blanket over Weldon's head. Behind Meven, a soldier covered another corpse.

"You'll clean him up before his father comes?" This came from Kalantha. "And take him outside this tent? No need for the elder Smithson to come into this horrid, smelly place."

The soldier looked to the King.

"Yes, clean him up," Meven said. "Put him in something not so bloody. He's about my size, so you can ask the steward for one of my tunics. Lay him in the palace entry hall if you'd like. Kal's right. His father . . . none of these men's families should see them in this place."

Meven stared at the blanket-draped form until Kalantha tugged on his arm. "We should go, Meven, and let these men tend the wounded. They're not working with you here."

Meven numbly concurred and let her lead him from the tent.

Kalantha breathed deep once the soldier closed the flap behind them. "Smells better out here. Will smell even better the farther we get from the tent. I think . . ." She spotted two more tents, smaller than this one and closer to the wall. She realized more wounded were in them. Between the tents was a tarp covering a mound of something.

"Bodies," Meven said, following her gaze. "They put the dead outside and cover them up until the families arrange for burial. And if there are no families, or if they can't tell who the dead are, they bury them in a mass grave near the cliff."

Kalantha continued to stare. "How many?" she asked finally. When he didn't immediately answer, she asked again. "How many soldiers have died?"

"Knights and soldiers," Meven said. "And some villagers who joined up along the way." His voice was flat. He glanced down at his hands and saw they were covered with Weldon's blood. The front of his richly embroidered tunic was blood soaked, too. "I don't know how many. A lot, I'd guess. Not near so many as Nasim-Guri has lost, the soldiers tell me. Too many, though. There are more dead and wounded in the villages between here and the Nasim-Guri border. Too many."

They didn't move and didn't speak for several minutes. The wind fluttered the edge of the tarp, revealing the bare feet of several corpses. A dog barked in the distance. Closer, a knight drilled a gathering of soldiers preparing to march to Nasim-Guri. They looked young and clumsy.

"How could I have wanted all of this blood, Kal?" He still looked at his hands. "How could I have wanted all this death?"

"Bishop DeNogaret . . ."

"He encouraged me to make war, Kal. But he didn't force me. He couldn't have forced me to do something I didn't truly want to do."

She vehemently shook her head and opened her mouth to argue. But she stopped herself.

"I wanted a bigger country, Kal. Maybe I still do, a part of me wants it. But I don't need a bigger country. Galmier is more than enough for me to rule." He let out a clipped laugh. "Too big for me to rule. Prince Edan should be alive and King. The crown falling to me is an accident." He finally raised his head and looked toward the palace. "I needed the Bishop's help to manage all of this . . . the estate, the city, the country, and the war. We're very close to winning, my advisors tell me. Nasim-Guri could be ours in a week or two, the capital falling. The Bishop—"

"Now you have me."

Meven smiled, honest emotion behind it. "I *will* need your help, Kal."

"Bishop DeNogaret, is he going to live?"

Meven pointed to a tower with an elaborately crenelated top. "He's high in the north wing, and I've a few servants tending him." He shrugged. "They think he'll live. But they think he'll be crippled. Rue crushed his legs and broke his ribs."

"A horrid man."

"Bishop DeNogaret raised you and me, Kal. I just can't imagine why he'd try to kill you. Maybe he went mad. Happens to people, you know."

"Have you seen him?"

Meven shook his head.

Kalantha closed her eyes and remembered their arrival yesterday. Rue was moving slowly because of his lame leg. She took him to the stables and was looking for a groom to see to him when Bishop DeNogaret appeared. He had a knife, and he tried to kill her with it, all the while raving that he should have done the deed himself in the first place rather than relying on his bird lackeys. She would have died, but Rue attacked the Bishop and slammed his hooves into the man's chest. Rue would have finished it, but she and Meven pulled the punch back. The Bishop was carried to the palace. She wondered if she should have let Rue kill him.

"I'm certain Bishop DeNogaret had something to do with the assassin-birds, the ones that tried to kill us . . . and tried to kill me on the way here. That book I brought from the Vershan Monastery, it has a picture in it of someone who looks just like Bishop DeNogaret. There are birds mentioned in the book, smart evil ones. You promised you'd look at the book, Meven. I think Bishop DeNogaret is far more powerful than we realized. He caused the war, I know it."

Meven watched the knight drill the young soldiers. "Not right now, Kal."

"I think the book could be important. You promised."

"What's important is you going back to the palace."

"No. I'm going to stay with you and—"

"Go back to the palace and pack a few changes of clothes. We're leaving today for Duriam in Nasim-Guri."

Her eyes widened in surprise.

Meven faced the tarp-covered mound of bodies. "We're going to see King Hunter Silverwood in Duriam. I'm going to put an end to this war, Kal. No more killing. No more mounds of bodies waiting to be put in the ground. I have to summon my commanders, tell them the war ends this minute. Then I'm going to make amends to King Silverwood. Somehow patch all of this up. I could win in a week or two, have a lot more land and subjects, but—"

"You're right to stop it now." Kalantha's smile reached her eyes. "I'll start packing right away, Meven. But the book. I really think you need to look at it, at least the part with—"

"We'll leave this afternoon, Kal, after the noon meal and before sunset, after I've met with the commanders. I'll send them out along the fields to help spread the news. Then there will be no more blood spilled because of me. Never again because of me."

"The book, Meven. You have to—"

"I'll read it later, I promise. A book is not nearly so important as putting an end to this war." He made a huffing sound, his breath fluttering the hair that hung down over his forehead. "I promise I'll look at the book when we get back from Nasim-Guri. After the war is done."

Kalantha decided it was an argument she couldn't win and headed toward the palace. Neither she nor Meven saw a thin crow hovering above the largest tent-infirmary. It flew toward the palace, reaching it long before Kalantha. Perching on the north crenelated tower, it cawed to a dozen blackbirds, which were quick to join it.

"Ninéon," the crow said. "I must find Ninéon and tell her of King Meven's intentions."

"Tentions?" a big cowbird asked.

"Intentions, plans," one of the blackbirds corrected. "What plans, Arlee?" Not all of the blackbirds were capable of speech, but this one was and the crow knew her to be overly curious. "What plans does the man-king have? Are they interesting plans?"

Two blackbirds with small red patches on their wings moved close to the crow, their dark eyes wide and shining. One bobbed its head and made a sound that approximated "what?"

"What, what?" repeated the blackbirds who could speak. "Arlee, what?"

The largest edged near the crow and met its gaze. "Interesting plans, Arlee, else you would not want to find Ninéon. Share what you know!"

The thin crow drew itself up to its full height and fluffed its feathers before it divulged its precious news. "It is about King Meven."

"The man-king," one of the blackbirds cut in. "The one who glitters like a peacock."

Arlee narrowed his eyes to needle-fine slits. "King Meven says he will end the precious war."

The blackbirds squawked, and the nearest shook its head. "Bad plan. Most unfortunate."

The crow clacked its beak. "Ninéon will be angry."

"Yes! Bad angry, Arlee," the nearest blackbird agreed. "Bad, bad angry."

"But Ninéon will not let it happen," Arlee continued. "Ninéon will come here, and she will find the Bishop."

"Bishop DeNogaret," one of the blackbirds supplied, pleased with himself that he'd recalled the old priest's name.

"Yes, DeNogaret. Ninéon will talk to the Bishop. The Bishop will dominate King Meven again, manipulate him like the soft mud of the riverbank. Then the man-king will make the war go on. On and on and on."

"On and on!" The smallest blackbird spread its wings. "We will find Ninéon for you, Arlee, and she will make certain the blood continues to flow."

2 · The Court Convenes

In keeping my charge safe, I have won nothing . . . but I have stayed true to my purpose. I was not born to succeed at my task, but I was born to strive for success.

~Patience, Finest Court Matriarch

Although the ache had lessened a little and the poultice was doing its work, Gallant-Stallion's lame leg still tortured him.

Never lame us, the jutland across the stable told him. *Sorry. Sorry.*

No. Never lame, a nearby noriker added. *Sorry, very sorry for you, big ugly, ugly horse.*

Gallant-Stallion appreciated their empathy, which they'd been occasionally voicing throughout the morning. However, he did not appreciate the noriker's "ugly" insult, intended or unintended. He could understand their nickerings, just as he could understand the languages of all the creatures of Paard-Peran. But sometimes he wished he did not hear the few who taunted him.

The pain is not so bad, he told them. *I have endured worse.*

The jutlands wuffled that they did not believe him. *Looks bad,* the smaller jutland returned. *Smells worse.*

Gallant-Stallion agreed that the poultice stank. Though the groom had first applied it several hours ago, the smell had not dissipated. Indeed, when the groom had returned and added more paste to the poultice and applied a fresh wrap of the salted water minutes ago, the odor had intensified. It lodged in the Finest's nostrils and throat, blocking out all other scents of the stables and making him feel light-headed and ill.

Bad. Smells bad, the smaller jutland repeated. *Smells worse than dead things. Take the bad smell away, big ugly, ugly horse.*

Gallant-Stallion decided to do just that, but not to appease the horses in the royal stables. He'd hoped to see Kalantha today before traveling to the Finest Court. But she hadn't stopped by yet, likely engrossed with her brother. If he hurried, he could leave for the Court now and be back to these stables tonight.

She might come by then, he hoped.

If not, he would certainly see her the following morning.

He closed his eyes and searched for something to distract him from the awful smell. The sparrow had flitted somewhere, and so its pleasant song could not help. The mice had quieted, too. There remained the clacking of the branches in the wind outside, and the voices of the norikers and jutlands—which continued to complain about the poultice smell while at the same time offering their sympathies. He focused on the clacking until he shut out everything else. He imagined that his heart beat in time with the branches, then he imagined leaving the stables, Nadir, and Paard-Peran.

The air had been dead in the stall, but now it swirled slowly around him, pleasantly cool and fresh smelling.

It teased his mane and tickled his back.

In place of the hard-packed stable floor a soft pasture stretched as far as he could see. Flowering pear trees and clumps of wildflowers dotted it, the scents of which teased some of the stench out of Gallant-Stallion's throat. The Finest had left the poultice behind when he made the mystical journey to the Court lands. Still, he hadn't quite managed to leave all of the smell behind.

Although it was nearly noon in Galmier's capital, it was shortly after dawn here in the land of the Finest. Down a gentle slope in the distance, Gallant-Stallion saw that the mist hadn't yet burned away. It coated the grass and wrapped around the trunk of a large flowering pear. He headed toward the old tree, as he knew there was a deep stream beyond it that had water sweeter than any he'd tasted on Paard-Peran.

He moved agonizingly slow, hobbling so that his right front hoof barely touched the ground. The mist was gone by the time he reached the tree, and he paused under its branches to rest. These lands had been shaped by the good powers, just as the Finest had been shaped and infused with the purpose of guiding chosen Fallen Favorites on the road to salvation. There was magic in this place, and it winnowed its way beneath his hide to heal him. He closed his eyes and let the breeze caress him, and without intending to, he fell quickly asleep.

Gallant-Stallion woke a few hours later, all trace of the lameness gone. He gingerly tested the leg to be certain it had healed, then he galloped toward the stream and waded into the center of it, where the water came up to his belly. He drank deep, chasing the last whiff of the poultice away, and he stood there for long minutes, muzzle raised high and breathing deep of the flower-scented air. Then he drank some more and scolded himself.

"I have been selfish, Steadfast." Gallant-Stallion knew the spirit of his mentor was not here, but he spoke as if talking to him anyway. "I have tarried and enjoyed this place. I have let it heal me while I should have sought the Court. It does not matter that Kalantha is safe and with her brother. What matters is that I be about my business here and return to her as soon as possible."

He tossed his head back, his mane whipping in the air. Then he struck out along the stream toward the lowlands, where he knew other Finest would be found. He hadn't traveled far before he came to a landais and a konik, both grazing on wild white clover. The landais was impressive, an old breed, shiny black with a small head and a stately profile. Muscular, it had sloping shoulders and pronounced withers. The konik was the size of a pony, looking tough and hardy, with dark brown dorsal and wither stripes cutting through its chestnut coat. Its small ears twitched at Gallant-Stallion's approach.

"Nightcrest." Gallant-Stallion acknowledged the landais, having met that Finest on a few previous visits. Then he looked to the konik.

"I am Fastrotter Summerfield."

"And you are called Gallant-Stallion, correct?" the landais said. "I remember you, Steadfast's apprentice. You have been gone from these lands for a long while."

"Too long," Gallant-Stallion mused. "Paard-Peran has beautiful parts, and features the Finest Court lands do not have. But . . ."

"The land of the Fallen Favorites has nothing so fine as this," the landais interrupted. "I know, I was a shepherd once many years ago."

"I promise that another time we will share stories," he said. "Where do the members of the Court gather this day?"

Fastrotter let out a low, long whinny and shook his head. "They are convened in the Shimmering Paddocks, Gallant-Stallion, a favorite gathering place. It is said they are listening to tales of the war. Good that war does not touch us here."

Images raced through Gallant-Stallion's mind. In Kalantha's company he'd seen dead and injured men along the road to Nadir, and he'd been wounded by flocks of assassin-birds he suspected were somehow tied to the war. There was so much blood in places the ground couldn't absorb it all. And he knew the scenes of carnage would always haunt him.

"Do you know of the war on Paard-Peran?" The konik edged closer until he was muzzle to muzzle with Gallant-Stallion.

"Yes."

"Have you seen it . . . the war?"

Gallant-Stallion nodded.

"And that is why you seek the Court today? To bring news of the war?" The konik's voice was thick with excitement.

"In part, Fastrotter Summerfield. I am here to report on my charge. And I came here to heal."

Both Finest looked at him quizzically, the konik walking around him to look for injuries and announcing that he found none.

"I was lame," Gallant-Stallion provided.

"Lame! Like a common horse becomes lame?" Nightcrest did not hide his surprise. "A Finest, lame? I did not believe that possible."

"I was lame," Gallant-Stallion repeated. "These lands have healed me, and now I seek the Court. Good day to you, brothers. Sweet fields and cool waters."

Ignoring more of Fastrotter Summerfield's questions, he galloped toward a rise, then raced across a stretch of flat ground that led to the Shimmering Paddocks. The simple act of running felt good. He heard hoofbeats behind him, and glanced over his shoulder to see Nightcrest following, the landais either not quite able to keep up or holding a respectful, polite distance.

Minutes later, Gallant-Stallion waded across a river and climbed a low hill. The Shimmering Paddocks came into view on the other side. Locust trees and clumps of birch trees pierced the flat land, and pink-flowered bunchberries bordered it and lent an ambrosial scent to the air. In the sunlight the tall grass and wildflowers glistened and stretched as tall as the hocks of the ponies in the assemblage. More than one hundred Finest were gathered before the Court. Gallant-Stallion had not seen so many in one place before.

It was a sea of color: white, gray, brown, roan, chestnut, bay, skeybald, dun, piebald, cream, and black. The Finest ranged from foals to a few that were several hundred years old. Gallant-Stallion noted tarpans, shaggy-coated bali ponies, thick-bodied bardigianos, heavy-headed bashkirs, diminutive bataks, attractive falabellas and long-maned fells. Pindos ponies were side by side with halflingers.

He was the only punch.

He trotted closer, past bretons, torics, akhal-tekes, barbs, and carthusians. Ten members of the Court formed a semi-circle at the front of the herd, a cluster of willow birch trees shading their backs. A handsome fresian stood before the Court. The color of thick fog, she had white stockings and a narrow black blaze that matched her mane and tail.

She talked about the war.

"The broken bodies of the young ones were the worst," she said. "Piled by the side of the road near the north border of the country called Nasim-Guri. The flies were so thick they made up a second coat of skin. And the smell. I cannot rid it from my memory."

She paused and closed her eyes. A halflinger several yards behind her snorted; that was the only sound in the Shimmering Paddocks. The silence was unnerving. Finally, she continued: "They are indeed Fallen, all of them, to wage war against each other and make a mockery of life. The ones with no promise of redemption are the most terrible. They seem to delight in the bloodshed and the killing. My charge, a Nasim-Guri soldier named Galvin, abhorred the fighting. But he believed in defending his country and his king, and so he gave his last measure. His heart and soul were pure!" She met the gaze of the Finest Court matriarch. "He died too young in a senseless fight over ground. No one should die because of ground."

The fresian bowed her head, signaling an end was coming to her report.

"I watched them take his sword and the few coins he had in his pockets. I watched them bury him in a common grave, with no marker for the names of the dead. Give me another assignment, another Fallen Favorite to lead along the path to salvation. But give me one far from Galmier and Nasim-Guri and the horrid, senseless war. Give me one I will lose to old age or some other malady . . . one I will lose after he or she has made some suitable contribution to Paard-Peran. One I will not see buried with a dozen other broken men."

When she raised her head, her eyes were filled with fire and tears. "Or give me another young, strong soldier, Patience, Gray. Give to me one who might slay the King of Galmier that started this horrid, sinful war."

Gallant-Stallion instantly thought of Meven, and of Kalantha, who vowed to help him stop the violence.

"My charge will end the war," Gallant-Stallion said. In that instant he realized he truly believed the girl could do just that. "There will be no more mass graves for soldiers."

3 · Secret Thoughts and Secret Passages

Things are hidden for complicated reasons, I've learned. The Fallen Favorites keep objects and plans secreted away in the shadows so only their fellows who avoid the light can find them. Nothing good comes of a secret.

~*Meara Swiftgate, in her first observations of Paard-Peran*

Kalantha spread four changes of clothes on her bed, one of them a cranberry-colored dress with pink ribbons at the waist and shoulders. She didn't know whom the clothes had originally belonged to, but she'd been presented with dozens of outfits yesterday. There hadn't been time for a seamstress to make new ones just for her, and what she'd tried on hung on her frame. Maybe they came from a local noble's house, his daughter having outgrown them. The previous King of Galmier had no daughters. Had Meven ordered these made in her absence? They looked like they'd never been worn.

She ran her fingers over the cranberry dress; it felt silky smooth and cool. She intended to wear it when they talked to the Nasim-Guri king and his attendants. She thought these clothes should be enough, though she didn't know how long they would be gone on their trip.

"How long does it take to stop a war?" she mused. "I don't even know how long it took to start it."

She could wear the tunics two or three times depending on how dirty they got, and wash them in a creek or a pond . . . or perhaps somewhere in the Duriam castle. She could take more clothes—she had several more dresses and tunics, leggings and an assortment of horrid hats to choose from. But she didn't want to put too much in the satchel.

She folded everything carefully, nesting the dress in the bottom as she wanted to protect it. The clothes practically filled the bag, but she managed to fit in a comb and brush, a small packet of scented powder, and she wedged a sheathed knife down the side. Ever since the assassin-birds, and then the bandits on the road, she'd felt the urge to carry something for protection. She didn't need to leave room for food, though she'd thought about it. She knew whatever soldiers and grooms Meven brought along would pack plenty. Still, she could fit in a few cookies—she intended to ask someone in the kitchen about that.

She slung the satchel over her shoulder, deciding it wasn't too heavy.

"Perfect," she pronounced, resting it on the floor against the bedpost.

Kalantha went back to her dresser and brought out doeskin leggings and a dark gray tunic. The leggings were plain and comfortable and would keep her warm. This early spring seemed to be unusually chilly. The tunic was made of a heavy cloth and had a slight pattern to it—elm leaves, she thought—with a few nubs in the fabric to hint it had been worn before. There was a little bit of embroidery along the hem. Not fancy, but certainly nice-looking, a step above commoner clothes. She knew she'd have to look acceptable in the company of King

Meven. She put them on and discovered the leggings were slightly baggy, like everything else she'd tried on, but would certainly do. The tunic's shoulders were only a little too big.

"Bet my brother'll fuss for an hour over what clothes to take and what to wear. And bet he won't be practical. He'll wear something that'll show the dust from the road." She smiled at the thought of seeing her brother in a fine outfit spotted with dirt. Her garments would get just as dirty as Meven's, but hers wouldn't show it as easily. "And he'll take far too many changes with him. He'll probably need two pack horses to carry everything. And another one just to carry the presents. He better give some serious presents to King Silverwood to apologize for the war." She sucked in her lower lip. "But I don't think there are enough presents in the world to make up for all the dead soldiers."

Finally, she retrieved a small walnut box from the top of her dresser, sat on the bed, and carefully opened it. The morning sunlight brushed the jewelry inside, setting it to sparkle. Meven had given her the box last night, saying these were some of her aunt's favorite pieces. Her aunt had been Galmier's queen. She died many years ago, and her husband kept the jewelry. Meven inherited the pieces along with everything else when he was crowned last year.

"These pieces of jewelry are now yours," he told her yesterday. Then he went on to say this certainly wasn't all of their aunt's jewelry. The other pieces he'd set aside for the next queen; he knew he'd be expected to marry in the next half dozen years. "But these are the best ones, I think. And they'll look good on you."

Kalantha selected a thin gold chain with a dozen small rubies spaced evenly. This one would be all right to wear to Nasim-Guri's capital of Duriam—pretty, but not gaudy. A polite show of wealth, she thought, and it would go very well with the cranberry dress. She put it on and closed the box, then opened it a moment later to look at the pieces again—necklaces, brooches, rings that were too big for her slender fingers.

It might be a couple of hours before they left for Nasim-Guri, since the commanders had to be gathered and Meven had to talk to them, so she had a little time to herself. She put on one of the brooches and draped two long strings of pearls around her neck. If she were younger, she would have called it playing dress-up. But at almost fourteen, she considered it simply trying them on. She managed to get a sapphire ring to rest securely on her thumb. An oval-shaped faceted stone circled by tiny pearls, it had one empty setting, and she wondered if a pearl could be found to fill it.

Kalantha put matching silver and onyx bracelets on her wrists, closed the lid, and put the box back up on the dresser. Then she stood in front of a narrow mirror to admire the jewelry. They looked out of place on her, given her tunic and leggings—and given the fact she'd never worn such before.

"If I was wearing a dress it would all look better." She wrinkled her nose; she didn't care much for dresses, but she considered the cranberry one an exception. "And if I had my hair all fancy with curls." She decided she would put all but the gold and ruby necklace in the box before they left for Duriam. But she'd wear the pieces for just a little while—why let them sit in an old box when they could be admired? "I'll show the cooks." She needed to go to the kitchen anyway, as the noon meal was near, and she needed to see about packing a few cookies for her trip. And maybe a cookie to snack on right now.

She hurried from her room and down a winding stone staircase.

The curving wall was festooned with banners decorated with various heraldic devices. The one she fancied, and the one that she paused by now, displayed a dark purple field with a single white mountain in the center of it. She made a note to ask Meven what it stood for. She guessed the purple stood for royalty, and the white, purity—that much symbolism she'd re-membered from her studies at the High Keep Temple and from something she'd read at the Vershan Monastery. There was a crest on the mountain rendered in light blue, and a piece of it formed a tear that dripped from the slope. Someone mourning a loved one perhaps? The device appeared much simpler than the others in the stairwell, but she considered it striking none-theless, and Kalantha wondered if she might ask for an outfit made of those colors for her birthday.

At the foot of the stairs she turned left, then spun to her right when she remembered a nearby statue faced the hall that led to the dining room and eventually to the kitchen and pantry. The soles of her shoes slapped against the marble floor, and she nearly lost her balance when she reached a section that had been recently polished. She slowed here and admired the paintings of various nobles, some of whom were likely ances-tors, though not a one had her red-brown hair or green eyes. Meven said there were no paintings of their parents, but she was hopeful he was wrong and that she would spot one any-way.

When she closed her eyes and concentrated, she could re-member her mother. Meven had told her on more than one occasion that she was too young when her mother died, and therefore couldn't remember well, that she pictured someone she'd simply made up. Kalantha was certain, however, that she could recall her mother's sweet face.

A few of the paintings in this hall bothered her. These were of elderly men with narrowed eyes and bushy brows. The angle of the poses made it seem like they were staring right at her, their expressions unkindly. Maybe she'd ask someone to hang those few paintings higher, or take them down altogether. The walls were tall here, oak painted a rich vermilion—fifteen feet high, she guessed, looking up to a ceiling that had been plastered and painted the shade of eggshells. Where the walls met the ceiling was a narrow strip of wood that had been carved with a scalloped pattern and painted a pale, dull green.

"Green leads to beans," she recalled. Meven told her the colors, like patterned tiles on the floor, would lead her to various places in the palace. Green led directly to the dining room. Brown, which started in a hallway to her left, would take her to the main library, where there were dozens of brown shelves and brown leather-bound books. She'd briefly been there yesterday, awed by all of the books and wanting to lose herself for days there. She intended to take a book with her on the trip, a small and not especially valuable one that no one would miss if something happened to it. One of the attendants told her there were three libraries; the smallest was devoted to religious manuscripts, and the other one held a collection of books and papers written by former kings, their relatives, astrologers, and neighboring noblemen. She had no plans to visit that latter place—all politics and stuffy subject matter. The religious library, maybe. The massive library, definitely, often, and probably for an extended visit on the very day she and Meven returned from Duriam. And the day after that and after that.

Kalantha loved books.

The libraries made her again think of the thick book in her room, the one she'd borrowed from the Vershan Monastery. She wondered if she should take the book with her now. Maybe Meven would have time to read it along the road and could make something of the reference to malicious birds.

"Doubt it. He'll be too busy. But I'll make him read it when we get back. He did promise." Not the whole book, just the section about the birds that had the picture of someone who looked uncannily like Bishop DeNogaret. She shivered when she passed the last picture before the hall opened onto the dining room. The picture was of the Bishop, and had been recently finished. The colors were more intense than in the older paintings, and the frame was heavy and thick, the wood etched with symbols of twisting vines and cryptic letters. Birds were nested at the corners. "Evil birds."

The dining room was empty, though she suspected the table would be set soon for the noon meal. She sniffed and picked up the scent of beef roasting with potatoes. Probably a stew, though no doubt a fancy one with vegetables that had been preserved in the pantry from the past fall's harvest. She circled the dining table, running the fingers of her right hand over the smooth surface and looking to see her face reflected in its polished top.

Kalantha didn't consider herself pretty, especially with the thick, ropy scar that traveled from her jaw down her throat. She'd been wounded by one of the assassin-birds, a big dark hawk, and the scar would forever remind her of that harrowing night and draw the stares of people who saw her. But she wasn't ugly, either, and she had only a dusting of freckles on her cheeks and across the bridge of her nose. A few years ago she had had a riot of freckles everywhere. She touched the large brooch and wondered what the queen wore with it when she used to dine here.

She heard pots clanging, and that drew her attention to the kitchen. She scurried from the dining room and down a short hall. One doorway led to the pantry. She hadn't looked in the other room before. That door hung halfway open now, and so she curiously peered inside. The heat of the steam struck her, and she wiped at her forehead. The room beyond was a laundry, filled with vats of water stoked by fires burning beneath them. Four women stirred the clothes in the vats with paddles. Another four were drying clothes on lines in front of a roaring fireplace. Two more women wrung out sheets.

"So hot," Kalantha whispered. She spotted one man in the room, the supervisor, Gervis Hull, who was standing as far from the fires and vats as possible and doing nothing onerous that she could see. "So very hot and so very unfair."

She retreated to the kitchen, where more women were working to prepare the noon meal. There was one man here too, and he seemed to be taking an inventory of the pantry. She would talk to Meven on the road to Duriam about the workers in the palace. It wasn't wrong that women had hot, difficult jobs. But it was wrong that men didn't share in those tasks.

"I'll talk to Meven," Kalantha vowed. "And things will be different after the war."

"What did you say, girl?" One of the cooks spotted Kalantha.

"I asked if you had any cookies. I'd like to pack some cookies for a trip Meven and me are taking. Just a few, please."

"You're his sister, right? Heard you came up from the Vershan Monastery." The cook beamed and wiped her hands on her apron.

"Yes, ma'am. My name's Kalantha."

"Sara Anne," the cook returned. Behind her two women were preparing a tray of soup and goat's milk. Kalantha knew it was for Bishop DeNogaret, and she thought about asking Sara Anne if she could deliver it. Because she wouldn't deliver it, she'd dump it somewhere and let him go hungry. It wasn't right that he was recuperating in a bed in the north tower, instead of being trussed up in a cell in whatever passed for the dungeon.

"Pleased to meet you, Lady Kalantha. I'm certain there are a few dozen cookies in the pantry. With raisins and sweetened oats. Is that all right?" Sara Anne reached into a cupboard and pulled down a linen napkin and a cord, went to the pantry and returned a few moments later with a tied bundle.

"Raisins are fine. Thank you!" Kalantha accepted the bundle and scurried from the kitchen. There wasn't quite enough room in her satchel for all of these cookies, unless she took one of the tunics out. But she'd eat one or two cookies now, maybe three if they were small. And any that didn't fit in the satchel would no doubt fit in the pockets of her cloak. "Thank you, Sara Anne!" she called again as she hurried down the hall and back into the dining room, where a young woman was setting the table.

"King Meven will not be joining you for the noon meal, Lady Kalantha," the woman announced. "His Majesty sent word that he's meeting with his commanders. He's expected to return to the palace early this afternoon."

Kalantha's shoulders sagged. That meant they wouldn't likely get started until late this afternoon, maybe not until sunset. Maybe if the meeting dragged out they wouldn't leave until the morning. "No." She shook her head. "He wants to stop the war, so we'll be leaving today no matter how late it is."

"Pardon?"

"How long until we eat?"

"Not long, Lady Kalantha." The woman finished with the plates and silverware and returned to the kitchen.

Kalantha took another course around the dining room. "Lady Kalantha. Lady Kalantha. I'm not sure I like the sound of that. Stuffy and . . . and . . ." She brightened and worked one of the cookies out of the bundle. "Lady Kalantha! It makes me sound older. My birthday is in a few weeks. I will be older. Maybe there'll be a party and . . . what's this?"

She stopped between a sconce and a painting of a wintry field. Something didn't look quite right about the wall. "What indeed?" She put her nose to the wall, sniffing, picking up the scent of smoke from previous guests and the fading odor of past meals that clung to the paint. It wasn't the smell that bothered her; it was a hairline crack. She ran her fingers along the wall, her nails catching in the crack. She pushed and heard a click, and a panel swung open.

"Oh my." Steep and narrow steps twisted down into the darkness. "Wonder what's at the bottom?" She'd have to get a lantern or a candle. There had to be one around here. She looked behind her at the set table. "Maybe after we eat I'll take a look. Before Meven finishes his meeting."

She closed the panel and poked her head in the kitchen again, confirmed that it was stew, and guessed that it would be several more minutes before things were ready. Time for a quick trip to the library. When she retraced her steps down the hall she walked slowly and ran her fingertips along the wall, looking for more cracks. She found one between two paintings of stodgy, square-shouldered men, the brass plates on the frames identifying them as uncles of the previous king. That would make them some distant relation to her. But they were just paint and ugly stares. She pressed on the panel and it budged only a little, the wood warped. She pressed it closed all the way.

"Definitely after we eat. How many secret doors are in the palace?"

Her course took her to the library. She reminded herself about borrowing a book to take on the trip to Duriam. Something small that she could manage to squeeze in her satchel or in a cloak pocket.

Between two shelves and behind a heavy thronelike chair she found another crack. She knew a casual observer wouldn't have noticed it. But she'd been looking for the hairline seams.

"Maybe before we eat. For just a few minutes." There was a candle on a shelf, set on a brass dish and surrounded by a glass cylinder to help it shed more light. She lit it and returned to the opening, holding the bundle of cookies under one arm. "Just to find out what's at the bottom." She opened the panel and crept down several steps, then returned to the top, pulling the panel closed behind her. Just in case no one was supposed to be here, she didn't want to be found. Could they punish her? She was some sort of royalty, right? She could go where she wanted. Still, she kept the hidden door closed—no use inviting trouble.

Kalantha took a deep breath and started down again. "Just for a few minutes," she repeated. "I won't be gone long."

4 · Blaming the Birds

I believe the war waged by King Meven Montoll cannot be won by either side. I believe it is no more possible to win a war than it is possible to win against a raging flood. There are only losers and plenty of bloated bodies for the crows to feast upon.

~Stoutspirit, of the Finest Court, speaking at the
Shimmering Paddocks gathering

Gallant-Stallion stood before the Finest Court. Not all the members were present. He couldn't remember a time when he'd seen all of them together. But there were ten this bright morning—more than he'd reported to in quite some time. The matriarch and patriarch, Patience and Gray Hawthorn, were in the center. Though all the Court members were larger and more impressive looking than their Finest brothers and sisters, these two were singular. Their coats shone and their muscles tensed, ears pricked forward to catch every word. Gallant-Stallion had never seen more beautiful creatures.

Also in attendance were the mares Firemane Stormwithers, Dreamchaser, Tadewi Sadgaze, and Meara Swiftgait; the latter two were the oldest of the Court members, practically ancient, tracing their roots back to the First Herd. The stallions included Blackeyes Longmane, Pureheart, Stoutspirit, and Rainfall Ironhooves.

Gallant-Stallion bowed his head until his muzzle brushed the grass, keeping eye contact with Patience. He let a moment of silence pass, then raised his head and began: "My charge, as you know, is Kalantha Montoll of Galmier in Paard-Peran. She is sister to Meven Montoll, the King of Galmier."

"The one who birthed the war." Stoutspirit edged forward, snorting and tamping the ground with his right front hoof. He was the color of polished walnut, save for the white stocking on that foot and a narrow blaze that ran from between his nostrils to just below his eyes. "I have little tolerance for the ones who start bloodshed. I consider them Fallen, certainly, but not Favorites. Greedy, power-hungry fools, the lot of their kind. And though we try to help, I doubt any of the good powers believe such creatures can be redeemed." Stoutspirit flicked his tail. "But the improvident King of Galmier is not your concern. Thank the good powers that his sister shows promise."

A few yards behind Gallant-Stallion a pair of tarpans nickered in whispers. Near them a bashkir snorted its agreement with Stoutspirit about Meven being a fool and one of the lowest Fallen Favorites.

Gallant-Stallion believed that Meven could find salvation—with Kalantha's help—that the young man simply had been swayed down a vile path by Bishop DeNogaret. But the Finest decided not to argue the point. Meven was not his charge, as Stoutspirit pointed out.

"Kalantha is wise for one her age, Stoutspirit. She is soon to be fourteen, young even for a Fallen Favorite. Still, she shows wisdom and maturity that many older people lack." He shook his head sadly. "Circumstances never let her enjoy her childhood."

"You truly think one girl will be able to stop the war?" Doubt was thick in Stoutspirit's voice. "One girl?"

"Of royal blood and with extraordinary determination." Gallant-Stallion looked from one Finest Court member to the next. "We are assigned Fallen Favorites to shepherd who might rise above their fellows and find redemption, and hopefully better the lives of those around them. There is indeed something special about Kalantha Montoll. I heard her tell King Meven that the war must end and that she would help him stop the fighting. I have confidence in her."

Stoutspirit snorted skeptically and took a few steps back. He was shoulder to shoulder now with Tadewi Sadgaze and Patience.

"And we have confidence in you, Gallant-Stallion-called-Rue." This came from Patience.

"I wish to learn more of this war." Gray Hawthorn was normally silent, leaving the questions to the other members of the Court. "Our brothers and sisters have lost more than a few charges because of it. And yesterday we lost a Finest pony."

"Roan Whiteshanks," Tadewi said. "He fell with his charge east of Ko's Point."

All the Finest closed their eyes at the mention of their lost brother, and the only sound was the wind teasing the tall grass and the leaves of a nearby birch tree.

After a suitable time passed, Gray Hawthorn asked Gallant-Stallion to continue. The tarpans started whispering again.

Gallant-Stallion described the aftermath of skirmishes, including the grisly sight of bodies awaiting burial, and of men picking through the possessions of their dead comrades. Neither he nor Kalantha witnessed much of the actual fighting. But they'd seen the results, and they'd heard tales from priests and stablehands while staying at the Vershan Monastery, and later from travelers along the road on the way to Nadir.

"Bishop DeNogaret played a role in the war," Gallant-Stallion said. "He was the guardian of Kalantha and Meven, and he was the King's advisor until . . ." The Finest paused.

"Until what?" Tadewi was known for her curiosity.

"Until he attacked Kalantha one day past. I defended my charge, and I may have killed him. For some reason, the Bishop considered her a threat."

Stoutspirit snorted loudly. "The girl a threat? Your charge a threat to a powerful man like a bishop?" The Finest tamped at the ground again. "Perhaps she is indeed worthy of your efforts, brother."

Gallant-Stallion nodded. "Kalantha believes that Bishop DeNogaret was responsible for the assassin-birds. These birds . . . they are not like their normal brethren. They seem to possess a keen intelligence and crave mayhem. They talk in the language of the Fallen Favorites."

The tarpans stopped whispering. Not a Finest in the gathering behind Gallant-Stallion made a sound, their eyes urging him to go on.

"The assassin-birds, the dark birds that walk like men," Gallant-Stallion added. "The birds that talk and slay without remorse. I have heard them. 'Death comes!' they cried during one of their attacks. They repeated it until it became so loud I could hear nothing else."

Tadewi Sadgaze reared back on her hind legs, front legs kicking at the air. When she came down the Finest behind Gallant-Stallion snorted anxiously. Tadewi was one of the second fourteen created by the good powers. Her eyes looked old and watery, but what marked her as such an august creature was her coat. It was predominantly white, glistening like the new-fallen snow Gallant-Stallion had walked through in Galmier's winters. She had a gray blaze on her head and a dappling of gray on her hindquarters. The good powers sculpted the first fourteen pure white, then realizing the Finest stood out too starkly amid the horses of Paard-Peran, added hints of color to the next fourteen. The Finest after that were all darker.

"I am old, Gallant-Stallion, and in all my years in these lands and in the realm of the Fallen Favorites, I have not seen such . . . assassin-birds, you call them." Tadewi glided toward Gallant-Stallion, the grass in the Shimmering Paddocks seeming to part for her. When they were muzzle to muzzle, she made a wuffling sound and met Gallant-Stallion's wide-eyed gaze. "But I believe you, Gallant-Stallion . . . because I believe you would not lie about such matters."

Patience tamped a hoof at the ground. "Neither have I seen such creatures." She paused, and all attention drifted to her. "But I've heard tales that the dark powers of this world favor birds and use them as symbols."

Tadewi snorted and bobbed her head. "Perhaps these birds have been beneath our notice, Gallant-Stallion, because their paths had not crossed a Finest's before."

"Or because no force had called them into play," Gallant-Stallion speculated.

Tadewi cocked her head. "You've told us of these birds twice before, brother, and nudged our curiosity then. Now you have the full measure of our attention regarding your assassin-birds. You said they slaughtered Steadfast, a prince, and all manner of men. You said they attacked you and your charge."

Gallant-Stallion stood motionless.

"I would see them, brother, these birds that walk like men, these birds that hunt and kill with apparent glee." Tadewi's wide eyes held his. "I would see them and look into their black hearts."

In a birch tree behind the Court members—hidden by a

clump of leaves—a small sparrow listened and watched intently. It had a black spot in the middle of its breast and a red-brown crown, with not a single dark feather on its head. And it had journeyed to the Finest Court when Gallant-Stallion opened the portal.

5 · A Meeting of Evil Minds

I learned best by being in the presence of Paard-Peran's worst. I discovered the beauty and value of quiet from power-hungry noblemen with loudly wagging tongues. I understood the depths of kindness by watching those who practiced cruelty. And I became more forgiving after observing those who did not have the capacity to forgive. Pity that the realm of the Fallen Favorites had so many teachers under which I could study.

~Mara, guardian of Bitternut, in a report to the Finest Court

The falcon flew so high that those below could see her only as a speck. The wind blew wintry cold at her lofty altitude, but when she concentrated, she became inured to it. She focused on the wind, which she relished when it passed above and below her wings and across her eyes. She listened to it, learned from it, and committed to memory what it taught her—in which directions cookfires burned, where men fought and died, how far she was from the sea, and how long before it would rain. At this moment it told her about soldiers being buried to the northeast and about a pack of wolves hunting in the woods beneath her—the scents of both rested delightfully on her tongue.

Her course followed the lengthy Sprawling River, which looked like a shiny blue ribbon twisted across a great piece of green fabric. The falcon's vision was so acute that she could pick out details far below—a half-sunken fishing boat, a doe drinking, a small raccoon washing a fish on the bank.

The raccoon sated the falcon's hunger and appeased her need to hunt.

The sun stretched at its zenith when the falcon glided over a stone wall and a row of evenly spaced spruce trees. She pulled her wings in tight and dove, opening them a few feet above the ground and skimming over a half moon–shaped bed planted with daffodils and other early spring flowers. She passed above a man-made pond ringed with circular stones and sculptures of long-legged birds. Then she banked toward the Nadir palace and started to climb.

The falcon circled the palace once, noting crows and black-birds perched under eaves and hidden by the shadows cast by stone gargoyles. A few called up to her: "Ninéon! Ninéon!" She acknowledged them with a throaty *skree,* and headed toward the north tower.

She sensed Bishop DeNogaret was there, though she couldn't explain how she knew that.

One pass around the tower and then she swooped in through a window near the top. She landed on the back of a chair and dug her claws into the ornately carved dark wood to purposely mar it. The falcon perched quietly for several moments, regarding the still form on the bed.

Bishop DeNogaret was thinner than last she'd seen him. He was propped up with several pillows, his legs and chest wrapped in bandages. His breathing was shallow but regular, and his eyelids and bony fingers twitched, as if he was in the midst of a bad dream. On a tapered table by the bed, Ninéon saw a bowl, a mug, and a piece of cake on a small plate. Eyes on the Bishop, she flew to the table and sampled the broth, finding it . . . interesting, but not fresh and hot like the raccoon had been. Neither was the goat's milk in the mug to her liking. But the cake was appealing. She nibbled at it for a few minutes, then she returned to the chair, deliberately flying inches above the Bishop so the flutter of her wings might wake him.

"Ninéon. Good of you to visit."

The voice had no power, and it had been his most commanding feature, she thought. It sounded frail now, like his broken body. But perhaps his mind remained strong, and that was what interested her today.

"I have a task for you my good friend, Ninéon."

The falcon made a soft skreeing sound and shook her head. "No. I have a task for you, DeNogaret."

The Bishop tried to raise himself further in the bed, but the chore was beyond him. "You serve me, Ninéon. You and—"

The falcon flew across him again, landing on the tray. She knocked the bowl of soup on the floor. "I serve myself, DeNogaret. I need you to summon your puppet-king."

The Bishop hissed at the falcon.

"Meven Montoll, DeNogaret. You will exert control over the young one again, work his mind like damp clay and get him to do what I want, what both of us want."

The Bishop glared. "How dare you, bird!"

"Oh, I dare, DeNogaret. And you are in no position to argue with me." The falcon nudged the mug toward the edge of the tray. "Now, about Meven Montoll."

The Bishop closed his eyes. "And what do you want with Meven?"

Ninéon took another bite of the cake. "As I said, I want what you want, DeNogaret—power. Mold Meven Montoll's mind like the mud along the banks of the Sprawling River and get him to continue this wonderful war."

"The war progresses, Ninéon. It—"

"Meven Montoll leaves soon to end it. This very day, he intends to ride. I don't want that. I don't want the bloodshed to end. I crave the conflict, DeNogaret, more than I crave a hunt.

There is more than enough carrion for all when the blood of men flows through the grass." The falcon paused to pick at a large crumb from the sweet cake.

"Meven has not come to see me. He knows I tried to kill his sister. I believe he suspects I was fogging his mind and manipulating him."

"Kalantha Montoll is his sister."

"Yes, Ninéon."

"Hateful girl on the hateful, ugly horse."

"I cannot control Meven if I cannot see him. The few servants who tend me whisper that the children will not come into this tower. Only two of the kitchen workers are allowed in this chamber. They bring me tasteless soup and tepid tea, souring goat's milk, and a piece of cake or a biscuit."

The falcon continued to pick at the cake while the Bishop talked. When only crumbs remained, Ninéon fixed the Bishop with an evil stare. "Then you will find a way to make Meven Montoll come into this room. The young one fears birds, DeNogaret. I cannot get close enough to control him. So I leave that responsibility to you."

"I can't. I'm hurt. I'm weak. When I'm a little stronger and—"

"You will find a way to lure Meven Montoll here. Now, DeNogaret. Meven Montoll must not stop this war."

Again the Bishop shook his head.

Ninéon pushed the mug off the tray. It landed on the floor with a dull thud, showering goat's milk on the braided rug.

"So you think to starve me, bird? I'll summon servants and tell them—"

"What? That a bird is trying to kill you? A talking bird? The servants won't believe you. Meven Montoll and his hateful sister would believe you, but they won't come up to see you—so you say." Ninéon spotted a silver bell on the table, near the Bishop's bed. The falcon pushed it just out of his reach.

"Find a way to get Meven Montoll here, DeNogaret. Find a way to control the King of Galmier once more and end his foolish plans for peace . . . if you want to live."

"His sister, Kalantha—"

"The hateful girl and her hateful horse are not your concern. And they may well be beneath my concern as well. We will see." Then Ninéon flew out the window.

6 · Bones and Dust

I believe that the Fallen Favorites who are most worthy of our aid are those who will risk everything—including their very lives. Only through great risk can one achieve greatness. Only by exploring uncharted lands and hidden places can the Favorites discover themselves.

~Hefty Thunderrun, Finest shepherd to Orlan Graman the Fourth

Just to see what's at the bottom. Just for a minute," Kalantha told herself as she made her way down. The stairway curved more sharply halfway down, at the same time widening, the steps becoming steeper. She doubted anyone had used them in quite some time, as grime covered the steps. "They're probably putting the stew on the table. I should go back and come down here with Meven after we're done stopping the war."

But her curiosity exceeded her hunger at the moment, so she went all the way to the bottom, telling herself she'd turn right around. The candlelight wasn't sufficient to reveal all of her surroundings, but the glass cylinder around the flame helped give the light a little more power—just enough to show that she was in a rather small room. She'd expected something cavernous, given the size of the palace above. Still, there were two doors off the room, and so she might find something immense behind one of them.

The room was walled by chiseled stone blocks that had been painted green, the paint badly flecking and looking like dried fish scales. The floor was smooth stone. There was a sagging cot draped in blankets and cobwebs, a nightstand by it, and a lantern, which she quickly discovered had no oil. A pewter mug on the floor had husks of insects lining the bottom. Perhaps the room had once served as a sentry's rest, she thought, as an adarga leaned against the nightstand. It was a small bladed shield fastened to a short spear, and Kalantha knew from watching enough soldiers that it was considered a parrying weapon. A few feet away lay a rotted aketon, a heavy quilted shirt usually worn under plate armor or long chain mail pieces. Neither looked serviceable any longer, and she wondered why someone hadn't thrown them out and cleaned the room up while they were at it. Perhaps she'd tend to that herself when she and Meven got back from the capital city Duriam. It would give her something to do.

She padded to the nearest door, finding nothing else interesting in this room. The doorframe was made of walnut and full of wrigglework—meandering carved designs of no particular pattern. The door handle was bronze, horribly filmy, and she almost didn't open it because she didn't want to get her hands too dirty before the meal.

"Oh!" She hurried back to the bed and carefully moved the blanket so as not to disturb too much dust and cobwebs. There was a thin pillow beneath, and she tugged the linen cover off it. The material smelled fusty, but would do. She used it to clean a spot on the nightstand, then set her cookies there. Returning to the door, she held the pillowcase against the latch and turned it, then pushed hard to open the door. It had swollen in the frame and resisted, but she managed to get it open just wide enough so she could squeeze through. She tucked a clean piece of the pillowcase under her belt so she'd have one hand free.

The old smell was stronger here, a moldy dampness she could taste. The room beyond was much bigger than the one she'd left. In fact, she couldn't see an end to it.

She started with the wall to her left. It was decorated with a smattering of parchment-thin pieces of jade, agate, and a pale orange-brown stone she couldn't identify. It took her a moment to realize it was a mosaic, and she traveled its length to see it all. The scene was a forest, with unnatural-looking trees, but only because the artist had left out the branches—rendering just trunks and clumps of green to represent leaves. A knight on horseback loomed large in the center, the rearing horse made out of pearl shavings, with too long and curvy of a neck. The knight was rendered in silver, and Kalantha thought all of it was quite valuable and that it should be displayed in a room upstairs where people could enjoy it. An old, wide wooden chair with arms and legs ending in carved claws was set back from the mosaic; likely someone used to sit here to admire the scene. But the chair hadn't been sat in recently—it was coated with a thick film of filth and dust, and spiderwebs beneath the seat were dotted with dried egg sacks that would never open. The chair rested on a rug that would have been considered ornate years ago. It showed red and black horses racing around its margin. Something oily had spilled on part of it, and Kalantha avoided stepping there.

She forgot all about the noon meal. The edge of the candle-light brushed a row of tall shelves, and she picked her way toward them over moldy piles she didn't care to examine and pieces of rusted metal that looked broken, perhaps the remnants of an elaborate weapon or a sculpture of some sort. Broken glass covered parts of the floor and the light caught the shards and caused them to shine. The shelf at eye level held a variety of interesting things, predominantly fist-sized brass figurines. Through a veil of webs she spotted a beetle, flower buds, a tailless cat, a clump of acorns, and several tiny bowls. A nearby hunk of crystal snared in the candle's light sent pink, green, and blue motes dancing across an assortment of other things—a bundle of quills, vials of ink she suspected were as dry as dirt, a rolled piece of parchment tied with a cord, and copper and brass slivers on an oblong crystal plate.

There were stacks of rolled parchments on higher shelves, and most of the lower shelves looked empty—save for the ever-present layer of dust. But the very bottom shelf had something in a gray drawstring bag. Kalantha squatted and put her candle on the floor. She hadn't noticed that it had burned down a little. She brushed aside a curtain of webs and tugged the bag out, opened it, and fell back in surprise, nearly knocking over the candle.

"Oh, that's just . . . awful." Still, she had to look closer. The bag contained a skull, and at first she thought it was a real one. But on closer inspection she realized the color was wrong, red-brown, and the eye sockets much too small. In fact, the sockets were set with smooth black stones. The skull had been sculpted from clay and missed the lower jaw. Kalantha could tell the jaw had been there at one time, but had broken off. It wasn't in the bag. The back of the skull was etched with a heraldry symbol she recalled seeing on one of the pennants hanging in a stairwell. "Truly awful. Whoever would make something like this?" She closed the bag and set it back on the bottom shelf, got up, and grabbed the candle. Then she went past the shelves and followed the wall, finding another mosaic, this one of a lion on a field of red and blue, looking over its shoulder.

She tried to guess what room in the palace she might be under, and suspected she was near the kitchen, as she saw a narrow set of steps that went up to what might be the panel between the pictures of the old men in the hallway. These steps were not so dirty as the ones she'd come down.

"Wonder why they hid the stairs?" Maybe they were simply hiding the darkness and dustiness of this place and not wanting visitors to know they stored old keepsakes and oddities under the palace, she thought, like the skull. "But they could have just locked a door to keep people out."

Another shelf, wider and taller and farther away, was filled with jars of colored sand, pretty goblets she thought should be used at the dinner table, and a couple dozen thin leather-bound books that were tied closed with twine. Again Kalantha set the candle on the floor and inspected everything. The books interested her, and she quickly discovered they were journals. Book after book she held near the candle, thumbing through them and seeing names she didn't recognize. Just as she was about to move elsewhere, she discovered a page that made her gasp. Names here were more than familiar, and a shiver passed down her spine when she read a little.

I have watched the priest DeNogaret with growing unease. Once, I admired the man. Now, he sends a shiver down my spine. Once, I believed he worked for the good of religion and the welfare of our King. Now, I believe DeNogaret has his own best interests at heart.

Today, when I walked in the gardens, I caught sight of DeNogaret praying . . . or so I thought. When I moved closer, I discovered he was merely talking to himself, speculating to a grackle that bathed in a puddle. He mused what might happen if the King's brother died. The heirs to the throne lessened, would he gain more influence? I shuddered and stepped away, but not soon enough. I watched his hand dart out of his robes and grab the grackle about its tiny neck.

The bird squawked once, then DeNogaret dropped its lifeless body in the puddle.

It had not crossed my mind that the priest might do something to limit the royal family. But then neither had it crossed my mind that in an instant he would slay a harmless, simple bird.

"Meven should see this." The book was heavy and twice the height of all the others. She thumbed through the pages and discovered there were only six or seven that she needed. Holding her breath, she tore them out, carefully folded them, then put them in a pocket. "Not right, my ruining that book." But taking the whole thing wasn't practical, and she wanted Meven to see this while on their way to Duriam. It was, perhaps, as important as the book from the Vershan Monastery. A smaller book caught her eye, on her family's history . . . or at least a part of the line. She managed to tuck this one into the pillow-case dangling from her belt. "Better go find him."

She held the candle high and took another look around. There was a room behind the second stairwell, the entrance a black door bound in polished brass and set into a stone arch-way decorated with round marble tiles the size of dinner plates.

"Find him after I take a look at this."

There wasn't near so much dust or so many cobwebs near the door, and so Kalantha decided someone came down to this part of the cellar once in a while. She paused only a moment before trying to open the door, candle in one hand. But she wasn't quite strong enough, and so she rested the candle on the floor a few feet away and yanked on the knob with both hands. The door was heavy and thick and resisted for a few moments before finally giving way. She grabbed up the candle and went inside, the odor in the wide hallway beyond hitting her like she'd been punched.

It smelled worse than the infirmary tent, like nothing she'd ever smelled before or could identify. She turned to run, then stopped herself, a morbid curiosity winning out. A quick look, she thought, then I'll leave and find Meven, show him the journal. He must see the journal!

"Just a quick . . . by all the good gods!" Lining the walls on either side of her were caskets propped up at steep angles. Lidless, they exposed the bodies inside. The ones closest to her were little more than skeletons draped in clothes that had once been opulent and wearing jewelry covered with a heavy film of dust and decay. Kalantha was horrified, but she forced herself to look further. At the foot of each corpse was a bronze plaque inscribed with a name.

Elandor Montoll, Sephraim Montoll, Jandiera Montoll-Kulu, Daphne Montoll-Porun, Condell Montoll, Feronimuth Edmure Montoll II.

The names went on, the bodies becoming less decomposed the farther she went. Some of the more recent plaques contained more information: Caldora Montoll, first daughter of Hiranth Montoll, fifth King of Galmier, died to the plague at age sixteen. Ira Montoll, second son of Hiranth Montoll, died in a fight with robbers on Halor Road.

"The family crypt."

So that's why there wasn't a cemetery on the palace grounds; the kings and their families were interred here.

She knew it was a customary practice to bury bishops and other high-ranking clergy deep beneath a temple, but she didn't know royalty did the same. It was amazing the entire place didn't stink from the dead, but the door had been thick and smelled of cedar, and it sealed well. So that explained it. Kalantha detested the reek of the corpses, but she wanted to see just how big the crypt was—as she didn't think she'd ever come back here. She breathed shallowly, thinking that might help, and she covered her nose and mouth with her free hand.

Kalantha was glad the candle provided just enough light that she could see where she was going and could see part of the bodies. More light would have revealed too many grisly details. As she neared the end of the hallway, she saw many open spaces where future Montolls would rest—including she and her brother, and any family Meven might have in the future. The last filled casket on her right had a bronze plaque proclaiming the deceased as Prince Edan Montoll. She'd been with his wedding party when the assassin-birds killed everyone but her and Meven. Edan's corpse was wrapped in a heavy brocade cloth. She knew the birds tore him up, and so presenting him would have been . . . "Horrible," she pronounced, turning away and walking to the last empty space. There was a round room beyond it, ringed by spaces where more caskets could be propped. In the center, a body was laid out on a thick marble slab.

She knew who it was without being close enough to see—the previous King of Galmier, her uncle. She approached slowly, stopping when the edge of the candlelight touched his face. The skin was drawn tight and was white, the eyes closed and fingers laced across a chest covered with a black silk tunic embroidered with gold thread. She cast her head down and prayed, thinking this an appropriate thing to do here.

Kalantha prayed long minutes for her uncle and Prince Edan, then she prayed for Rue and that his leg would heal soon. She wanted to talk to Rue before she and Meven went to Nasim-Guri to stop the war. Rue wouldn't be able to go because of his leg, and though she would miss him, it was important she go with Meven.

Rue would have to stay behind.

Finally, she prayed for Meven, that he could indeed make peace with King Silverwood of Nasim-Guri and find a way to make amends for all the death. She prayed for her brother to be a good, strong ruler. She prayed for her old friend Morgan, the gardener of the High Keep Temple. But she stopped herself from praying for Bishop DeNogaret. Someone needed to pray for him, she knew, but it wouldn't be her. Not today.

"Better go," she told herself. "Ouch!" She finally noticed that the candle had burned down to a few inches and that hot wax was spilling out a crack in the glass cylinder and over her fingers. "Oh, I'm awfully late!" She realized she'd been caught up in her explorations and that no doubt the noon meal had been served and anything left over picked up. Meven was probably finishing his meeting with the commanders and would be ready to leave soon—maybe right this minute—and was looking for her. Good thing she had the bundle of cookies, since she'd missed the meal.

She nodded to her uncle's body, thinking she should say something beyond the prayer, but not knowing what was customary. She wondered if she should bring flowers down here when more bloomed later in the spring. She'd talk to Meven about it on the trip to Duriam.

She retraced her steps down the hallway, looking at the floor this time and avoiding the corpses. Then she pushed the door closed, finding that every bit as difficult as opening it.

There should be just enough candle left to get back to the stairway that led up to the library. But she'd need to hurry, as the flame was flickering and the wick growing perilously short.

"This way, I think." She paused, her heart suddenly pounding. "No, this way. This way." Her light more feeble now, she couldn't see more than five or six feet. She walked quickly toward where she thought the murals and the chair were, and the shelves with the interesting things and journals. She was holding the candle plate with only three fingers, cringing when more wax spilled down over them.

Kalantha passed by an alcove she hadn't noticed before, then brushed against a wardrobe closet that stretched taller than her light reached. She let out a breath she'd been holding. A dozen more steps and she saw a large, familiar shelf. Beyond that was a smaller shelf filled with the brass figurines and rolled parchments. The mosaics weren't far now, and beyond them the room with the stairs.

Something caught her attention and she blinked, seeing a speck of light in the darkness to her right. She blinked again when the light moved, like a firefly floating on the breeze on a summer night. Someone else was down here. There was the faint click of heels against the stone floor.

"Who's there?" She stopped herself from saying anything else. She should call out again, and loudly, she told herself— someone was obviously looking for her, using a candle or a lamp to find their way. Maybe Meven had sent someone. But no one was in the library when she opened the panel and slipped through, and the light wasn't coming from the direction of that secret stairway. So who would know she was down here? Had someone seen her use the secret stairs? Had someone been following her around the palace? Whoever searched over there, they'd come down another stairway than the one she used.

It had to be someone looking for her, she thought again. She opened her mouth to call out, and she took a step in that direction.

Or maybe someone came down here to tend to the family crypt.

The light became larger and brighter, indicating that the person holding it walked toward her. But something didn't feel right, and she had so very little candle left. So she turned from the glow and headed toward where she believed the mosaics stretched. She was rewarded by the crunch of glass shards under her feet. "That's it," she whispered. "The chair."

"Kalantha? Lady Kalantha?"

The glow got larger still.

"Who's there?" Kalantha didn't recognize the voice, but

there were so many workers in the palace, and she'd met only a handful of them. She certainly couldn't be expected to re-member them all.

"Lady Kalantha. Stay where you are and I'll come to you."

"Who's there?"

"I'll take you out of this dark, wretched place."

Three times she'd asked the name of the man, and he hadn't answered. She swept past the chair, her candle almost out now, a stub with a whisper of a flame. It took her a few moments to find the door to the sentry's room and to squeeze through, and in that time the glow behind her had gotten big enough so she could tell it was from a large lantern held by a tall man. His clothes were too dark and the lantern held too far from his face for her to recognize him.

I'll get out myself, thank you, she thought. "I'm fine. I know the way out," she told him.

She saw the bundle of cookies and didn't pause to grab them. She started up the steps, just as the man yanked the door open wide enough for him and came into the sentry's room, too.

"Kalantha, stop!"

If he wanted to help her get out of the cellar, he wouldn't be asking her to stop, she knew. Maybe he wanted to chastise her for coming down here or for entering the family crypt. If that was the case, he could scold her just as easily upstairs, where she felt more comfortable. She climbed nearly to the top step when her candle went out. She dropped it, heard the glass break and the little plate hit the stone, then she pushed on the panel.

It didn't budge.

She threw her shoulder at it, figuring it was simply stuck. But it moved only a little. Faint light spilled in through the crack she'd made, and peeking through the crack she saw that some-thing had been wedged against the panel.

The thronelike chair!

"Hey!" she hollered into the crack. "Hey!" She started hitting the panel, then heard footsteps pounding up the stone steps behind her.

Whirling, she saw the figure coming closer, lantern held low and away from his body, light bouncing with each step.

7 · Black Memories

I am ancient, brothers and sisters. I have seen so many years that I can no longer remember the times of my youth. There may be few days in front of me, but I anxiously gallop into them with my head held high. Dying is such an easy thing to do, leaving behind the flesh and casting your spirit into the cool breeze. I do not fear death. But I fear what lies at the end of nightmares and at the bottom of memories.

~*Tadewi Sadgaze of the Finest Court*

Tadewi Sadgaze considered herself a dalusian, and her pale coat carried the slightest hint of a mulberry shade. She had a wheat-colored mane and tail that were slightly curly and luxuriant, and her elegant head looked almost hawklike in profile. Her eyes betrayed her age, for they were watery and there was a faint milky covering over the pupils. They looked up into Gallant-Stallion's wide, dark ones.

"You said your chosen Fallen Favorite calls you Rue."

Gallant-Stallion nodded, his eyes never leaving hers. "Meven Montoll named me, saying I was a rueful-looking horse."

"And your chosen Fallen Favorite accepted the name?"

Gallant-Stallion heard some of the Finest ponies in attendance nicker in fun at the name. "Kalantha said the assassin-birds would rue the day they crossed my path. And when she says my name, it sounds like music."

"A good name then," Tadewi decided, "though not so proud as the name the Court gave you. Rue . . . I hear music in it."

A shake of her head told Gallant-Stallion the pleasantries were over. Tadewi Sadgaze's coat glimmered like the grass and the wildflowers, and the Finest gathered around them fell silent. Each Finest possessed a gift. Gallant-Stallion met a mountain pony who could heal others with a touch, and an old horse who shepherded a village who could look cryptically into the future. His own gift allowed him to communicate with his Fallen Favorite.

Tadewi's gift was to vividly recall memories, but only the unfortunate ones.

Her eyes bore into Gallant-Stallion's, as she delved into his mind and retrieved a horrible experience.

SUDDENLY IT WAS NIGHT, THE CLOUDS THICK OVERHEAD, with only a few gaps in them to let the stars shine through. The wind gusted chill, and rain pelted against everything. Gallant-Stallion could smell a worse storm brewing and could hear Meven talking to Prince Edan and Kalantha. Horses in the entourage were nervously whinnying, and one of the soldiers barked orders to his fellows. They were all on a road paralleling a branch of the great Sprawling River to the east and the Galmier Mountains to the west, heading toward Nasim-Guri where Prince Edan would be married to Princess Silverwood.

Gallant-Stallion knew it wasn't really raining, and that he was in the Finest Court and not on a night-dark muddy trail. He knew Meven and Kalantha weren't here and that Prince Edan was dead. But it felt so very real. He listened intently, trying to hear Tadewi or the other Court members. But all he heard was an odd noise, something steady and muffled. As it grew in intensity it sounded like the thundering of horses' hooves pounding across the ground. Kalantha heard it, too—though she in truth wasn't there—and Meven and Edan and all the attendants. They were all trying to spot the approaching herd, twisting in their saddles and cupping their eyes from the now-hammering rain.

Steadfast was there, too, at Gallant-Stallion's side. His coat was blackest black and shining, not the ghost image from the royal stables.

A herd races toward us. Gallant-Stallion heard himself talk to Steadfast, though he in fact wasn't saying anything, was standing silently in the Shimmering Paddocks. The words had been pulled from his mind by Tadewi, and they swirled loudly around his head. *How many horses? The shadows and the rain hide their numbers! Has something frightened them?*

Perhaps they are merely running for the joy of it, Steadfast returned. *Maybe they try to outrace the storm. I tried that once, a long time ago, with a daring astrologer on my back.*

In a heartbeat the shadows behind the wedding party separated. A sudden flash of lightning revealed a wave of black—dozens of dark men on dark horses headed right at the Prince's procession. Black cloaks flapped angrily and fought with the sound of the thundering hoofbeats.

The soldiers tried to outrace them.

"Death!" came a strangled cry from somewhere in the mysterious charging forms. "Death comes!"

Gallant-Stallion had noticed nothing unusual in the growing storm, no distant whispers of the black-clothed men. He decided they'd done something to cover their scent, as he couldn't smell them. There was only the fresh scent of the rain, the mustiness of the ground, and the odors of the people and horses he'd been riding with.

The attackers were like ink spilled from a bottle, spreading out to surround the wedding party and moving in with terrifying speed. The night continued to hide their details—even from the exceptional senses of Gallant-Stallion. All the Finest could see were the vague forms of men, likely more than one hundred, swords coated with weapon black and slashing at the wedding party.

Lightning flashed, the ground rocked with thunder, and Gallant-Stallion's heart pounded wildly.

Gallant-Stallion, we must run! Steadfast called in the hidden speak. Moments later: *Flee! Protect your charge.*

He did just that. Meven was securely on his back and reached down to grab Kalantha. Gallant-Stallion sped away with the children, tossing his head back and looking behind him, seeing only the black, indistinct forms of men on horses.

"You saw more than shadows, Gallant-Stallion-called-Rue."

He blinked to clear his senses and saw Tadewi's eyes wide and locked onto his. He felt dizzy, as if he'd been whisked from that storm-drenched night and dropped in the Paddocks.

"You just didn't realize what you were seeing." Tadewi's eyes were mirrors reflecting his own, growing to show him the dark shapes she'd pulled from his memories.

Away from the terror of the battle, things were clearer. Gallant-Stallion saw birds, hundreds of them, all black with black shiny eyes filled with malevolence. Crows, starlings, blackbirds, and more, a few bats in the mix. Their bodies were pressed so close together that only the flashes of lightning revealed beaks and claws and the smallest of gaps between beating wings. Their formations resembled men on horseback, and because of the storm and the night none in the wedding party could tell otherwise.

"Even had I known then what they were, nothing would have changed," Gallant-Stallion said. "All those people and horses . . . and Steadfast . . . still would have died." He paused and pawed at the ground. "But I might have done things differently to protect the children, and I would have known to keep watch for the birds."

He recounted how nights later the birds came again, looking like riders on horseback spilling over a rock face and descending on Meven and Kalantha. He'd fought them off then, and once more.

"But had I known what they were that first night, I would have come to the Court straightaway and sought your guidance."

"Are they still a threat, Child of the Great Grassland? Do these evil black birds still menace your charge?" This came from Patience, who glided forward until she was even with Tadewi.

A silence slipped between them, the only sound the rustling of the grass and wildflowers around their hooves.

"I do not know," Gallant-Stallion finally answered. "And I don't know why."

8 · Warriors and Peace

My Fallen Favorite is a very large man, a merchant who sells worthless baubles out of the back of a wagon so heavy it threatens to crush its own wheels. But he and his overloaded wagon tread ever so lightly on Paard-Peran. He knows a truth, and I reveal it now to you: Paard-Peran was not made for my Fallen Favorite, nor did he inherit any land or goods from his parents. What he possesses was given to him by future generations . . . and he knows to take good care of it for them.

~Prudent-Flehmen, shepherd to Bartholomew the Bold
and Sir Scuddles

The three knight commanders were difficult to distinguish from one another with their helmets on. Each was clad in a suit of plate armor, the breastplates scratched and pitted from skirmishes, but polished and gleaming in the noon sun. Swords with matching pommels hung from leather belts embossed with lion heads, and kite shields lay on the ground near their feet. The wind fluttered the hems of their blue cloaks, which were King Meven's colors.

Meven approached them slowly, looking toward the large infirmary tent, where two bodies were being carried out on planks.

"Sire." One of the knight commanders stepped forward and removed his helmet as he bowed. "We came immediately in reply to your summons." Despite the cool air a sheen of sweat glistened on his face, evidence he'd been working hard drilling the soldiers north of the royal stables. "Commander Farote is still in the field and beyond the Nasim-Guri border camped outside Giaia."

Meven watched as one of the bodies was carried to the palace, as he'd requested. He looked down at his hands that were still bloodstained. "Commander Marno." Meven finally nodded to the knight. "Word will be sent to Commander Farote that the war is ending. I will send a squire when we are finished here. He is not to march into Giaia."

Marno didn't bother to hide his surprise. "Sire, Duriam has surrendered? King Silverwood would not—"

Meven shook his head. "You are correct, Commander Marno, King Hunter Silverwood is too proud to surrender. His soldiers . . . what is left of his soldiers . . . will defy us to their last breath."

"Then I don't understand. Why is the war ending?"

"Commander Marno, I am calling a halt to all of this."

The knight commander sucked in a breath and raised an eyebrow.

"Too many of your men have died, and certainly far too many of the Nasim-Guri soldiers." Meven dug the ball of his foot into the ground and sighed. "I should not have started this war, Commander Marno. But my sister made me realize just what evil I've wrought. And now I definitely should end it."

Another commander removed his helmet, a shock of sweat-soaked, wheat-blond hair spilling out. He'd sparred with Meven last spring when the young King of Galmier wanted to learn swordsmanship, and so he felt at ease speaking. "A week, or a little more, Majesty, and we will crush the last of the Nasim-Guri forces. Scouts report that their soldiers are spread too thin and that all of their experienced commanders are dead. Farm boys are taking up swords, townsmen being recruited or pressed. We scattered their largest unit three days ago and broke through the Miachi Wall. If we . . ."

Meven dismissively waved his hand, and the knight stopped

in mid-sentence. "Commander Bradmark, I am well aware that we are winning this war, and that within a matter of days Nasim-Guri could be ours. But, my friend, it *should* not be ours."

The third commander removed his helmet and rubbed his thumb across his belt. Disbelief was apparent on all of their faces.

"I understand your confusion, gentlemen. I must admit that I am a bit befuddled myself. But my mind is clear now. This war has been a dreadful, sinful mistake. So many people have—" The image of the soldier who died in his arms flashed in his mind and he clenched his fists, fingernails digging into his palms. He was close to tears, but he couldn't let his knight commanders see him cry. That would be a show of weakness that would be difficult to recover from. "I want no more blood spilled because of me."

The commanders stood silent, waiting for Meven to say something else. When he didn't, the one with the blond hair spoke.

"Aye, King Montoll, the war ends now as you wish." Bradmark wiped a hand across his forehead. "We will ride into Nasim-Guri and inform all the soldiers along the way."

"As you wish, Sire," Marno added. "We serve at your behest. It will be done."

The third knight commander simply nodded.

"Gentlemen, I am—" Meven stopped when he heard the skree of some bird. He glanced around and frowned to see several crows perched on a palace eave. Then he looked to the large infirmary tent, where another body was being carried out. A crow flew a course parallel to the body. "I am having declarations of peace drawn up now, and they should be ready before sunset. I will sign them, then you and your soldiers will distribute them to villages in Galmier and Nasim-Guri. You'll inform the troops stationed along our border and into Nasim-Guri.

They will no doubt need to see the declarations, as word of the war's end might be . . . difficult . . . for them to believe."

"We will leave at first light tomorrow," Marno said.

"You will leave as soon as the declarations are ready," Meven said more sharply than he had intended. "You will travel through the evening, exchanging horses in villages when necessary. I suggest you rest for a few hours now."

Meven waited a moment, expecting them to leave.

"Sire?" Bradmark risked a comment. "We will do as you say. But to come so close to winning a war . . . and to walk away . . . the soldiers will not take it well. They've fought hard for you, and they've watched their friends and brothers die. Many of them, maybe all of them, will be angry to have a prize in front of their faces disappear. And they will not want to simply walk away. The wives and fathers who've lost family, they will think the sacrifice wasted. You will become unpopular."

The other knight commanders quietly voiced their agreement.

"You need to realize the ramifications, Sire," Bradmark continued. "There will be unrest."

Meven squared his shoulders and thrust his chin out. "The declarations will be ready by sunset. You have your orders."

"Aye, King Meven. It will be done." Commander Marno turned with military precision and walked toward the main gate. "Bradmark, Javal, let us get a few hours rest."

Meven watched the men go. They would do precisely as he wanted, and he knew full well they wouldn't be happy doing it.

"I'm losing my mind," he whispered. He stumbled toward the large infirmary tent and dropped to his knees in the long shadow it cast. He ran a bloodied hand through his hair when he heard a wounded man moaning on the other side of the canvas. He prayed to the good gods to forgive him. It seemed he'd been swallowed by a nightmare and that he was falling into some horrible black pit. He sobbed and cupped his face with his hands. "I am winning. I could win." But victory would be madness, he knew, the eternal black nightmare. And he doubted he would be able to live with himself if more men died. Still, more men were dying—this very moment—in the infirmary tents and on the battlefields.

"By all that's holy, what have I done?" He struggled to his feet and hurried toward the palace, intending to make his scribes work faster.

A crow followed him, and Meven saw its shadow on the ground. He stopped at the south tower and gestured to the nearest sentry.

"Archers," Meven demanded. "However many of them are in the tower and practicing on the field. Roust all of them now and direct them to shoot every last bird on the parapets and eaves, on the infirmary tents, on the stable roofs. Kill all of them."

Several minutes later he paced in one of the dining rooms, urging his scribes to write faster. He pulled literate cooks and attendants in to help, and sent word to the stable to find any literate grooms to join them.

"Drucalla," Meven cringed when he realized he got her name wrong. There were just so many workers in the palace—nearly two hundred—it was difficult to remember all of the names.

She placed more inkwells on the table, and smiled wanly at him. "Drucilla," she said softly.

"Drucilla, would you find Weston and have him pack several changes of clothes for me?" Meven had intended to see to that himself, wanting to be particular about the outfits he chose. But he was in too much of a hurry now for that.

"Of course, Sire." She gathered up the empty bottles, stopping when he put his hand on her arm. It was an uncharacteristic gesture for him, to touch one of his servants, and her eyes widened in surprise.

"And when Weston is finished with that, tell him to fill a chest with gems and the most valuable trinkets from the treasury. I will need a peace offering for King Hunter Silverwood of Nasim-Guri."

"Yes, Sire." She hurried from the room, and Meven went in search of Kalantha.

She wasn't in her room, though he saw her packed satchel and had it taken to the royal stables. He sent two women polishing the floors to look for her. Then he went to the kitchen, thinking his sister was probably gathering food for the trip—even though she should know one of the attendants was taking care of food for the entire entourage.

Meven was so intent on finding Kalantha that he wasn't paying attention to his surroundings. He soundly smacked into the laundry master when he rushed down the hall toward the kitchen and knocked the man down.

"Gervis! My apologies." Meven extended a hand, and the man was quick to accept the help up.

Gervis brushed at the bottom of his trousers. "No apologies needed, Sire. I should have heard you—"

"Have you seen Kalantha? My sister? I introduced you to her yesterday and—"

Gervis shook his head. "No, Sire. I haven't seen your sister all day."

Meven brushed past him and hurried into the kitchen. The pleasant clatter of plates and mugs being washed and the conversations of the cooks buzzed around him. Something baked in the oven, honeyed bread from the smell of it. Meven hoped it would be done in time to take some with him. He looked around for the head cook.

"Sara Anne—" She was easy to remember, as he saw her often, bustling from the kitchen to the pantry, and occasionally to the dining room to sneak a look to see if guests enjoyed her fare. "Sara Anne, have you seen my sister? I think I might have introduced her to you yesterday. Kalantha."

"I know Lady Kalantha, Sire. I haven't seen her at all today. I suspect she was at breakfast and at the noon meal, but I've been very busy preparing food for your trip. I'm sorry. I just haven't seen her."

9 · Mystery in the Dark

Surprises, how I love them! They are the best part of shepherding a
Fallen Favorite. The Finest Court is beautifully predictable. But Paard-
Peran . . . ah, the world is a precious mystery. One cannot say how a
Fallen Favorite will act or what dream she will pursue. One cannot
know how all the others in the land will treat her. One cannot guess
the weather or the temperament of the seas. Forever give me Fallen Favorites to guide, so I cannot predict my future.

~Joyous Barkbiter, shepherd to Grella Tantis,
high prelate of Dea Fortress

Kalantha shivered at the top of the hidden staircase, watching the light come closer, held by a tall, dark-clad man.

"Take care, girl. I'll help you get that door open."

But for some reason she didn't think he would. She made a
last effort to open the secret library panel, called out once
more, then took a deep breath and ran down the stairs toward
the mystery man. She barreled into him, though that wasn't
her intent, sending him tumbling down the steps in front of
her, the lantern flying from his hand and breaking. She nearly
fell off the steps herself, then tripped over him.

Suddenly, the world was inky black.

"Girl! How dare you!"

Kalantha scrambled up and away from him, stood indeci-
sively for a moment, listening to the man gather himself up
and grunt. She suspected she had hurt him, but there was no

way to tell how badly. Her heart hammered wildly in her chest and her breath came fast and ragged from fear. She hated the dark and she hated being suspicious of people.

"I'm sorry," she whispered.

She'd gotten a glimpse of his face just before she'd knocked him off the steps. He was vaguely familiar, meaning she'd seen him somewhere in the palace. What if he'd really been trying to help her? What had she done? Was he seriously hurt? He could have broken a leg or an arm . . . or worse . . . because of her. She stepped to her left, as she knew he'd fallen to the right. She forced herself to breathe shallowly so he wouldn't hear her. She heard him moving around in the blackness, then, after a moment, climbing the steps. By his tentative footfalls she could tell he was going slow, forced to feel his way and maybe trying to find her at the same time, not knowing she was moving farther from the hidden stairs.

"Kalantha! Come here, girl. Let me help you."

She shook her head. Maybe she was too suspicious of people. Maybe he really did mean to help. But a shiver passed down her spine, and she pulled the pillowcase loose from her belt, set it gently on the floor and got on hands and knees. She started crawling, the musty smell of this place stronger so close to the floor. A sliver of glass lanced into her palm and she almost cried out. Her fingers gingerly danced forward and she felt more pieces of glass and oil from the broken lantern. She was careful to crawl around them, fingers tentatively feeling in front of her and to her sides, brushing webs and the coverlet on the bed and getting a better idea of where she was.

Kalantha heard him coming back down the stairs. He hadn't tried to push the panel open—she would have heard him do that. He shuffled, an irregular step that made her wonder if he'd indeed hurt his leg and limped. She heard a crunching sound; he was stepping on the broken glass. Then there was a *clunk,* and she guessed he had stepped on the metal of the lantern. She crawled faster, fingers finding the nightstand and the weapon propped against it, catching the table when it started to tip. An idea sprang into her head and she grabbed the base of the lantern and flung it to her right with as much strength as she could manage. She didn't hit him with it, but she wasn't trying to. It clanged against the opposite wall of the small room.

Let him think I'm over there, she thought.

Faster she went, her hand guiding her along the wall until she reached the end of it. She fumbled around until she found the door and crawled through it.

"Kalantha!"

He was still in the small room looking for her.

"Kal . . . ugh!"

He toppled over something and muttered a string of curses, most of them aimed at her. Then he paused when he bumped into something else—the nightstand or the bed, she suspected. He was quiet for a moment, and Kalantha didn't move, listening and hearing only the pounding of her heart, seeming almost deafening in the complete blackness. After what seemed like an eternity, she heard him moving again and heard the glass of the broken lantern crunch. Then he was going up the stairs, this time pushing against the panel. It took him two attempts, then she heard the creak of wood and something large being moved, no doubt the thronelike chair.

Kalantha saw the blackness lighten almost imperceptibly, light slipping in from the library at the top of the steps. And since she didn't hear him any longer, she guessed he was staying upstairs. Should she turn around and follow him? Was that what he wanted her to do? Before she reacted, she heard a thump and the catching of a latch, and it was pitch-dark again. He'd shut the panel behind him.

She could find her way back through the door and into the small sentry's room, then make her way up the steps. Maybe he hadn't pushed the chair back against the hidden door. Maybe she could get out. She started to turn around, then stopped herself, deciding to trust her first instincts about him. He might be waiting for her in the library, and he might mean her harm. So she continued to crawl forward, following the wall until her fingers brushed the first mosaic. She stood and placed her palm against the stone chips, shuffling along until she felt something cooler and realized it was the silver horse. She traced the metal chips, the legs, head, and mane.

"Rue," she whispered. "Rue, why did I come down here? Why didn't I trust that man?" She wondered if the grooms had been tending to his lame leg, and if he was feeling better. She told herself that she would go to check on Rue soon—as soon as she got out of here. Then she edged forward again. The chair on the red and black rug was to her right, she remembered, and all around it were the pieces of broken metal. But she didn't want to lose her place along the wall.

Several long minutes later, the wall curved and she came to a tall shelf. She never knew anything could be so absolutely dark as this cellar under the palace. Cellar? she mused. Cottages had cellars where people stored vegetables and fruits. "Cellar" wasn't an appropriate word for this massive place under the palace. And dark? This was more than dark. The blackness brought back memories of being surrounded by the assassin-birds. But that was a suffocating blackness; here at least she could easily breathe. She felt the objects on the shelf, the small figurines she'd noticed earlier. Higher up were stacks of scrolls. She used the shelf as a guide, finding the larger one beyond that. She tried to remember where she'd explored before, then tried to shake off the memory of the skull sculpture in the bag and the bodies in the crypt.

When she reached the end of the last shelf, she stopped.

Where should she go? She knew another set of stairs stretched not too far from the crypt, and they probably led to the hallway near the dining room. But could she find them? She tried to visualize the room, not that she'd ever seen much of it to begin with.

Why did she knock that man off the stairs? What if he really did want to help her? What if— She held her breath and cocked her head. There was a soft tapping, and it took her a moment to recognize the sound as footsteps. The sentry's room and the steps the mysterious man had come down were both a good distance away—the noise could be coming from there. She heard voices, and she strained to make out what they said. Kalantha couldn't catch it all, but she gleaned snatches.

"Troublesome girl, she—"

"—last see her?"

"—find her."

"We need to—"

"Put her . . . family crypt . . . forever."

Body? In the crypt forever? The mysterious man had indeed meant her harm! A shiver shot down Kalantha's spine and made her heart race again. She frantically fumbled with her boots, tugging them off and carrying them now so her heels would not click against the stone floor. She could hear the men approaching, their heels clicking, but they couldn't hear her. She waved her free arm in front of her, hoping to find furniture, something that she might remember from when she had a candle, and she walked faster than she wanted. She was afraid she would stumble over something and make noise, but she was also afraid that if she didn't find a place to hide quickly, they'd find her and kill her.

The blackness didn't seem quite so dark anymore, and she knew they'd brought candles or lanterns with them. How many men were looking for her? Two at least—she'd heard two different voices. Why were they after her? It had only been the assassin-birds before. And then Bishop DeNogaret. She gasped. The Bishop! Had he sent them after her? No, he was hurt and in a tower.

"Bert, look here."

"A pillowcase. What can—"

"I saw the girl with it, Bert. She must have dropped it."

"Something's in it."

"I don't care what's in it. Leave it be. We just need the girl."

The voices were getting louder, and she distinctly saw two yellow-white glows, one of them brighter and larger than the other and obviously coming from a good-sized lantern. She was dizzy with fear. It was worse than fighting off assassin-birds, she thought. Then she'd been outside, and she saw where she was going and had a chance to get away. Here she was trapped, and in the utter dark she hadn't a clue where to go.

Move! she told herself. She gripped her boots tighter and forced herself forward, arm out to her side now and fingers stretching to find something, anything, that could help hide her.

Their footsteps came closer, the clicking heels more distinct, the voices louder, and the light of the lantern brighter. It turned the air in front of her gray, and suddenly a large shape loomed in front of her.

Yes! She knew where she was now. A moment more and her arm brushed up against the wardrobe closet she'd seen earlier. Another moment and she had the door open. She crawled inside, careful not to bump anything or drop her boots. She tugged a garment down on top of her and silently pulled the door closed.

"I thought I heard something over here. You hear something, Bert? Bert? Bertrum! I said, did you hear anything?"

There was a shuffling sound outside the wardrobe.

"Thought I did. Thought I saw something moving over here."

"Cobwebs. Look. They're all over."

Bertrum grunted noncommittally. He lowered his voice to a whisper: "Need to find her and make sure she stays down here."

"Forever," the other man said.

Why? Kalantha continued to wonder. What have I done?

They were saying something else, but she could only make out a buzz. Her own breathing was too loud and it seemed to echo against the bottom of the wardrobe. She made sure the garment completely covered her and her boots, and she curled into a tight ball. She wasn't trembling any longer; she'd managed to calm herself.

Kalantha told herself that she'd been through worse . . . fighting against assassin-birds, fleeing from wolves, surviving in the wilderness. Two men searching for her under the palace? She could deal with this, too. They'd give up eventually, she thought, and she could wait them out. She was safe here, hidden at the bottom of a wardrobe closet. They wouldn't find her.

But she hadn't planned on waiting so long in the cramped space, listening for the click of their heels against the stone and their indecipherable words. And she hadn't planned on falling asleep. When she finally woke, she was at the same time rested and sore. Her legs and arms were stiff, and she carefully uncurled herself, not wanting to make any noise in case they were still out there.

Kalantha didn't know how much time had passed. But it was long enough that she was truly hungry. Her stomach growled as she pressed her ear to the door. Her legs cramped worse, and she finally stood, cringing when she disturbed other clothes hanging in the wardrobe. Something fell to the bottom with a *clunk*.

After another several minutes, she cracked the door open. There was no hint of gray from the men's lanterns, but she knew the space under the palace must be vast, and they could still be down here, just out of sight of her hiding place.

She sucked in a deep breath and climbed out of the wardrobe, then felt around behind her for her boots. Holding them in one hand, she felt about with her free hand until she found a wall. She tripped over something, a crate or a barrel she guessed, and minutes after that she knocked over a large piece of pottery that loudly shattered. She held her breath and pressed herself against what she guessed was a cabinet. If the men were down here, they would have heard the racket. She peered into the utter black, expecting to see the glow of a lantern, but seeing nothing.

"They gave up on me," she whispered. "Maybe thought I'd gotten out of here."

She had no way of knowing that they thoroughly searched for hours, and that they'd passed by the wardrobe more than once and with more men to help them. Bertrum even had his hand on the door latch, then was distracted by a dripping sound and pursued that. She couldn't know that indeed they had given up and assumed she'd found her way out and were now looking for her upstairs.

"Brrrr." The stone beneath her feet held the spring cold well. She'd been standing so long in one place that her feet, and now her legs, were chilled. She sat, sucking in her lower lip, when she bumped against the cabinet and made noise. She put on her boots and felt her belt, remembering that she'd left behind the pillowcase with the small journal in it. She wanted that journal, and she wanted Meven to read it. But she doubted she'd be able to find it in this complete darkness. At least she still had the journal pages in her pocket. She wished she hadn't dropped the pillowcase and hadn't set the cookies on the nightstand. Her stomach growled.

"Can't see anything." This must be what it is like to be blind. She'd seen a blind priest at the High Keep Temple a few years ago. He traveled with other visiting priests from Uland, and she found him a curiosity because he seemed to get around on his own quite well.

"I couldn't do what he did," she said. "I can't do it." She was frustrated and still nervous, and she was getting angry that she couldn't figure out her location. She slammed her fist against her hip. "Meven has to be looking for me so we can leave for Nasim-Guri." But he wouldn't know to look here. He probably doesn't even know "here" exists. "He's going to be angry that he had to wait for me."

She kept talking to herself, though softly in the event the men crept back down and were looking again and might hear her. A part of her hoped someone would come down, as she hated being alone in the dark.

She fell over a rolled-up carpet, and when she picked herself up she tripped over something else and scraped her arm against a piece of metal. She stayed on the floor, thinking and fuming, and then praying for a way out. She kept praying as she started to crawl again. She crawled in a spiral, for several minutes finding nothing but the cold stone floor, then finding a small table, stacked chairs, a barrel, a spiderweb that coated her face and got in her mouth. She spat and spat and felt the web dissolve on her tongue, leaving behind a horrid taste in her mouth and small crunchy pieces she feared were dead insects.

She didn't know how long she'd been crawling, but she started sweating and her arms and legs ached by the time she finally found a set of stairs. She climbed them slowing, feeling ahead for each step and expecting them to go straight up. The stairway that led to the hallway by the dining room and kitchen was straight. But these steps curved, though not as sharply as the ones she came down from the library.

Just how many secret stairs were in the palace?

10 · Running

I passed nearly a century in the land of the Fallen Favorites. In that time my most perplexing charge never rode me; he always ran at my side until his legs gave out. Then he would rest until he could run again. It was good for him that my form was not a particularly fast one. He was certain that endurance of the body was gained through adversity and demanding physical trials. I considered it fortunate that he was always running to something instead of running away. Had something been chasing him, no doubt he would have been caught. My charge's physical endurance had limits. His mind, particularly his imagination, however . . . now that was nigh limitless.

~Portly Carthusian, in his second chronicles to the Finest Court

These steps went somewhere other than to the hallway or the library. She didn't care where . . . she just wanted out of here. At the top she pressed her ear to the panel. She heard someone walking quickly; a moment more and two people passed by. When she didn't hear anyone else, she pushed against the panel, half expecting it not to open. But the catch slipped noiselessly, and the hidden door opened into a shadowy room filled with suits of plate mail, statues, and paintings. She blinked, then rubbed at her eyes. She couldn't see very well, everything in the room being shadowy and indistinct. At first she thought it was difficult to see because she'd been in the darkness for so long. But then her eyes adjusted and she spotted a window, and what little light came through it colored the sill orange.

The sun had nearly set! She'd been downstairs since late this morning! Six or seven hours had passed, maybe more. No wonder her stomach grumbled with hunger. And no doubt Meven would be furious that he'd had to wait on her this long!

She dashed from the room, brushing webs from her hair and shaking dirt off her tunic. She knew she must look a fright! She'd have to wash before they left, put on something clean and tuck away the beautiful pieces of jewelry. The hallway was lit by lanterns burning, and she immediately looked up to find the color of the wood trim where the ceiling met the wall. Gray . . . she tried to remember. Where did the gray trim lead? She didn't know, and she wasn't sure if she'd even been in this part of the palace before. Meven gave her a tour yesterday, but they didn't have time to see everything.

"Hello?" she risked. "Anyone here?"

No answer, but she hoped someone worked nearby, as she'd heard footsteps. She picked a direction and ran, finding the hallway long and opening into a sitting room and then a music room. Why did her brother need so many rooms? Around a corner she found a study. Around another corner was one of the smaller libraries Meven had showed her. At last something was familiar.

She knew where she was now, and one more turn down a wider hall put her heading toward the dining room and kitchen. She heard the clatter of pans and plates ahead and snippets of conversations about clothes and relatives. She glanced in the dining room as she passed it, but it was empty and the table was bare save for a few candles that burned. So they'd served the evening meal and had picked up already.

"Sara Anne?" Kalantha burst into the kitchen and with great relief spotted the portly cook.

"Gracious, Lady Kalantha! What happened to you?" Sara Anne gasped as she looked the girl over from top to bottom, eyes lingering on the pieces of jewelry that looked so out of place. "Where have you been? King Meven has been worrying terribly!"

"She's filthy," muttered an overly thin woman who scrubbed furiously at a pot. "Been rolling in the dirt somewhere like a peasant child. Heard she was wild."

Sara Anne hurried toward Kalantha, wiping her doughy hands on her apron. "Girl, you're a mess. And you're hurt." She pointed to Kalantha's arms, which were scratched and were showing the beginnings of bruises from her falls and scrapes. "King Meven was looking for you and—"

"My brother. Where is he? I've got to get cleaned up and ready. We're—"

Sara Anne shook her head. Strands of graying hair came loose from under her cap, and she thrust her fingers at them to poke them back under. "King Meven left with some soldiers for Nasim-Guri right after dinner. About an hour ago, I'd say."

"No!" Kalantha cried. "I was to go with him. He wanted me to go. He—"

"Looked for you, girl. He sent servants to looking, too. He was so terribly, terribly worried. Where were you?"

Had she been wrong about the men downstairs, misinterpreted their conversation about putting her in the family crypt? Killing her? Were they simply looking for her? Had she missed her opportunity to help Meven make peace with the King of Nasim-Guri by staying in the huge cellar?

"I'm supposed to go with him, Sara Anne. I packed clothes and . . . and you gave me cookies for the trip . . . and—"

"King Meven was in a bad way, Lady Kalantha, worried dreadfully sick that you couldn't be found. But he said he couldn't wait. He had something very important to attend to."

"Yes, stopping the war." Kalantha forced back a sob. "I need to help him."

"Girl, we didn't know where you were. He left with the soldiers and ordered his attendants to keep looking for you. Even sent someone to the stables, thinking you might be out there with your horse. I told him I'd seen you earlier, gave you cookies. I thought maybe you were going to give one of those cookies to that big horse of yours."

Kalantha shook her head and dragged her fingers through her tangled hair. "Oh, I never should have gone down there. Should've waited to eat the noon meal. Should've waited for Meven. Should've—"

"Calm down, Lady Kalantha. This is what you get for getting lost under the palace." Sara Anne put a hand on Kalantha's shoulder, the gesture tentative because of the webs that still clung to her tunic. "He'll be back as soon as he's done with his business. He said that when you were found we were to give you a thorough tour of the palace and arrange a better room for you. I suspect he'll give you an entire wing, seeing as how you're his sister and of royal blood."

Lost under the palace? How could Sara Anne know she'd gone down a secret stairway and was underground? Sara Anne had asked where she'd been, but Kalantha hadn't answered. Someone must have watched her go down the secret steps in the library and told Sara Anne! "I have to find Meven. I need to help him." Kalantha spun and started to head back down the hallway, but Sara Anne gripped her arm, nails digging in hurtfully and holding her in place.

She tugged Kalantha to her and looked down into her startled eyes. All traces of kindness were gone from Sara Anne's face. "I said, folks have been looking for you, girl." The words were heavy. "You're not running off, hear?"

Kalantha shook her head. "You don't understand. Meven needs my help, and—"

"And Silas and Bertrum will be pleased I've found you."

Bertrum! That was the name of one of the men downstairs.

Sara Anne pulled Kalantha toward the far end of the kitchen, where a door was cracked open to the outside.

"Bertrum?" Kalantha looked around the kitchen, trying to

find someone sympathetic to help her. They were all absorbed in their tasks, pointedly ignoring her and Sara Anne.

"Yes, Bertrum. He's been looking for you, girl. For hours. Missed dinner because of you. Put him in a bad mood."

"Who's Bertrum? One of Meven's attendants?"

"He's outside, still looking for you. On the grounds, now. Turning over every bush and rock." Sara Anne clicked her tongue against her teeth. "Yes, I suppose, Lady Kalantha, that Bertrum is one of King Meven's attendants. But he's a servant your brother assigned to Bishop DeNogaret."

Did the glimmer of something dark and amused flicker in Sara Anne's eyes? Kalantha's mouth dropped open and she rammed her heel down hard on the cook's arch. The surprised cook released her grip, and Kalantha ran back through the kitchen and down the hall. She fled past the dining room and the portraits of Bishop DeNogaret and the old men who must have been some relation to her. She glanced down one intersection and then the next, finding the right color of trim and the right pattern in the marble floor tile. She bolted past surprised servants she hadn't met and paused only to throw open a door and rush outside. She was near the south tower, and she looked up to see its beige stones tinted gold by the disappearing sun.

Her feet slapped over ground where soldiers had drilled this morning. It was bare of grass, though in places clumps of stubborn weeds persisted. Near a barracks she spotted three archers, bows at the ready and eyes trained on the palace roof. Another time she would have asked them what they were looking for, but now she let the question settle at the back of her mind. To her left were the infirmary tents, and two men were carrying a body on a plank out of the largest one.

Instantly, Kalantha didn't blame Meven for leaving without her. The war had to end now! She just had to catch up to him. Running past the smallest of the three infirmary tents, she cringed to hear the moans of a man in pain. A horrid, horrid thing, this war!

There was a shout, and first she looked to the tents and then over her shoulder, never slowing. Two men were coming out the same palace door she'd used. One was tall and dressed in blacks and grays and was limping a little, making her think it might be the Bertrum who had looked for her downstairs. She grabbed her side, which was aching from the exertion, and threw all her effort into running faster still. The royal stables were not far, and she needed to see Rue. Even lame, she knew he'd protect her from the men—he'd protected her from all manner of threats since she first met him a few years ago.

A groom was outside, walking one of Meven's prized norikers. Another was coming out of the stables carrying tack. She saw a third washing out feed buckets. She ran past all of them and through the stable's open door.

"Rue!" she hollered.

Behind her one of the grooms called: "Wait, girl!" likely not knowing her name.

"Rue!" She couldn't run in the stables, as there were buckets and rakes, coils of rope and mounds of hay. She hurried past the norikers and came even with Rue's stall. "Rue?"

A coal-black noriker with a thin white blaze nickered. Kalantha didn't know he spoke in the horse tongue, saying: *Gone. The punch is gone. Somehow gone.*

"Rue!" She pulled down the rope stretched across the stall's entrance and stepped inside. He was lame and he couldn't walk far, she knew. Maybe one of the grooms had moved him— there were two other stables on the grounds, though she remembered Meven telling her those were for the horses of knights and high-ranking soldiers. She quickly checked the rest of the stalls at the back, finding one other empty and no Rue.

She looked to the two jutlands, but one was absorbed in his feed pail and the other pawed at something in the hay.

The black noriker continued to nicker at her as she retraced her steps, looking at every horse as she passed. A groom stood in the doorway.

"Can I help you—"

"Kalantha," she supplied.

"You're King Meven's sister." He stood practically at attention.

"I'm looking for Rue. He's been moved to one of the other stables. Have you—"

The two men who'd run from the palace were closing in.

She wanted to catch up to Meven, and for that she'd need a fast, hardy horse. One of the norikers would more than do. None of them were saddled, but she'd never ridden Rue with a saddle or used any tack. Rue was special, and she might need a saddle with another horse. And by the time the groom got one of the fresh norikers saddled, or even led him out of the stable, Bertrum and the other man would be on her.

"Kalantha!" The one she thought was called Bertrum waved and limped faster. "Carson! Hold her! By order, she must be detained!"

By whose order? Kalantha wondered as she dodged the groom's hands and ran past the man washing buckets. She hurdled a bench and headed straight toward the southern gate.

"Stop her! Don't let her escape!"

Other men started hollering, the words smearing together into something unintelligible. There were four sentries at the gate, and they were watching her, puzzled, but waiting. As she neared the gate, two of them moved to block her way.

She veered away, her legs and lungs burning and her breath coming uneven and hot in her throat. Horrid thoughts swirled as she ran—what had she done to make the men chase her? Did they really want to kill her? Where was Rue? Which stables? Had the men done something to her magical horse?

A trellis for emerald ivy stretched against the wall. Only the brown stems from last year clung to it, the spring still too chilly for the plant to start. A glance over her shoulder showed she had a significant lead on the five men now chasing her. Behind them trailed two of the gate sentries—seven altogether. By the good gods, what had she done?

Her hands closed on the trellis rungs and she skittered up it as fast as she could, as the rungs snapped beneath her feet. At the top of the wall, she turned to look at them, pointing and yelling and closing. Then she leapt off the other side and rolled.

Kalantha cried out when pain shot up her right leg. It had been a drop of at least a dozen feet. She stood and cried again when she put weight on it. Was this how Rue felt being lame? Was she lame, too?

The palace sprawled separate from the city, and the wall around its grounds kept the townsfolk out. But the southern part of the wall was nearest Nadir proper, and Kalantha hobbled toward it, fixing her eyes on the tile roofs shining like embers in the setting sun. Nadir was the largest city in Galmier, and Kalantha had seen only a little of it. She didn't know what section she was heading for, but she prayed it had stables that hadn't closed for the day. She would use a piece of jewelry to pay for a horse, then she'd ride out of Nadir before the sentries stopped her. Then she'd use another piece of jewelry in a village to the south to buy clothes and food after she'd caught up to Meven.

She was terribly hungry, but she didn't want to stop for something to eat in Nadir. She needed to find Meven and his soldiers. She'd tell him about the small book in the pillowcase beneath the palace, about the pages in her pocket, and about Bertrum and the other men looking for her, about Sara Anne acting oddly, and about Rue missing. She'd make him read the pages in her pocket and help him stop the war, and then together they'd come back to Nadir. To the horrible city of Nadir! He'd put Bertrum and the others in their place, help her find Rue, and then she'd be safe.

"There she is!"

A shrill whistle cut through the air. Glancing behind her, she spotted two sentries climbing over the wall, one with a whistle in his mouth. They'd somehow got ahead of her other pursuers, and they leapt to the ground with far less effort than it had taken her. It was obvious neither one of them got hurt in the process. They'd catch her, she realized, as she was so tired and her leg slowed her. But she refused to make it easy on them. She wasn't about to simply give up.

Reaching the city just before they did, she darted between two old, leaning buildings. It wasn't the best neighborhood, as the buildings that loomed up on either side of her were made of wooden planks, all weathered and bowed, weeds growing up their edges. Fortunately the shadows were thick here, and she pressed herself against the side of one building and hobbled along it until she reached a street. She took it, not caring where it went—only that it would be away from the sentries.

Then she took an alley off it, then another street, limping more pronouncedly now. The buildings were close together here, and the smells of the city were strong. People cooked dinner, fish and stew and who knew what else, all melting together and seemingly revolting. The scent of animal dung wafted up from the road, as no one here apparently cleaned up after the horses and stray dogs. She could smell sweat, too, her own, and the rankness that clung to her clothes. Her stomach roiled from all the odors.

She heard a dog barking, the whistle of the sentries, children laughing, men yelling obscenities. She leaned against a stack of crates to catch her breath and rest her leg, then she spotted another alley and slowly made for it. She'd stay out of sight for just a little while, like she had beneath the palace.

Then she'd find a stable—with all the horse dung in the street there had to be a stable nearby. She'd get out of the city and find Meven.

"Lookit here, Hallory. Look at the dirty girl."

Kalantha froze as a rag-draped woman stepped out from the shadows of a boarding house.

11 · Casualties of War

A country without peace is akin to an eagle without wings—it will never achieve its lofty reason for being, and it will never climb to the heights the good powers deemed it to reach.

~*Gray Hawthorn, Finest Court Patriarch*

Knight Commander Beldar Javal led a company of twenty soldiers south along a swollen branch of the Sprawling River. The hours he'd spent riding had done nothing to quench his ire. He'd been silent when King Meven announced the war's end and when the peace declarations were signed and affixed with the royal seal. He'd stood at attention when a dozen such declarations were carefully rolled and tied with ribbons, blue to match King Meven's colors, and were placed in a pack resting behind him on the rump of his horse. He'd nodded when the King told him to distribute eight to the villages along the way, the last in Cobston before he crossed the border of Nasim-Guri, and to give the remaining four to knights stationed with soldiers there. Knight Commanders Bradmark and Marno had been given similar orders, but from their words Javal could tell they were taking this turn of events much better.

As the youngest of King Meven's commanders, Javal had worked long and hard to gain his position. The son of a nobleman who owned a considerable stretch of land between the river and the Galmier Mountains, he stood to gain his own ground in Nasim-Guri when the last of its army was crushed. He was also the youngest of four brothers, and therefore he would gain little inheritance when his father died. No victory in war . . . no land in his future. His anger grew the farther south he rode. Javal needed the war.

He'd spoken little to his men, and then only to give them an occasional order and to give them permission to stop and water their horses and relieve themselves. And he'd shared with none of them his plan—to not pass out the declarations to the forces in Nasim-Guri. Oh, he intended to follow his orders regarding letting the Galmier villagers know of King Meven's plan for peace. But he'd let the fighting go on across the border—they were so very close to winning. If he did nothing to stop the soldiers, victory might be had before King Meven could do anything about it.

There could be consequences if King Meven discovered his insolence, and he intended to mull over all the ramifications on this journey. But his dreams of property and power were too ambitious to give up just because a boy on the throne had changed his mind about a war.

The evening sky was filled with stars, and when Javal cast his head back and trusted his horse to follow the trail he could make out several constellations. There was a thin slice of moon, and it helped light the way. He let the breeze play across his face; it cooled him, but it did nothing to quench his fiery temper. He listened to the night sounds, thinking they might soothe him: the throaty *whoooot* of an owl perched in a tall elm; the scratching of small animals hidden by the tall grass along the riverbank; the splash of a fish in the water; and crickets chirping endlessly. Behind him a soldier's horse made a wuffling sound, and at the far edge of his hearing came the howl of a wolf or wild dog.

He thought about the noblemen of Nasim-Guri, and whether they had young and beautiful daughters. He would need a wife when he gained his land, and one from a rich family would provide needed wealth to aid in the construction of a manor house and the hiring of servants. The richer the woman, the less comely she would need to be. He didn't intend to spend much time at home anyway, as a noble knight would have matters to attend to elsewhere—especially if he wanted to expand his holdings and influence.

Javal didn't notice the crickets stop chirping, or that the small animals along the bank fell silent. He'd closed his eyes and didn't see the moon disappear and the stars wink out as a curtain of black cut across the sky. The darkness was absolute when one of the soldiers cried out.

Javal's eyes snapped open and registered nothing but blackness. The pleasant scents of the river and the trees were instantly replaced with a strong mustiness that threatened to choke him. The soft evening sounds had been replaced by nervous whinnies from the horses, questions from the soldiers, and a thunderous noise he couldn't at first place.

"Sir! We are attacked!"

Javal's hand flew to the pommel of his sword, gripping it tight and pulling the blade free.

Wings! The deafening noise was the flapping of hundreds of wings.

"Birds, Commander! We are—" The rest of the soldier's words were drowned out by the caws of dozens upon dozens of crows.

"Death comes!" cried a blackbird that dove toward Javal. "Death comes for you!"

There were other cries in the descending sea of black: "Sweet death; make them bleed; we slay for Ninéon." Within moments the falcon's name became a chant that sounded like the buzz of a locust swarm.

A few of the soldiers threw their hands over their ears. Others swung their swords wildly into the blackness. The soldier nearest Javal fell from his horse, which spooked and galloped down the bank and across the river. A cloud of blackbirds enveloped the fallen man and began tearing at him.

Javal heard the soldier scream, and he leapt off his horse. He cursed when the horse reared back and plunged through the blackness and down the trail they'd been following.

"Evil beast!" Javal called to it. "Vile birds!" His sword sliced through a large crow and cut down several smaller blackbirds. He remembered hearing King Meven speak once about assassin-birds, but he hadn't believed the tale—it had been too preposterous and spoken by a boy-king Javal had little regard for.

But now the tale was all too real, and Javal swung like a madman, cutting through birds and batting them away with the flat of his blade. Blood rained down on his face, and he closed his eyes. All he could see was the unending black, so his eyes served him not at all. He felt claws and beaks digging at the exposed skin of his neck and hands, and he whirled and continued slashing.

He heard the wheeze of one of his soldiers, and knew that the man was dying. A scream added to the cacophony.

"Death comes! For Ninéon we slay! For Ninéon the war continues!"

"Who is Ninéon?" Javal cried.

"Ninéon, Ninéon, Ninéon," the birds chanted.

"Face me, Ninéon!" Javal continued his maddened swordplay.

There was another scream, and another. One soldier hollered for direction and was answered by one of his fellows: "Just kill them!"

"Kill the men slowly!" The voice was clear and mellifluous, and Javal instinctively knew it came from whomever—or whatever—Ninéon was. "Savor the battle!"

The pace slowed all around Javal, and he risked opening his eyes again. There was still the blackness, but there were bands of gray intruding, gaps in their wings, he guessed. He heard a loud *thump,* and knew a horse had fallen. Hoofbeats and splashes told him other horses were getting away across the river.

"Call to me!" Javal yelled. He waited heartbeats before he repeated the order.

"Andlow!" a soldier answered.

"Wildenson!"

"Kent!"

Three. Javal's heart raced. Only three soldiers remaining. "Fight toward the river!" He hoped the birds were afraid of the water and would fly away. "Follow me!"

But how could they follow him? he realized. A cocoon of black again surrounded him. Still, he pushed through it, his free hand held up defensively, his fingers being painfully shredded by the birds. One speared his palm and he screamed. It was echoed by the cry of another soldier.

"Call to me!" Javal's voice had lost some of its strength.

"Kent!"

"Andlow!"

"Death comes! Death comes!"

"Kill them slowly! For Ninéon!"

Javal was certain he was making headway toward the river, as the ground was sloping a little, and the grass was getting higher around his legs.

"Call to me!"

"Kent!"

Javal was sucking in great gulps of air. The mustiness of the bird feathers was filling his mouth. He fought to keep from gagging and to stay on his feet when a swarm of birds struck him in the back.

"Death comes!"

"Call to me," Javal croaked. He fought forward a dozen more steps, then slipped on the grass at the river's edge. "Call to me! Sound out!"

There was no answer this time.

He tried to stand, but the birds were all around him, a feathery prison he couldn't escape. He felt one bite through a finger, and his scream was lost in the flapping of their wings. His sword fell when more attacked that hand. Then they went for his face.

Ninéon watched the battle from her perch in a tall elm. She was drunk on the carnage and disappointed her flock hadn't drawn out the confrontation so she could better savor the men's terror. When it was over she dove toward the trail and landed on the carcass of one of the soldiers. She watched the crows feast and the blackbirds circle overhead.

Ninéon had no way of knowing that Commander Javal wanted what she did—for the war to continue. She only knew that she had stopped one of King Meven's peace patrols, and because of that she was pleased.

"We fly!" she called to her flock when she believed they were suitably sated. "There are two more knight commanders to find and stop. They must not spread the boy-king's decree."

"The war continues!" a large crow returned. "For Ninéon the war continues!"

"Yes, the blessed war continues," Ninéon said. Then she pushed off the corpse and struck out to the east, the cloud of black following her.

12 · Ropes and Dashed Hopes

Only two years did I shepherd an aging priest from the great city of Dolour. He lived and worked among the poorest of the Fallen Favorites, and he died from the hardness of his life. He was the wisest of all the charges I guided through the decades, and I often looked at Paard-Peran through his eyes. He believed that those whom kings consider wretched and insignificant are the closest to the good powers of the world. Those sad-seeming people know how to harvest happiness from grief.

~Twist-Tail Glimmercoat, in her chronicles to the Finest Court

Gallant-Stallion willed himself to return to Paard-Peran. The long sweet grass and delicate wildflowers that teased his shanks faded away. The air that carried the scents of the other Finest and the nearby river were replaced by the musty odors of the royal stables.

The jutlands immediately started nickering.

The punch is not here, then here. How?

Gallant-Stallion thought they hadn't been paying attention when he left.

Gone and back with no rider. How?

Yes, how is the punch here?

He didn't answer them until their questions persisted. *I left through the back of my stall,* he finally said. *Where the boards do not meet tightly.* He wasn't used to lying, and so he wasn't very good at it. Still, it managed to satisfy them.

The boards are strong in our stall, and we cannot break them. The larger of the jutlands seemed to grow sad because of that. *We do not leave this place often enough. Not enough grass beneath our hooves.* He moved to the edge of his stall and looked forlornly down the aisle that led to the door.

A small sparrow with a red-brown crown flew from behind Gallant-Stallion and to a beam above one of King Meven's prized norikers. Neither the Finest nor the horses paid it any attention. It chirped musically and settled in its nest.

How do you leave when you are lame? The larger jutland started pawing at something in the hay. *Lame, you cannot walk. But you walk. Curious.*

My leg feels well, Gallant-Stallion returned. He did not appreciate the jutlands' curiosity, and he wanted them to stop asking questions. *The* . . . He searched for a term they would understand. . . . *medicine of bad smells healed my leg. The lameness is gone.*

The jutlands tossed their heads and whinnied their approval. *A good man cared for you, punch.*

Gallant-Stallion decided to question them now. *The good man . . . did he come back while I was away?* That wasn't what he really wanted to know, but he started with it.

The jutlands said no.

Did other people come? The girl with the green eyes? Did I miss her?

Only the good man who feeds us came tonight. He did not leave food for you. Our food is gone.

No food for you tonight, the larger jutland said. *You must back out of your stall by the weak boards and feed on the grass.*

Gallant-Stallion wuffled that he wasn't hungry. He eased back in the shadows intending to rest until the morning, when he was certain Kalantha would come by. But a noriker changed his plans.

Ugly punch, your girl was here, the noriker said. *After the food came, she was here.*

Ah, yes, the smaller jutland said. *I remember now that a girl looked for you. Did not see the color of her eyes. I was eating and waiting to be brushed.*

Eating, the other jutland echoed. *Eating is important to you.*

More important than the girl, it is.

Gallant-Stallion grabbed the rope in his teeth and tugged it away from his stall's entrance. He caught the wide-eyed expression of the jutlands, and ignored their questions. The noriker was a few yards away, eyes closed and resting.

Your girl was as nervous as a foal in its first storm, another noriker said. *Running like a rabbit and breathing quickly like a mouse. She was dirty and rude, not stopping to give us sugar or brush us. I think she was looking for you. How were you not here?*

You did not pass by us, punch, a third noriker said.

The punch did not leave. This came from the horse in the stall nearest the door. *I would have seen him leave, a big ugly horse like that. The girl was a frightened foal, she did not see the ugly punch at the back of the stable. She did not look hard enough. Maybe she was looking for a different horse.*

Gallant-Stallion stamped his hoof, wanting to silence them.

She was fast, said the noriker directly under the sparrow's nest. *In a hurry, like a frightened fox.*

How long ago? Gallant-Stallion's tone was demanding.

How long what? a noriker mare posed.

The Finest let out an exasperated snort. *How long ago was the girl looking for me?*

Not long.

Long.

Before food.

No, after food.

Yes, after food, after full.

Gallant-Stallion pushed the stable door open and trotted out onto the lawn. He didn't know how much time had passed in the Finest Court. Time passed differently there. Here, it was early evening, and the twilight sky had taken on a purple cast. The first stars winked into view.

The girl was in a hurry. The girl was terribly, terribly frightened.

Gallant-Stallion looked down and saw a mouse at the edge of a mound of hay outside the stables.

I understand fear, big horse. The girl ran into the horse-house, then ran out.

A girl with red-brown hair and green eyes? Gallant-Stallion asked him.

The mouse raised up on its hind legs, whiskers twitching and black eyes wide. *Brown boots, dirty legs, smelly. I did not see her eyes or hair. Too high for me to look. I worried that she would step on me as she ran.*

Gallant-Stallion doubted Kalantha could be dirty and smelling foul—not since she was staying in the palace. There were other young women and men on the palace grounds. Some other girl, then, had come to the stable.

The mouse pawed at the air to get the Finest's attention. *She called and called a pretty word. Roooooo.*

Gallant-Stallion whinnied in concern for his charge.

Men chased her.

Where, mouse?

Many men, pound, pound, pound with their feet.

Where did they chase her, good mouse?

Away. They went away where I could not see. One so small as I and so close to the ground cannot see far.

Over the wall, she went. This came from a brown and white

speckled hunting dog tied on a long lead to a post by the stables. *The wall far away by the climbing vines. Over she went. I saw. She ran fast.*

To the south, Gallant-Stallion guessed. *Show me where she went, dog.*

Stump. I am Stump.

Gallant-Stallion noticed that's what the dog had for a tail, as if someone had whacked it off to a nub. It must have hurt. *Show me, Stump.* Gallant-Stallion reared up then came down hard, his front hooves slicing through the lead and freeing the dog. *Please, please, Stump. It is very important to me.*

Bored here, the dog said. *And I am full.* He made an exaggerated stretching motion, rump in the air and front paws reaching toward the post. He yawned and shook his head, ears flapping. *I will show you, big horse. A horse never talked to me before. I will show you, and then I will sleep after they beat me for being bad because I am loose.*

Help me find the girl, Gallant-Stallion repeated. *Now, please!*

Follow me, big pushy horse.

The dog loped across the grass at an easy pace that annoyed the Finest. He wanted the dog to hurry, yet he was careful not to make another demand. He was unfamiliar with the dog and worried he might anger it.

I can smell her, the dog continued. *It is not a good smell. Good that it is bad, I can follow it with ease.*

The Finest wondered what had happened to Kalantha that would make her flee the palace. There was no sign of the black birds, and he'd heard from the norikers that archers were shooting birds on the infirmary tent and stable roof. And what had she gotten into that would make her stink? He would ask her when they were reunited. He told himself there was no doubt that they would find each other.

Steadfast, I need to find my charge. I was a fool to tarry so long with the Finest Court. Gallant-Stallion trotted after the dog, at the same time searching for the spirit of his mentor. All trace of his lameness was gone. He trotted past a groom carrying a saddle, so lost in thought he paid no heed to the loose dog and horse. Then they went past a quartet of soldiers walking toward their barracks. There were sentries stationed at the southern gate, but they didn't stand in the pair's way. Stump and Gallant-Stallion sprinted past them and down the road that led from the palace to the city.

The dog's nose brushed the ground, as he turned immediately to the south and paralleled the palace wall. He searched for where the girl went over and mumbled about all the smells he had to sort through. Gallant-Stallion was about ready to give up when the dog stiffened and raised his right front leg, as if he were pointing to a rabbit an archer might target.

The girl who smells bad came down here, Stump said, though Gallant-Stallion figured as much from the dog's posture. *Fell down here.* The dog angled away from the wall and headed toward the city proper. Gallant-Stallion saw candles and lanterns burning in the windows of homes and in the upper floors of buildings that likely served as businesses.

Two men follow her, big horse. She must have been bad. They beat me when they call me bad. They will beat her. They will call me bad for breaking the leash. They will beat me when I go home. I will hurt because of you, big punch of a horse.

Gallant-Stallion didn't reply.

The dog stopped near the edge of a squat building made of stones mudded together. Gallant-Stallion fancied that it looked a bit like a turtle, round and with a dome roof. It was in the best repair of all those in the neighborhood. The other homes were made of wood planks, weathered and uneven, only some of them painted.

Gallant-Stallion pawed nervously at the road, but said nothing. Steadfast had tried to teach him patience, and he employed as much of it as he possessed.

A moment more and the dog let out an unsettling baying sound, then padded down a street that narrowed and went from dirt to cobblestones. The stones were smooth from the decades of travel across them. The street was lined with buildings so close together no more than a man's hand could fit between them. Pans hung from hooks on a wall outside of one, the seller only starting to put them away. So it was a business district Kalantha had ventured into, Gallant-Stallion decided. From the building on the opposite side he picked up an unusual combination of odors: garlic and cinnamon and a smoky scent he guessed was meat. Refuse was strewn along the sides of the buildings, and he could see where chamber pots had been emptied and not cleaned up.

So it wasn't the best of neighborhoods she'd chosen, Gallant-Stallion decided. But if she had run from men, she would not have had time to be selective. The dog continued down the street, pausing again when he caught sight of a haggard-looking trio arguing which of them would enter a tavern first. When all three squeezed through the doorframe, the dog continued and turned down an alley. Stump moved more slowly here, and the Finest was certain the dog found it difficult to pick through all the smells. There were dead birds, rotten heads of cabbage, clothes that were too raggedy to wear, crates filled with things he had no desire to look inside.

Bad place for someone to be, the dog mused. Its nose was to the dirt. *Bad, bad, bad. Blood from fights, I smell. Things here smell worse than the girl, worse than anything. I should go home, get beaten for being bad, and go to sleep.*

I will not let anyone hurt you, Stump. Though the Finest wasn't sure he could keep that promise, he certainly intended to try.

Stump took little persuading, finding the city . . . *interesting,* he said. Smells he hadn't known existed waited to be discovered. Halfway down the next alley, he found something interesting to roll in. When an offensive green-black smear coated his right hind leg, he was off again on Kalantha's trail.

The next street grew even narrower; a man standing in the center would be able to touch the buildings on either side. It was growing darker and the shadows were thick here, making the Finest nervous. This wasn't a place for a girl like Kalantha. Candlelight shone out of a few windows, but it wasn't enough to reach into the small gaps between buildings. The night could hide assassin-birds and ill-tempered people. The Finest studied overhangs and listened carefully, hearing only the *clop-clop* of his hooves against the hard-packed ground and the sniffing and snorting of the dog.

This, too, was a merchant district, though there were residences in the mix. Nails on the outer walls hinted that people displayed their wares openly during the day. The doorways were rounded at the top, as were arches that linked rooming houses. Latticework and intricate carvings above windows suggested that the people who lived here were originally from other countries.

Under other circumstances, Gallant-Stallion might have found the neighborhood interesting and worth tarrying in. Now he only wanted to be through it and with Kalantha. He'd always prided himself on his strong form . . . even though other creatures called him an ugly punch. He was too big to enter the buildings and search for Kalantha; he was severely limited by this form he cherished. He could only look in windows and listen for her voice. There were conversations, but none of the voices were familiar, and the topics revolved around work and being poor.

Is she near? The Finest hadn't talked to Stump for several minutes, not wanting to interrupt him.

Close, very close, Stump answered. *Her very bad smell is stronger here. She rolled in something interesting to smell so. I would like to roll in something this interesting, too.*

The Finest wasn't sure how the dog could smell Kalantha after he stunk so bad from rolling in whatever it was. Kalantha could not smell worse than that.

Close, big horse! There was excitement in the dog's voice, and his stumpy tail started wagging.

They passed through an intersection. The light was better here, with a gap between buildings letting the starlight filter down.

So very, very close! The dog took off running, and Gallant-Stallion galloped after him.

Stump cut down another alley without pause this time and started baying joyfully.

Gallant-Stallion had trouble negotiating the turn, but only fell back a few yards. It was a narrow alley, and he had to vault over crates that had toppled. His keen senses let him pick through most of the shadows and keep the dog in sight.

Close, big horse! I will find your girl! Much softer, the dog growled: *And then I will go home to be beaten.*

One more turn, and the street widened just a little. The buildings here looked like a strong wind could turn them into slivers. Gallant-Stallion lengthened his stride, then was jerked back when a rope dropped around his neck, and then another and another. Three strong men started pulling him. He reared back in anger and flailed out with his hooves, as the men came out of the gaps between buildings.

They were tattered men with skin darkened by dirt. Their grins were crooked, and one man had no teeth. But their eyes shone in the starlight, and they were strong.

"Holfers will be pleased we've caught such a big, big horse!" one of the men shouted.

"Color of mud, he's not worth much. Short legs," offered a squat man with upper arms the size of summer melons. "Get some coins, though. For the dog, too."

Gallant-Stallion saw that a fourth man, this one little more than a boy, had snared Stump and looped a rope tight around the dog's neck. He was pulling the dog farther down the street, which is where the men were pulling the Finest.

Gallant-Stallion knew he could break free from the men, but probably not without hurting them, and he wouldn't have that. These were poor men who'd captured a stray horse. To injure them would be heinous. It was bad enough Gallant-Stallion had injured and killed innocent hungry wolves in the forest southwest of this city. Bad enough that he had battered Bishop DeNogaret, even though the man was vile and was trying to hurt Kalantha.

No, the Finest decided he would let the men put him and Stump in a pen, then he would break out and resume the search for Kalantha. Besides, it looked like the men wanted to go in the same direction Stump had been searching. After he and the dog were free, they would find his charge.

But they didn't put Gallant-Stallion in a pen. They tugged him into a huge decrepit-looking barn and forced him into a stall, where a man the Finest didn't see in time wrapped chains around his back legs. It was difficult to see, as only one lantern was burning. But the Finest had keen senses and stared through the shadows until he could make out other creatures on the far side of the barn. More horses, a goat, a pony, and a couple of big shaggy dogs tied to a post.

"Strong horse, this one is," the man with melon-arms said. "You'll need the chains or he'll break the stall down. Break the whole barn down from the looks of the muscles in his legs." He laughed and slapped Gallant-Stallion on the side. "Maybe we can get a pretty coin for you. Pull a lot, I'll bet you could."

They threw Stump in a wire cage that was little bigger than he was.

The hunting dog looked hopelessly at the Finest.

Worse than a beating, Stump said. *I wish I had never helped you, big horse.*

13 · Conflict with Interests

Most of the creatures on Paard-Peran are simple beasts . . . and therein they are beautiful. They care about eating and sleeping, running for joy, drinking from cool streams, and finding companionship with others of their kind. They do not worry about tomorrow, and they do not dwell on the past. Tomorrow and yesterday are unknown concepts. Today . . . today is what they live for. Perhaps the Fallen Favorites should follow the example of simple beasts.

~*Fencebiter Whitemane, in her last observations to the Finest Court*

Meven was aware of the soldiers around him, and that they were talking. But he paid no attention to their conversations, nor could he tell which men were in front of him and which behind. He was only vaguely connected to everything—feeling the cool breeze that fluttered the sleeves of his tunic and stirred the mane of his horse so that the hairs brushed against the backs of his hands and tickled. He heard birds singing, jays from the sound of them, and nearby came the rush of water from a fast-moving stream. He registered everything, not taking time to enjoy any of the sensations—which he considered interesting but unimportant—and relegated all of them to a corner of his mind.

The clopping of the horses' hooves sounded rhythmic and lulling, and this he concentrated on as his conflicting thoughts whirled.

He recalled his early days at the High Keep Temple. His

parents recently dead, his uncle the King too busy to take him and Kalantha in, Bishop DeNogaret stepped in and was named his guardian. The Bishop became like a father to Meven. Indeed, it was so easy to picture that kindly face and imagine the feel of those hands on his shoulders. Only good memories lingered of the days at High Keep. And only good images of Bishop DeNogaret flitted before him.

"Why couldn't I still be there, at High Keep?" He spoke the words so softly they didn't carry to his companions. "Why couldn't things be like they were?"

Nothing had worried him at the High Keep Temple. Meven followed a schedule each day with little variation: prayers, breakfast, studies, work, prayers, dinner, and the evening to himself before the end-of-day prayers. He embraced the blessedly simple existence.

Everything planned for him, Meven had few decisions to make. Happiness never eluded him at the High Keep Temple, and when he was there, he had no real desire to be anywhere else. It wasn't an easy existence, as the bed was not so comfortable as what he had in the palace. The food was simple fare, though filling—and there were special meals on religious holidays and when important people came to visit. The chores were just strenuous enough to make him work up an appetite. The religious, studious, simple life pleased him.

"Why did things have to change?"

He remembered being excited about traveling with his cousin Edan. His cousin was to be married to the princess in Duriam. He remembered drinking everything in, and not minding the mud and the wind along the trail. Too, he recalled with vivid intensity the attack of the assassin-birds, his and Kalantha's escape, and later discovering Edan's shredded body. He recalled taking Edan's ring and putting it on his own finger, as he became the prince of Galmier that horrid day.

And it wasn't long after that he became King.

The simple, religious, studious life had been ripped from him.

At first being the Prince of Galmier, and then the King, had been thrilling. He relished the responsibility thrust on him. Never before had he been responsible for anything beyond himself. And the authority! Never before had he had power over anything or anyone. Each day presented new challenges and opportunities. Above all of that, Meven admitted that he enjoyed the fine clothes and food and being waited on by so many servants he couldn't recall all of their names.

But he could not have managed all the responsibility without Bishop DeNogaret.

As always, the elderly priest was at Meven's side to guide him and help him through difficult decisions—to tell him what to do. Bishop DeNogaret was the true power in Galmier, Meven realized. The priest didn't physically wear the crown, but he might as well have.

The Bishop selected which nobles and merchant houses Meven met with, wrote decrees for Meven to sign, and oversaw the day-to-day operations at the palace by assigning tasks to various people. Meven had nothing of real consequence to deal with, except for the war. And then even that wasn't under his control.

"Not my idea," he whispered. "Not really, was it?" Wasn't it Bishop DeNogaret who suggested Meven increase his holdings by sending soldiers into Nasim-Guri? Meven tried to recall the conversations about the matter, but the clearest recollections were of the great map board with all the equisitely painted miniature soldiers on it. He moved them around like it was some great game.

But it wasn't a game. The men dying in the tents on the palace grounds proved that. And the Bishop, tucked away in a bed in a high tower room, would not get any of the dying soldiers' blood on his age-spotted hands.

It had been the Bishop behind all of it, planning the war and ordering men trained, suggesting Meven exercise with the men and learn how to properly use a sword. The Bishop plotted the army's moves and sent spies into Nasim-Guri. The Bishop met with landowners and raised coin to pay for the war.

But all the while Meven went along with it, dreaming about an even bigger kingdom that he couldn't manage on his own. Bishop DeNogaret vowed to help him, though. Together, they would make Galmier the largest and most powerful country in all of Paard-Peran.

So blind, Meven thought. How could I possibly have wanted this war? Why did I want a bigger kingdom? Oh, it might all have been Bishop DeNogaret's idea, but I went along with it. I even liked the notion of men fighting! I just hadn't thought about the blood and the deaths and the grieving parents and wives left behind.

"I was a fool."

Meven closed his eyes and bowed his head, the wind whipping the horse's mane against his face now. He prayed for the Bishop to get well, as the man had been like a father to him, had taught him and advised him. The Bishop hadn't truly forced him to start the war. Encouraged, yes. Suggested strongly. Nudged. But the Bishop had forced nothing on him. He prayed for Kalantha, and lastly he prayed for himself . . . that if he could end this war and return to Galmier, he might find someone else to advise him.

Meven knew the burden of kingship was beyond him.

14 · City Streets

The great Sprawling River cuts through the hearts of Galmier and Nasim-Guri. I count it the most impressive feature in Paard-Peran. The current is strong, like the people who live along its banks. It is wild and beautiful like the animals who come to drink. And it is capricious like nature should be—raging at times and flooding, slow and rambling and sometimes smooth like a mirror. I have watched it sweep away villages, provide a bountiful harvest, and cool children in the height of the summer. I am grateful my charge is a holy man who meanders with the river. I am grateful my Fallen Favorite does not care for cities. I have heard they are dirty and ugly, and the magnificent Sprawling River refuses to wend its way into any of them.

~*One White Stocking, shepherd to Alan Fachett, river monk*

Kalantha instantly hated this city. She hadn't liked it before, particularly the poor sections with the stench and the depression and the utter hopelessness that swelled on some of the most rundown corners. But now she truly hated it, looking at the woman and the young man, all raggedy and dirty and staring at her. The shadows were getting longer, and she knew the criminal element flourished in the dark . . . at least so she'd heard from the priests at the High Keep Temple where she'd lived a few years ago, and so she'd heard from her brother and some of the servants in the palace. Common sense told her that, too.

"We got us a lost girl, Hallory." The woman made a sound that was not quite a cackle, then she rubbed her double chin and pulled at the wobbly flesh. "Doesn't belong to this neighborhood, that's for certain. Look at all the sparkles on her, Hallory. A fancy little girl."

Kalantha's fingers flew to her neck. She'd forgotten about all the jewelry she'd put on before she discovered the secret stairway beneath the palace. Of course she would stand out here.

"Mama, she didn't come from nowhere near this neighborhood." The young man shuffled toward Kalantha, and she turned to flee. "So she's lost, Mama, like you say. Maybe we need to help her."

Kalantha froze at the word "help," faced the raggedy pair, and took a good look at them. Their faces didn't seem to hold secrets or malice, and kindness flickered in the doughy woman's eyes. Instead of running away, she limped toward Hallory.

"I need to find a stable, sir."

"Sir, ha! That's something nobody's called me before. What would you want with a dirty animal-place like that, girl?" The young man scratched his head, and Kalantha noticed that his hair hadn't been combed in a long time and probably served as the home for an assortment of bugs. He looked over his shoulder to the woman. "Well, Mama? I don't never pay attention to horses or such. A stable? Is there one around here?"

"I need to buy a horse," Kalantha explained.

The woman waddled closer, stopping to keep a respectful distance between her and Kalantha. She cleared her throat and spat a gob of phlegm.

Kalantha could smell the woman even from a couple of yards away. The pungent odor made her eyes water and made her wonder if the woman hadn't bathed in years. And over that the woman had applied some sort of too-sweet cologne that added to the olfactory misery. Kalantha realized she'd smelled nothing pleasant since venturing below the palace: her dead ancestors rotting in the family crypt; the stench of herself from crawling on the floor and tangling with old cobwebs; the redolent odors of the poor neighborhood; and now this woman who clogged her senses.

"Child, there's a stable in the neighborhood, not terribly far from here. Though I don't know if they sell horses or if they just keep horses for the few folks around here who can afford to rent stalls. They might sell you one, though, for one of those shiny sparklies. Sell you an old horse." She quickly rattled off directions, repeating them to make certain Kalantha understood, and gesturing toward a steeple that rose above the rest of the buildings, looking dark turquoise in the failing light. "These streets aren't the safest. Child, I could send Hallory with you if you'd like. He'd look out for you, and—"

Kalantha shook her head. "Thank you, good woman. Thank you, Hallory. But I can find my way now." She offered them a smile and hurried down the alley as fast as her sore leg would move, glancing once over her shoulder and seeing that the woman and the young man had disappeared.

She was angry with herself, thinking that they'd meant her harm just because of the way they were dressed and because she was in a poor quarter of the city. It's what's on the inside of the person, the quality of his or her heart, not what's on the outside, she scolded. "Look beneath the surface. That's what Morgan taught me." She wondered what made her think of Morgan now, the gardener at the High Keep Temple. He was old when she left . . . did he still live?

She turned right at the intersection and tried to walk quickly, fearing the stables might close soon—if they hadn't already. People milled around in this block, looking not quite so scruffy as the woman and her son, but with so much dirt on their faces and hands she suspected it would never wash off. They watched her as she passed by, and she could still feel their eyes on her back and wondered what they were thinking.

At the next corner she saw a dozen boys playing a game of roll ball in the street. They'd outlined goals with sticks, and a gangly youth with torn trousers madly kicked a pig bladder— filled with peas, she suspected—toward her. She stepped up into the doorway of a closed butcher shop to keep out of the way. She thought it a vicious game, and had watched it played once in a village near the High Keep Temple. The participants were adults then, and one man had been carted off the playing field with a broken leg. The boys seemed to be just as rough, judging by the scraped knees and bloodied cheeks. When someone on the opposing team stole the ball, she hobbled past the intersection, curious how they could be so happy living and playing in such squalor. There were two girls observing the game, sitting on crates for safety. The smallest shouted suggestions and held a small basket filled with fabric scraps and thread spools. Despite the failing light, the older one mended a man's shirt. She had more clothes folded next to her—either already finished or waiting to be tended to.

The smile disappeared. Even male children had more freedom than girls. Indeed, Kalantha realized that except for the doughy woman who gave her directions, it was only men she'd seen out on the street—and most of them were going to taverns. Even in the poor quarter men could revel and boys could play while the women no doubt were home working and taking care of the babies.

Kalantha would talk to Meven about this, too, when she bought a horse and caught up to him. As King of Galmier, he could do something about the situation and give women a better lot. Oh, he couldn't wave his hand and turn the poor district into a gleaming, prosperous one—at least not immediately. It wasn't within his power to cure all of Nadir's woes. But he could work to improve things, and he could walk through this neighborhood with her and see the unfortunate living conditions. She thought about the women working in the palace laundry. It wasn't right that women were relegated to the worst jobs. Then she thought about a woman who ran a bakery in the village of Stilton, inheriting the business when her husband died—would that women all over could have such stature. Would that the girl mending shirts could be playing roll ball, and one of the boys take her place with the needle and thread. Kalantha knew she was blessed to have royal blood, and therefore more choices.

She put on a petulant expression as she struggled to pick up her pace and leave all the children behind.

Yes, she would talk to Meven about all of this.

At the next intersection three men huddled on the corner, breaking their conversation to stare at Kalantha, one of them pointing. She instantly wished she had asked Hallory to accompany her. Then she wondered if she should return to the palace and wait for Meven to come back from Nasim-Guri. Her leg ached terribly. Was she being foolish to try to catch up to him . . . she might not be able to find him . . . might take the wrong road out of Nadir . . . might get lost in the poor quarter before night settled in . . .

"Horrid place." She hated this neighborhood, and this city that smelled awful and made her feel suspicious of people because they were dirty and poor . . . made her so suspicious of everyone. She told herself that she shouldn't fear the people on these streets, and she was just as safe here as in the palace— safer, as someone who looked for her in the cellar clearly meant her harm. She couldn't trust people in the palace, ought to instead trust the people here—ought to trust someone.

"I will find the stable. And I will catch up to Meven." She smiled at the three huddled men, and one smiled and waved in return. Then she turned left, recalling the woman's directions: "Follow your right hand for one block, then follow your left for two, then left again for another one. Look to your right and there is the stable."

At the end of the street, a block away, she spotted a large wood-plank building, all weathered and crooked-looking as if it might fall over, with a thatch roof that had gaps in places. The turquoise tower rose behind it, and Kalantha guessed that it was probably blocks away and was no doubt a temple to one of the good gods. Peran-Morab was often depicted dressed in blues and greens. A hint of the evening's near-full moon was appearing above the turquoise tower, translucent and promising that when the sky grew darker still, the moon would be gold and beautiful.

She touched the brooch and decided that would be the piece to give up for a horse. "A fast horse with good legs."

A light glowed from the only window she could see in the big building, which she figured had to be the stable from its size and the woman's directions. So someone worked still, likely cleaning stalls or feeding and watering the horses, and the brooch would be more than fair trade for the best horse there. They certainly wouldn't have a noriker, as she'd remembered Meven saying the only norikers in Nadir were in the royal stables and belonged to him, some of the knights, and to visiting nobles from the north. Norikers were valuable and powerful. She hoped she could find something other than a heavy draft used to pulling carts and plowing fields. Something fast—maybe even a big pony. She was small enough she wouldn't present a problem for a pony. And when she came back to Nadir after the war ended, she would release the pony and find Rue. If catching up to her brother and helping to stop all the killing wasn't essential, she'd be looking for Rue right now.

Halfway down the block, she heard a slapping sound behind her, odd and rhythmic and prompting her to turn around.

Stretched across the street behind her were four youths, three in trousers too small and straining the seams, and one in baggy leggings that hung on his hips and stretched to the dirt; nothing fit properly, and nothing was clean.

"Girl, girl, girl," the tallest sneered. He'd been clapping his hands—that was the sound she'd heard. He continued to clap, and the three other youths clapped, too, slow and in time with their footfalls.

They stalked toward her.

She whirled and nearly fell over as pain shot up her injured leg. She'd intended to bolt to the stables and the welcoming light in the window, but she saw two more young men closing in from that direction.

"Girl, girl, girl," the tall one repeated. "Fancy girl with all the sparkles."

She spun back at the last word, her mouth wide in surprise to see Hallory standing behind the quartet. A trap! Hallory had alerted the young thugs that she was coming, probably scampering a shorter way to set her up, knowing she couldn't travel fast because of her leg.

"You give up all those fancy pieces of jewelry, girl, and your fine and fancy clothes . . . if you want to see the sun come up next morning."

15 · Reflections and Revelations

The same is true of Fallen Favorites and Finest. Give every measure of yourself every day. Perform every task as if it were your last. Though you can never be perfect, by that dedication you can attain perfection.

~Steadfast, veteran Finest

Two soldiers rode in front of Meven, though the notion of not being out front festered in the young monarch. He'd intended to lead the retinue of nine south to Nasim-Guri, and he'd chosen the largest of his norikers to ride. The highest-ranking soldier in the entourage, a lieutenant, rode at the back to observe and give orders and undoubtedly to escape Meven's icy gaze. He demanded that the King of Galmier be shielded, front and back, by his soldiers.

Meven initially countered that, saying that as King of Galmier, he gave the orders and everyone was to obey them.

"But His Majesty has ordered an end to this war," the lieutenant risked, "and so it would be better if he not become a casualty to it before he hands out his decrees. If I am to serve you, Sire, you should accept my counsel in this matter."

Lieutenant Rendell was a loyal, wise man twice Meven's

years and obviously unafraid of punishment. Meven was thankful to him and brooding at the same time, and decided to reward him when all of this was done with a piece of eastern coastal land. It took a soldier of courage to stand up to royalty—or it took someone like his sister Kalantha. He thought about Kal. Where had she managed to get herself lost? He had no doubt that's what had happened, her curiosity sending her exploring while he met with his knight commanders. He knew his sister, and he knew the palace was big enough to become lost in. He'd done it himself on more than one occasion.

Please let someone have found her, he prayed. She's probably feasting on Sara Anne's sweets at the table in the kitchen or reading a book from one of the libraries—maybe the book she'd brought from the Vershan Monastary, the one she'd been so insistent I read. I should have searched for her myself, and at least looked at the book to make her happy.

"She's all right," he whispered so softly that none but his noriker could hear. "She's truly all right. But maybe I should have waited for her." After a few moments of thought: "Maybe she's safe with that ugly horse of hers." Meven's horse reached sixteen hands high with a coat that gleamed like polished walnut and a mane and tail so black they looked like they'd been dipped in ink. He'd named the stallion Nobleborn, and he liked that it held its head high and often tipped its ears forward as if searching for signs of trouble. He considered all the norikers alert and striking, this one especially so—as beautiful as Rue was unsightly.

They rode in silence until the sun set, painting the chips of rocks in the road orange like the dying embers of a fire. The trees were still, the breeze dying with the day, and the rustling leaves gave way to insects chirping. Meven listened to water burbling, suspecting there was a creek behind a row of birch, one of the threadlike tributaries seeping away from the

Sprawling River. He heard the flapping of large wings, probably a heron spooked or a great owl searching for prey.

Meven gritted his teeth; he hated birds.

The trees thinned out close to the road with the coming of twilight. Many of the smaller ones had been cut down for firewood for the soldiers camping here on their march south. He could see fresh mounds of earth to the west, several yards away, and was thankful the shadows hid most of the details. There were no markers that he could see, but nonetheless Meven knew they were graves. The men bringing back the wounded talked about burying their fellows who died along the way in mass graves between villages. Only the common soldiers would be resting there, no stones or blocks of wood to record their names and ages and where they were from. Sons of noblemen or knights, or the rare peasant-hero who'd distinguished himself in the eyes of his commander, were taken home to receive proper burials. Meven swallowed hard and tried to guess how many soldiers were buried there.

Because of him.

Too many, but considerably more in Nasim-Guri, he told himself. Very many more. More orphans and widows and grieving parents in the country he'd made war with. The casualties on the other side of the war were staggering, his spies reported. Places in Nasim-Guri were drenched with so much blood that streams ran red. Days past, before Kalantha returned from the Vershan Monastery and brought sense to him, he had counted the enemy dead as a blessing. Now it would forever remain his curse.

Music intruded on Meven's misery as they continued, and to the east he spied a home perched on cut-off oak trunks. He knew there was an entire village, Stilton, built on top of stumps. He'd been through the place once. In the spring and fall when a wide branch of the Sprawling River flooded, the roads disappeared around the village, and the people moved from home to home to businesses on rafts. Perhaps the people in the lone house on the oak stumps feared flooding from the nearby creek, or perhaps they just enjoyed a lofty vantage. Someone in the home was playing a flute, and as Meven listened, the first musician was joined by a second with a stringed instrument, and then a third person tapping his hands on a drum. It was not so refined or complicated a tune as what the musicians in his palace played. But it was splendid in its simplicity and eased his mind, and Meven found himself humming along. Too soon they were beyond the music, and all he could hear was an occasional snort from one of the soldier's horses and the shrill chirping of crickets.

A falcon or a hawk, so fast he couldn't make it out, cut across their path and banked and climbed to the northeast. It was gray, not black, and so not a threat. Meven closed his eyes. He truly hated birds, all of them. But most of all he hated the black ones that too often filled his nightmares. He tipped his head back and felt the cool air take the nervous sweat from his face. Worse than anything, he hated the war he'd started.

IN THE BACK OF HIS MIND HE SAT IN HIS WAR ROOM HIGH IN the west tower of the palace. An intricately rendered map of Paard-Peran rested on a long, low table, with raised areas for mountains and hollowed-out lines and depressions for the river and lakes. He moved carved soldiers around on the map, expertly painted down to their eyes and weapons and dressed in his colors. The Bishop's colors, he corrected himself. Blue, two shades—one a bright, dark hue, like the sky before a spring storm, the other, in less prominence, a watery tone that bordered on gray—were the Bishop's colors at the High Keep Temple. They became Meven's colors at the coronation when they moved to Nadir. Meven thought he had selected the colors to honor the Bishop. Now he wondered if it had been his idea at all.

Bishop DeNogaret sat in the war room, too. The elderly priest had given Meven the miniature soldiers and commanders, and only recently had presented him with knights mounted on horseback—the most exquisite figurines of all. The Bishop said the artist was making additional miniatures—of Meven and his advisors.

"And one of you?" Meven asked.

The Bishop looked surprised and humbled and shook his head. In retrospect Meven realized it was an act, feigned modesty.

Meven insisted that the Bishop be graced with such a figure—one more magnificent than all the rest. Bishop DeNogaret relented after a mild argument and agreed to have one commissioned immediately.

The war room also featured a tapestry of Galmier and Nasim-Guri that took up an entire wall. Embroidered by the greatest seamstress in the city, metallic threads highlighted the capital city of Nadir. Meven found himself admiring it often, and wondering if red threads should be added here and there to mark the scenes of the greatest battles, and if the seamstress could alter the map and cut the threads that said "Nasim-Guri" so the entire map became Galmier. At the war's end he would own both countries.

"You'll talk to the artist about crafting a miniature of you?" Meven reminded the Bishop.

The elderly priest nodded and left to attend to the matter.

Less than an hour later, Meven took a stroll in one of the courtyards to think about something other than the war and his soon-to-be-expanded kingdom. Instead, the war intruded, as he heard two people talking about a particularly fierce battle waged at the center point of the border to Nasim-Guri. He crept closer to listen, and peering around a thick cedar he spotted the Bishop, alone, continuing to talk. Someone contin-

ued to answer and to provide details about Nasim-Guri sur-
vivors and the strength of the enemy forces along the eastern
part of the border. The Bishop faced a statue of Peran-Morab,
and so Meven guessed the speaker stood behind it. But he
didn't see a second man's shadow, only the statue's . . . and he
eventually noticed a falcon perched on an upraised marble
arm.

The Bishop spoke to the bird, Meven realized. The notion hit
him as hard as if he'd run into a stone wall. And the bird answered in a feminine voice that sent shivers down Meven's
spine. Meven started to edge away, but Bishop DeNogaret spied
him, and in that instant the falcon flew away.

"Your Majesty, come here please," the Bishop purred.

Meven shook his head but stepped closer and closer, his eyes
locked with the Bishop's. It was as if the priest's gaze pulled
him. The old man's eyes normally looked rheumy and weak,
but they were bright and piercing now, and they were all Meven
could see.

"You did not see a bird in the courtyard, Meven."

Meven opened his mouth to argue, but nodded in agreement.
"No bird." What bird? he wondered. There'd been no bird.
No bird at all.

"No, Bishop. I only saw you."

"And you heard nothing."

"Nothing but the wind playing with the leaves."

Bishop DeNogaret smiled, and Meven felt pleasantly warm
and good. Meven returned the smile, then returned to his war
room to plot future moves against Nasim-Guri.

MEVEN CHEWED ON HIS LOWER LIP. WHY WAS HE REMEMBER-
ing all of that now, about the falcon with Bishop DeNogaret?
He'd seen the Bishop with an owl before, once at the High

Keep Temple and another time at the palace. But the details were all muddy, though he could recall the intensity of the Bishop's stare easily enough and recall being told to forget. Why could he remember these things now? On this road? Because he was away from the palace and the Bishop? Because he was truly on his own? Because no one was making suggestions?

"You did not see an owl," the Bishop had said.

"No owl," Meven replied.

"You did not see a falcon," the Bishop said on two occasions. "You did not see birds."

"No birds," Meven had answered.

"The war is a good idea, Meven, and it is all your idea."

"My idea." But was it? Meven had told Kalantha that the Bishop might have suggested he go to war with Nasim-Guri, that expanding Galmier was the correct thing to do. But was the war all Bishop DeNogaret's plan? Only the Bishop's plan? Was it only the Bishop's notion to send Kalantha away?

"Was I only a puppet?"

"Beg your pardon, Sire. What did you say?" This came from the soldier behind and to his left. The soldier was only a year or two older than Meven.

"Just talking to myself . . . Horcort." Meven was gratified he'd remembered the young man's name. "I do that sometimes, just talk."

They slowed when it grew darker and some of the horses showed fatigue. Nobleborn could have kept going at the faster pace, but Meven didn't want to push the smaller norikers, particularly since they were burdened by soldiers in chain mail and with weapons and supplies. The two packhorses were plodding now, and foam flecked at their lips.

Lieutenant Rendell rode up until he was even with Meven.

"Sire, there is a village not far, Lornsby. We could get fresh horses and ride through the rest of the night."

Meven stared at the backs of the soldiers in front of him. "That's what I said I wanted to do."

"Or we could rest there for a few hours, and rest our horses. Then move on before first light."

Meven didn't say anything for a few minutes. In the quiet that stretched between them he heard the cry of some night bird and the shush of something moving in the brush beyond the line of trees, something small and likely of no consequence.

"Perhaps I should make you one of my advisors, Rendell." Meven kept his eyes on the soldiers' backs. "If we rest these horses, we likely would make better time. The norikers are the best Galmier provides, and whatever stock we could acquire in the next village would likely be swaybacked plow horses."

"Then we stop to rest in Lornsby, Sire."

"Yes, Lieutenant Rendell. We'll stop to rest."

The moon was nearly full and well illuminated the road that widened as they neared Lornsby. Two or three more miles to go, Rendell estimated, before he drifted back to the rear.

Meven yawned and looked down, seeing ruts in the road from wagon tracks. He would relish a few hours' sleep; he was so tired he'd find a dirt floor comfortable. He yawned again, deeply, then wrinkled his nose. Something smelled out of place.

The lead soldiers pulled back on their reins and raised their right hands, signaling a stop. Meven was slow to react, but his horse stopped just in time. The packhorses snorted in confusion, as the soldiers in the back whispered questions.

"I smell something . . . odd," Meven hushed.

"I smell it, too," Horcort said. He slipped from his horse and passed the reins to the soldier opposite him. Then he looked to Lieutenant Rendell. "Shall I investigate?"

Rendell pointed forward, and Horcort took the center of the road, drawing his sword and moving as quietly as possible in his armor.

Meven slid to the ground and stretched, grateful to be standing for a change, but instantly nervous. Night cloaked the assassin-birds, and he listened for the flutter of wings, his nervousness turning into fear. He touched the noriker's neck and waited.

A few minutes later Horcort returned, no longer bothering to be quiet.

"Report." Lieutenant Rendell rode to the front of the party.

"The smell is what I feared, sir."

"Death?" Rendell shook his head. "How many dead?"

"All of them."

Meven rushed forward, propelled by fear and anger and the curiosity that seemed to run in the Montoll blood. He heard the lieutenant calling to him, then heard the steady clop of horse hooves as Rendell passed him by and followed the road around a curve.

Meven expected to see all of Lornsby dead—a few years past, he and Kalantha had seen the remains of villages attacked by assassin-birds. While the scene the moon highlighted was horrid, it wasn't on the scale of a village. But it struck Meven just as hard.

Meven dropped to his knees and fought for breath, his chest feeling like someone in armor was sitting on him and trying to suffocate him. He heard a great pounding and numbly recognized it as the sound of his heart.

"Knight Commander Javal," Meven whispered. "They were less than an hour ahead of us." He fell forward, caught by his hands, and he shook and retched.

Javal was not far off the road, on his back with his arms and legs spread like someone had posed him. The declarations of peace were shredded around him, held to the ground because they were soaked with blood. Seven soldiers stretched from the center of the road to the tree line, all being picked at by crows. Rendell and Horcort worked to shoo the birds away, clapping and yelling, and finally drawing their swords because the birds were so defiant.

"The war goes on for Ninéon," Meven thought he heard a crow say as it flew away.

16 · The Finest Livestock

The worth of a Fallen Favorite is measured by his or her ability to shape a better world. The worth of a Finest is measured by his or her ability to shape a soul.

~Mara, Finest guardian of Bitternut

Eleven horses, four dogs, two mules, one cantankerous goat, and more chickens and pigeons than Gallant-Stallion bothered to count were in pens and stalls inside what he believed had once served as a warehouse. Too tall and massive to have been built as a stable, nails and discolored bands on the walls indicated where myriad shelves had been. Depressions and gouges in the floor showed where heavy objects had once rested. Rusted pulleys hanging from rafters on thick, frayed ropes might have been used to move things from one end of the building to the other. Bridles and saddles, most all of them in poor repair, hung from hooks on posts. Beyond the animals, where no lanterns hung, barrels and crates reached halfway to the ceiling. The shadows were deep, so the Finest couldn't see what else was stored there. Perhaps the place still served as a warehouse.

Gallant-Stallion smelled the old wood that surrounded him, moldy straw, and animal dung. The few high windows and two holes in the roof weren't sufficient to bring in enough fresh air to clear his lungs. His senses were keen, and so everything smelled uncomfortably strong. He could make out the individual odors of most of the livestock and could tell that a few men were somewhere in the shadows. They talked in conspiratorial tones, and the Finest could not pick out enough of their conversation to make sense of it, as the mules snorted and brayed at inopportune times. By the time the mules stopped making noise, the men were done talking.

He thought the chickens and pigeons oddly quiet, and after watching their listlessness and noting their wide eyes realized they were fearful. Feathers stuck to congealed blood outside their pens revealed that some of their brothers had been killed in front of them. The goat alternately complained about being tied with a too-short cord and chewed on a slat in his stall.

Caged, this is worse than a beating. Stump directed this to Gallant-Stallion. *I should not have followed the smelly girl, big punch. You should not have cut my leash. I should be home. Safe and fed.*

Gallant-Stallion didn't argue; the dog was probably right. The Finest doubted anything good was slated for the animals kept here. The place had a pall about it that clung to the floor and rafters and that the animals wore like a second skin. He felt it dampening his already sagging spirits.

If I get free, I will not help you again, big punch. The dog punctuated this with a growl. *I will find my way home and stay away from you.*

Gallant-Stallion studied the horses. He could see all of them when he strained the chains and stretched his neck so he could look around a thick post. There were four cutting horses the color of sand and dusty from either working a herd or trudging across dirt roads. From the angle of their teeth and the grooves and hooks in them, he could tell the horses were between ten and fifteen years old. Two dark brown cobs, each with rear white stockings, had cropped tails and manes and vacant looks in their wide eyes.

How long have you been here? Gallant-Stallion asked the cobs.

One continued to stare, but the other shifted his attention to the Finest. *Three suns,* he answered. *Not enough food here, not enough sweet air. No sweet air ever.* He echoed the sentiment of Stump: *I want to go home.*

Where is home?

Away from here, the cob answered after a few moments. *In the barn of a swaybacked man. A comfortable barn of good smells.*

Gallant-Stallion cocked his head in question.

A wrinkly, wrinkly, wrinkly man with pale sky eyes and cobweb hair. His barn. Good food there. Good man who brushed us. But one morning he did not come to feed us. Not that night. Not the next morning. My belly burned from hunger when the dirty men came and took us away to here. I knew the wrinkly, wrinkly, wrinkly man was dead. I miss him more than I miss good food.

The Finest knew then that the vacant look in their eyes was grief, not the numbing fear the fowl evidenced. He lowered his head in respect, then looked to the remaining five horses. An iomud, an ancient breed with akhal-teke blood used primarily for riding, dozed directly across from Gallant-Stallion. Her small, alert ears twitched in her sleep. Her thick gray coat suggested that she came from the north or the mountains, where cold weather still held sway. One other gray, several shades darker, nickered softly in the last stall—this a cracker horse with a mane that draped below the chestnuts of her front legs. The cracker had blunt, jutting teeth that marked her at near thirty years, old for a horse. Her deep chest and muscular neck, with stripes of hair worn to the skin, told the Finest she'd been used for pulling heavy loads.

Thrown away, the cracker told Gallant-Stallion. *Old, my people threw me away. Too old to pull so much.*

The final two ponies, huculs, stood twelve hands high. *Taken,* they said in unison, answering the Finest's unspoken question. *Stolen in the night.*

Stolen, one of the mules brayed. *The dirty men are thieves to steal us and bring us here.*

And garbage grabbers, they are, the cracker said. *Grabbing horses that are thrown away like spoiled oats. Grabbing us garbage creatures.*

The goat raised its voice, complaining about the men and the nickering horses, not able to understand what the horses were saying.

Stolen, Gallant-Stallion whispered. *Stump and I were stolen, too.*

The Finest retreated as far as possible into his stall. He was angry that he had allowed himself to be dragged into this reeking, morbid place. He should have fought the men on the street. He shouldn't have worried about hurting them; they were not innocents after all, and holding these animals here was sinful. Would the animals find new homes? Would they be sold? Or would they be butchered? Desperate people ate horse-flesh, he'd heard.

Steadfast . . . Steadfast . . . Gallant-Stallion waited, but the spirit of his mentor did not come. *Steadfast, I should have escaped on the street. I will escape now.* Breaking the chains would take some work, but it was not beyond him. The wall would likely give before the rusting iron, and the noise would draw the men. He could charge out of the stall and through the shadows, racing past the men he knew still milled there, and crashing out the door to freedom.

But there was an easier way. He wouldn't be able to take Stump with him, and he felt bad about putting the hunting dog in such a sad situation. But the dog would no longer help him find Kalantha—Stump had said so more than once in the past several minutes, and so at the moment the dog was expendable. Gallant-Stallion would have to find his charge on his own.

So he would retreat to the Court lands. Already he was closing his eyes and picturing the green pastures with luscious grass and fragrant wildflowers. He imagined the shallows of a clear river swirling around his shanks and a refreshing breeze combing his mane and tail. In a few more heartbeats he would be there, then he could return to Paard-Peran—but not to this hole. He would return to the royal stables, or perhaps in the alley near where he and Stump were caught. He'd search for Kalantha again. Search and search until he found her. She was his responsibility.

He felt the air stir, and his quivering nostrils picked up a hint of jasmine. He felt the irons around his shanks fall and watched everything become hazy and out of focus. A heartbeat more and he would be in the Court lands, then he . . .

Do not leave, brother Finest. There is work we must do here.

He immediately stopped his journey, his eyes snapping open and searching the visages of the horses. Their images were still blurry, and he concentrated to pull himself back—though not exactly in the same position. Gallant-Stallion had no desire to be in chains again.

Together, we can win this day, brother.

The heads of the horses were getting clearer and sharper, and the last trace of jasmine from the Court lands was replaced by the malodorous tang of animal dung and moldy straw.

The iomud met his stare.

You are a Finest, Gallant-Stallion said in the hidden speak she'd been using.

She snorted at the obvious.

And you are without your charge.

As you are without yours, she returned. *We shall mourn them together, my brother.*

Gallant-Stallion shook his head. *My charge is not dead.*

Mine is. A great sadness filled the iomud's deep brown eyes, a grief as deep as the cobs showed. *The one I shepherded for the past eight years died two nights ago.*

Who?

Lord Garald, a minor noble from Duriam. On my back he slipped into this city, trying to approach the palace and gain an audience with the young warlord, the King of Galmier. Garald collected coins and gems from other Duriam nobles, and several small historic pieces of estimable worth from his family vault—all of it to be used as a bribe to the warlord.

An effort to stop the fighting.

She wuffled long and low. *In his heart Garald doubted it would work, though he did not voice such. But he felt he needed to try. He'd lost his father and brother to the war, and friends who served in the army. He'd written a speech he memorized on the way to this city. Quite stirring, one of the most elegant pieces he'd ever penned. It begged for peace.*

But he died before he could deliver it.

Ambushed by vile men, the ones in the shadows beyond the crates, and more. We chose a wrong road to come to the palace, trying to avoid the main street where by his colors and heraldic device he might be recognized, turned away, or captured.

And these men, the ones who brought me here, and you . . .

These men and some rough-looking youths. They killed my Garald when he refused to part with his bribe. If he surrendered the baubles, his bribe to the warlord would be lost and his purpose for coming to the city would be foiled. He fought them with a thin-blade that belonged to his father. And I fought them with everything in me.

Gallant-Stallion noticed slashes along her left side. He couldn't tell the extent of her wounds from the angle she stood in the stall, and the foul scents of the place were too strong to smell if she was still bleeding. Why hadn't she returned to the Court lands to heal? Why hadn't she reported on the death of her charge and asked for a new one?

We were nearly away, she continued, *but one cowardly, wicked young man threw a knife and struck my Garald in the back. He fell from me and I stopped. I prayed to all the good powers that I could help him, but he died within moments. He cried—not because of his imminent demise, but because he could not find peace between Galmier and Nasim-Guri. I suppose I should have fled then, made my way clear of the city and returned to the Court. But I stayed over his body, and the men roped and chained me and put me in this foul-smelling place. They caught you, too, though your charge obviously escaped them. I do not know what has become of Garald's body.*

Gallant-Stallion let a respectful silence lapse, then he quickly explained that he'd been caught while searching for his charge, who'd fled the palace grounds.

So you shepherd royalty . . .

Gallant-Stallion. My charge calls me Rue. She is sister to the King of Galmier.

Sister to the warlord who has caused so much bloodshed.

Gallant-Stallion did not reply to that.

I am Honest-Stormchaser, though I am fond of the name Garald called me—Cornsilk. He was a good man, Rue, best among all those I shepherded.

It was the first time a Finest had called him only by his Fallen Favorite name.

He should not have died in a dirty alley. And thieves should not have stolen his glittery dreams for finding peace.

Gallant-Stallion studied her for several long minutes. He listened to a mule bray and the cantankerous goat bleat and complain about the taste of the wood. He heard Stump pine for home, and he caught another piece of conversation from the men at the far end of the building. They talked about the cobs, and a potential buyer. A faint light from beyond the crates indicated they'd lit a lantern.

You should not be without your charge, Rue.

Gallant-Stallion wuffled at her. *I was leaving for the Court when you stopped me, intending to come back elsewhere, free of this place, and search for her. Indeed, that is what I will do now, and you should come to the Court lands, too.*

To heal.

Yes.

And to request another charge.

Yes.

No.

No? I do not understand, Honest-Stormchaser.

I have important work to do here.

Gallant-Stallion ticked his ears forward in puzzlement.

Before you arrived, Rue, I made a promise to all of the creatures here that we would leave this building together. I said I would rescue them, and I welcome your help in this most worthy endeavor.

You are injured, Honest-Stormchaser.

Hurt when my Garald died, but I have been slowly healing here. Though I still ache terribly, I am well enough now to attempt this.

You could have healed in the Court pastures.

Stormchaser's nostrils flared in anger. *I promised not to leave these creatures until they are free in the woods south of this wretched city.*

Gallant-Stallion continued to argue. *Your responsibility is to the Court and your next Fallen Favorite, not to a barn full of animals. These creatures hold your sympathy, obviously, but they should not overly concern you.*

She shook her head, her long, pale mane flying away and looking like the silky tassels on summer sweet corn. *You are wrong. I have decided that these animals are my responsibility, Rue. We Finest have long lives, and so I will have plenty of time to return to the Court lands and ask for another Fallen Favorite to shepherd. And another after that.*

The Court . . .

Will have to understand. At the moment, all of these creatures are my charges.

Not possible, the Court . . .

I have free will, Rue. Other Finest have not waited for the Court to name the ones they are to shepherd.

Gallant-Stallion instantly thought of Mara, an old pony he had met in a stable in Bitternut. She considered herself guardian to the entire village. Gallant-Stallion doubted the Finest Court gave her the appointment.

He looked away from Honest-Stormchaser and to the creatures in the building—ten horses, four dogs, two mules, one still very cantankerous goat, many chickens and pigeons, and a skinny black and white cat he hadn't noticed before. It crept across a rafter in pursuit of a sparrow, but the little bird ever stayed out of its reach.

Gallant-Stallion didn't watch the sparrow long enough to see that it had a black spot in the middle of its breast and a red-brown crown, with not a single dark feather on its head.

My devotion is to Kalantha Montoll, Honest-Stormchaser. And I will journey to the Court and return elsewhere to renew my search for her. I wish you well in your plan to help these creatures. May the good powers give you strength.

She snorted and tamped her hoof against the hard-packed ground. Then she retreated as far into her stall as she could, ears pointed up in defiance.

Gallant-Stallion closed his eyes and concentrated, once more picturing the pristine Court lands filled with sweet grass and wildflowers, clear rivers and . . .

Two men tromped past the crates and stopped in front of

the first mule. The largest pointed a thick finger at several stalls, then gestured to the cobs.

"Got us a buyer for these two, a merchant who'll take 'em to the south to resell in one of the villages. And the goat, too. He wants it for milk."

"The rest?"

The big man shook his head and slapped his hip. "Like the last batch, Ben, we'll have to sell the rest to the butcher. He'll be here before sunup, wants to have them rendered right away. Thought we'd have us a buyer for that riding horse, but not this go."

Gallant-Stallion nickered to Honest-Stormchaser: *I will help you, sister. But only if we act now.*

17 · Friends and Other Enemies

What is worse ... madness and anger and a bitter welling in the soul ... or the fiery incidents that brought those things about? I think it is the end result that is far more heinous. The end result mars a pretty face.

~Fancy Moondancer, Finest shepherd to Alaine Cooper,
third daughter of Windswept's first mayor

No!" Kalantha screamed the word. "You'll not steal from me!" Her stomach churned with rage. The jewels belonged in her family, and she needed at least one of them to buy a strong, fast horse so she could catch up to Meven. Stopping the war was more important than anything to her right now, and she wasn't about to let these foul boys keep her from that goal.

The one who'd started the clapping stopped and raised a hand to his fellows. He was obviously the leader of the gang. He grinned wolfishly, then laughed. "Girl, girl, girl. You have less sense than a chicken in a rainstorm. They drown, you know, the chickens. They look up, beaks gaping open. Farmers say water fills their lungs 'cause they don't bother to look back down. You're just like that."

"These are mine!" She grabbed at the brooch and the necklaces, her face heating up and breath coming faster. "I need these!"

"So do we." He waved his arm to indicate the neighborhood. "We need to eat, girl. And those pretty pieces are going to feed us for a very long time."

She spat at him, something she'd never done before, and shook her fist in defiance. She glanced around the five in front of her, noting the rickety wooden walkway on one side of the street, glanced behind her at the two boys who'd moved up a little. Her swollen ankle felt hot and awkward inside her boot, and she knew she couldn't run very far on it.

"Don't want us to hurt you, do you, girl?"

She shook her head, her eyes venomously aimed at his. She could tell him who she was—sister to the King of Galmier, warn him that when the King came back to Nadir, he'd punish them all for threatening her. She opened her mouth to do just that, then swallowed the words. Kalantha was wise beyond her years and instantly realized announcing herself would make the situation worse. They might try to ransom her.

"The war," she whispered. "I have to help stop the war."

"What was that you said, girl?"

Hallory edged up between the quartet and thumped the leader on the shoulder. "She can't run, Thorn. She's got a bum leg. See how she favors it? This'll be nearly too easy."

Kalantha fumed, then she screamed. Not a scream for help, but a scream of anger. She hoped it would draw the attention of someone nearby, adults who might shoo away these ruffians.

"Now that did it!" Thorn rushed her, his gang closing behind him.

Kalantha limped toward the sidewalk, but she didn't make it that far. Dirty hands grabbed at her arms from behind, pinning her. She kicked back with her good foot, as hard as she could, the heel of her boot digging into her assailant's shin. He let go, surprised she fought back, and she rammed her elbow into his stomach. The other youth kept a tight hold, and though she struggled against him, she couldn't break free.

Thorn was on her a heartbeat later, his nails digging into the skin of her free arm, his heel slamming down on her foot. This time she let out a shrill, ear-splitting scream and kicked backward again, striking another leg. The youth yelped.

"Fights like a rabid dog, she does, Thorn."

One of the boys behind her tried to clamp a hand over her mouth, but she bit down, drawing blood and getting a taste of dirt and sweat in her mouth. Another yelp from the youth, who then punched her in the back and kicked her swollen ankle.

Kalantha buckled, supported by Thorn and one of his thugs. They kicked her again and again, and then punched her in the stomach. One of them stuffed a rag in her mouth to silence her. Thorn drew his face close to hers.

"Little wildcat, no one's gonna come running no matter how much you scream. No heroes in this neighborhood, girl. No one cares." He had one hand free, and he used it to pluck the brooch from her tunic. He stuffed it in his pocket and ogled the other pieces of jewelry. "I'd say you're every bit the thief I am. Raggedy muffin like you doesn't come by things that sparkle honestly. I'll be teaching you a lesson . . . not to flaunt what you steal . . . and not to visit my neighborhood."

His rank breath competed with the smell of stale sweat and smoke that clung to their tattered clothes. He gave his wolfish grin again, displaying his yellowed teeth and a gap where a few were missing.

"Bet we could sell you to some merchant heading to a port, girl. He'd sell you again to a ship—profit all the way around for your sorry carcass. There's good coin in slavery on some of the islands. You get that leg healed up and someone'd buy you to scrub chamber pots and floors. Get lots of years out of you . . . thief."

Kalantha could hardly breathe, the hand across her face covering her nose, too. She squirmed and managed to kick Thorn, which only served to make him madder. He kicked back at her sore leg and pushed her to her knees. Hands on her shoulders kept her down.

"Don't know who you stole these from. They're worth a lot, little thief." Thorn spat the last word, a gob of spittle hitting her cheek.

"We really going to sell her?" This came from Hallory, who looked only mildly sorry for setting up Kalantha. "My ma wouldn't approve, you know. She figured we were just gonna rob her. Mama wants that ring."

"Well, your ma's not here, is she, Hal?" Thorn tugged on a necklace, the thin gold chain with the little rubies. The clasp broke and he dangled the necklace in front of Kalantha.

Tears streamed from her eyes, though not because of the treatment the ruffians were giving her. She was thinking of Meven and the war, thinking that she would never be able to help him now and never find Rue.

"You stole from royalty, girl. Some high and mighty baron or something. Rubies like this, royalty for certain."

"Thorn, bet she stole from the King. Bet she's some kitchen help who helped herself to those sparklies." Hallory leaned in close. "We ought to let her go. She might be valuable to somebody."

"No!" One of the other thugs argued. "I like the idea of selling her to some merchant. I know a couple of 'em who work the trade on Dorchester Street. One of them'd take her to the coast. We could get a pouch of coins for her, so young."

"I think I know just the merchant who'll . . ."

A loud stomp cut Thorn off. He looked to the wood plank sidewalk and snarled, "Get out of here, Sean, Talbot, this isn't your business."

"No one's going to be taking that girl. Let her go!"

"You heard him, Hallory. You let that girl go now!"

Kalantha spied two men through a gap in the thugs' legs. They stood on the wooden sidewalk, and one of them pointed a kitchen knife at the cluster of youths.

"Hallory, I will tell your ma!" This came from the one with the knife.

"Mama already knows!" Hallory returned.

The man with the knife stepped off the sidewalk and started toward the group. "Your ma doesn't know you're beating up a little girl. Stealing's one thing, Hallory. Beating? That'll send your soul to a very bad place." He thumped the handle of the knife against his palm. "And I will give your soul a head start if you don't—"

The man didn't have to finish the sentence. Hallory spun away from Thorn and the rest and ran down the street and around the corner, one of the other youths following. The remaining five ruffians held their ground as the second man approached. This one didn't carry a weapon, but it didn't look like he needed one. Not much older than the youths, veins stood out like vines growing on a tree trunk on his short, thick neck. His upper arms were massive with muscles, and his hands were calloused and filthy from hard labor.

"You be about your own business, Sean, Talbot." Thorn had a measure of respect in his voice. "We won't hurt her bad. She's just got some things that belong to us. Teachin' her a little lesson—not to be rude to me. Takin' some things that are mine."

Sean thumped the knife handle again. "Now does she have stuff of yours?"

"Yeah, she does, Sean."

"Does that pretty necklace you're holding belong to you, Thorn? Funny, I haven't seen you wear it before." He stepped closer, only two or three yards away now, and drew the knife back over his shoulder as if to throw it. "You might outnumber us, Thorn, but you know who's stronger. Do we need to fight again?"

"No need to be mean about this." Thorn released Kalantha and stuffed the necklace in his pocket. He inched back from the girl and nodded to his friends. "I guess this'll do, Sean."

"It'll more than do, Thorn. Get your sorry selves out of here before I help your souls find that very bad place."

The youths sneered, but complied, swaggering away slowly to show that they hadn't wholly lost the confrontation.

"My soul's got a warm, cozy spot already reserved, Sean," Thorn taunted over his shoulder. "Right next to yours."

Then the gang turned the same corner Hallory had moments ago, and the muscular man named Talbot gingerly helped Kalantha up. He brushed at the spittle on her cheek and tucked her hair behind her ears, his calloused fingers scratching her face.

"You all right?" Talbot's voice fit his frame, big and coarse. "Not like them to actually hurt someone. I used to run with their kind a few years back. They're mostly talk."

"Used to be all talk anyway." Sean stood, one fist set against his waist, shaking his head, watching the corner to make sure the gang stayed away. "Hard to blame them. This is a desperate place and you do what you have to sometimes." He looked over his shoulder at Kalantha. "But you wouldn't know that because you aren't from the neighborhood."

"No." She futilely brushed at a spot on her tunic and studied her hands, not wanting to meet the gaze of the men who'd rescued her. She didn't want them to see the pain in her expression. Her leg hurt worse than ever now because the boys had kicked it, and her ankle felt burning hot and terribly squeezed inside her boot. "I came from the Vershan Monastery.

I lived there for a while." It wasn't a lie, she had lived there for more than a year. It just wasn't the complete truth—she'd no intention of telling them she'd just come from Meven's palace.

"And if you're a thief," Sean continued, "you're not a very good one. Thieves don't wear what they take, least not in public. All that glittery stuff, you were asking for trouble—in this neighborhood or most likely any other."

She tested her ankle and gritted her teeth when pain shot up her leg. But she was able to stand on it. "I'm not a thief."

"No, I don't expect you are. You don't have the looks of one." This came from Talbot. "You're a filthy mess, but under all that dirt your clothes are in good repair. Marks you coming from a better street than this one."

They waited for her to say where she was from, but Kalantha didn't explain. "The jewelry belonged to my aunt." Another true statement. Kalantha figured they didn't need to know her aunt had been the Queen of Galmier. "I shouldn't have put it on."

Sean finally turned away from the corner. "Where are your folks? We'll walk you home. It's getting pretty dark, and more people like Thorn and his bunch'll be out. Foul people I've not got the mettle to challenge with an old kitchen knife."

She didn't answer for a moment, caught between whether to tell him the truth or make something else up. She opted for neither. "I was going to a stable. Some woman gave me directions. I think that's the stable." She waved a hand to the end of the street and the big rickety building.

Sean raised an eyebrow and bent to take a close look at Kalantha. He had a careworn face and gray-brown beard stubble. There were wrinkles at the edges of his eyes, and when he opened his mouth to talk again, she smelled bitter ale.

"What's a girl want a stable for?"

"I need a horse," she blurted. In the same moment she took

a step back, crying out when she put too much weight on her injured leg. Talbot picked her up.

"She's hurt, Sean. Thorn and them beat her pretty bad. I can take her to Rosalynn's. See if she can do some mending."

Kalantha shook her head. "I thank you, but I don't have time for that. Please put me down. I have to get to the stable. I have to buy a horse."

Talbot shrugged gingerly and set her down, big hands under her armpits holding up some of her weight. "You can't walk far on that leg—"

"Kalantha." She guessed giving them her name wouldn't hurt.

"Good-sounding name," Talbot returned. "Might have a broken leg there, or an ankle. Rosalynn's good about mending folks, Kalantha. And she'd probably take you in for the night. She's a kind soul, she is."

Kalantha's face relaxed. "I don't have time, but I thank you again." She started to limp toward the big building. "Thank you for everything."

"That's not a stable." Talbot's coarse voice hit her like a fist. "Don't know who told you it was, but that's no place you want to be going. It's a rendering place, and they tan hides there. Only horses you'll find there are dead ones."

Kalantha clenched her hands, fingers biting into her palms. It felt like her stomach was rising into her throat. "Where can I find a stable? Please." Her voice had a tremor to it. Nothing right had happened today: the cellar beneath the palace, being chased, not finding Rue, getting wrong directions from a foul woman. "Is there one nearby?"

She faced the big building, and so she couldn't see Talbot scratch his head and shrug his shoulders again and look to Sean. But she heard him. "Sean, we ought to hoist her up and carry her to Rosalynn's."

"Rosalynn's healing don't come free," Sean returned.

"That girl could give Rosalynn one of them strings of pearls. That ought to pay for the mending and a meal, a place to stay tonight. Pay for a lot more than that probably. I got to be getting home to Sinda and the baby. Could take her by Rosalynn's on the way."

"No." Kalantha's voice regained its firmness. "I need to find a stable."

She heard Talbot and Sean come up behind her, Talbot resting a hand gently on her shoulder. "Kalantha, this isn't a good neighborhood for you. Rosalynn could . . ."

"Probably help me just fine," Kalantha returned. "But I've . . ."

Sean cleared his throat and came around to stand in front of Kalantha. The starlight wasn't bright yet, and his features were indistinct. The sky had a twilit cast to it, and there were wispy clouds to the west.

"I know of a stable, four blocks south of here," Sean said. "And you can probably use one of them bracelets to buy you a horse."

"That's just what I intend to do, sir."

Sean chuckled. "I'm not no sir, girl. Don't know what I was thinking acting all chivalrous a moment ago. Don't know what at all I was thinking." He reached out and grabbed her arm and pulled her close. She stumbled on her sore leg. Talbot protested, but Sean ignored him and pulled the two strands of pearls over her head. He stuffed them in his own pocket and dug his fingernails into her shoulder when she struggled. "And while I don't count myself a thief, I don't mind taking a few things now and then."

"Sean—"

"Hush, Talbot." He grabbed the sapphire ring off her thumb, then took one of the bracelets. The latter he passed to Talbot, and he smiled when the big man accepted it. "That leaves you a bracelet for a horse, girl. Consider that you just paid us for saving you from Thorn and his bullies."

Kalantha stared, dumbstruck. These men had helped her! And now they were robbing her! She said nothing, a part of her mollified that they'd left her a bracelet. And she still had her life.

"Should think about a mule instead," Sean continued. "They ride more even, better for a girl, I'd think. My mom had a mule once."

"Wh-where's the stable?" she managed. She looked down, seeing the tips of her boots and the tips of Sean's. She definitely didn't want to look the man in the eyes.

"Next street over, to the west, then three blocks south. But it's night, girl. You won't find anyone there but some skinny stable boy. And I doubt he's got the authority to sell you anything." Sean took a step back and stroked the stubble on his chin. "And since you can't buy anything tonight, you won't need this." His hand shot out and grabbed the other bracelet, her last piece of jewelry.

"Sean!" Talbot grabbed the bracelet away from his friend.

Kalantha thought the big man might give it back.

"Sean, you already took the best pieces, let me have the bracelets." Talbot patted Kalantha on the shoulder, the gesture so strong this time it sent her to her knees. "Sorry." His voice held no apology. "Should've let me take you to Rosalynn's when I had a mind to."

"You were never going to take her to Rosalynn's, and you know it." Sean made a clucking sound. "You were gonna rob her the moment I got out of sight, take it all for yourself."

Then the men took the opposite corner the youths had, leaving Kalantha alone amid the growing shadows.

She choked back a sob and inwardly cursed the men. Then she stopped herself. They hurt her, they were wrong to steal from her . . . but they weren't evil . . . not like the birds or Bishop DeNogaret. Desperation, the need to survive in this squalid place, drove the men to what they did.

"Not evil. They weren't evil." Saying the words helped her believe it. Kalantha well knew what desperation could cause people to do.

18 · Freedom Beckons

When I open my eyes in the hush before dawn, I realize what a marvelous gift I have—life. These are precious things: to breathe in the cool air; to dream about what the day will hold; to run for the sheer joy of running; to learn great wisdom from an old mongrel; to drink in the majesty of a starry sky; and most of all, to love.

~The Old Mare

Perhaps because Honest-Stormchaser appeared slighter than the other horses and seemed obedient, the men hadn't bothered to chain her. Perhaps she hadn't put up any fight and went with them willingly, standing docilely in her stall, secretly conversing with the livestock and plotting an escape. She had only the wood gate to contend with, and she was smashing at it now with her hooves. At the same time she called out to the cobs:

Break free! As we planned! All of us together!

And to the mules: *Pull on your ropes. Free yourselves and follow me!*

She shattered the last slat that barred her way and charged out into the aisle between the rows of stalls. She reared and spun on her hind legs, front hooves battering the gate on the stall of the cracker horse. *Run with everything in you,* she told the old horse. *Run as if a thousand fires were roaring behind you!* Then she started on the gate of one of the ponies.

Considerably larger and stronger than the iomud, Gallant-Stallion made quick work of his gate, charged out, and struck the slats of a hucul's stall. The pony raced out, and the Finest whirled to deal with the two men. Honest-Stormchaser had caught them off guard, and they stood shocked like frightened deer, mouths open and eyes trying to take everything in.

The smaller man was the first to react. He leapt away from his fellow and toward a bank of stalls, putting himself between a cob and Gallant-Stallion. He thrust his back against the gate and waggled his fingers, shouting at the punch to stay away and calm down. The rest of his words disappeared in the chorus of whinnies and the sound of wood splintering as two cutting horses broke out of their stalls.

"Ben, look out!" The big man finally moved, waving his arms wildly. "Ben! Ben!" He called again and crouched, trying to grab a rope around the shank of the iomud. Honest-Stormchaser eluded him, however, flailing away at the gate of a mule's stall.

Gallant-Stallion reared in front of Ben, chasing him away from the other cob's stall. The Finest's hooves cleaved through the slats and the cob ran out, turning down the aisle and trampling the smaller man.

From amid the ruckus, Gallant-Stallion's keen hearing picked up the sound of bones breaking, and he didn't have to look to know that the man was seriously injured or dead. The Finest felt sorry for the man, even though he'd helped kill Honest-Stormchaser's charge and stole who knew how many animals. Death gave no man the opportunity to repent.

"Ben!" The big man raced away from the stalls and to the spot where the stack of crates started. He reached for something Gallant-Stallion couldn't see. The Finest slashed at the stall of a cutting horse.

The aisle filled with rearing horses, all of them neighing and snorting loudly and, under Honest-Stormchaser's direction, breaking open the stalls of the animals still trapped. Through the cacophy, Gallant-Stallion heard all their voices.

Free! called one of the cobs. *Cornsilk freed us! Follow her!*

Yes, follow, brayed a mule. *Follow her away from this bad place.*

Free the others, the cracker urged. *Let none of us stay here.*

The goat could not understand the horses. He complained about the shrill, endless noise and the dust, and he bleated that one of them should chew his pen so he could escape, too.

The chickens and pigeons squawked in fear, though a capon in the midst screamed to be released.

Gallant-Stallion reversed his course and charged the opposite way down the aisle. One of the cobs brushed by him and whinnied that the punch was going the wrong way; the doors were beyond the crates. In a heartbeat Gallant-Stallion was at the fowl cages, bending his head and using his teeth to cut through the wire and wood. A heartbeat more and chickens were flying out, feathers like snowflakes filling the air. The pigeons and the capons followed.

After me! Gallant-Stallion said in their language, though he realized they weren't paying attention. Their clucking and shrieks added to the noise, as they flew to the rafters and in all directions. Then suddenly a high-pitched whinny cut through everything, and Gallant-Stallion reared so he could see over the horses.

The big man had a pitchfork and had used it to stab a hucul. The pony thrashed in pain on its side, as the man stabbed her again and again and then waved the pitchfork in an arc to keep the rest of the horses back. It didn't work; the horses were intent on escaping and in their panic were rushing at the man.

He swung the pitchfork, catching a cob in the side, the tines digging bloody grooves. Then he swung it again, cutting across a mule's neck and sending it to the floor next to the dying hucul.

The man leveled the pitchfork again, this time wielding it like a spear. He clipped the cracker horse and drew the pitchfork back to stab with it again. But his feet got tangled in the rope that trailed from Stump's neck. The hunting dog, perhaps intentionally, bumped into the back of the man's legs, causing his knees to bend. At the same time, the old cracker reared and brought her hooves down on the haft of the pitchfork, breaking it in half and knocking it from the man's grip. She galloped by him, into the shadows beyond the crates, where the iomud had run moments before.

The remaining mule brayed loud and long and hurled himself into the big man, knocking him down and stamping on his chest, breaking his ribs and arms, and stamping again and again. Splattered with blood, the mule kicked at the body with his rear hooves now, braying that the man's death was justice. The man had killed the mule's brother.

Gallant-Stallion herded the rest of the horses and ponies toward the crates. Honest-Stormchaser called to them from the shadows.

The way out is here, hurry! There was anguish in her voice. *Mourn for your brothers and sisters when we are free.*

There was a crashing sound, and Gallant-Stallion suspected the iomud had battered open the door.

Cries of *free!* and *we escape!* filled the air. Behind Gallant-Stallion, the mule continued to bray its loss, and the goat complained that there was too much in its way and it could not move.

Come with me now, Gallant-Stallion said in the mule's tongue. *There is nothing you can do for your brother, save shed tears he can no longer see.* To the goat in its tongue: *Stay here or follow me. No matter what you choose, stay silent. I tire of your wagging, wicked tongue.*

He heard Stump baying from the shadows, and heard all the horses whinnying, a mix of confusion and elation in their voices. He heard, too, men shouting, and knew that more of those who had captured the animals were trying to stop them from escaping. He couldn't make out the words, as everything was a jumble of sound, but he could hear the intent.

Galloping past the crates and barrels, which smelled strongly of old ale, Gallant-Stallion saw the soft glow of a lantern through the legs of the cobs and a hucul. He could tell that this barn indeed had been built as a warehouse, and was one of the largest buildings he'd seen in Paard-Peran. Much of it looked empty, but along one wall stretched several cots and crates full of rubbish. Two unlit lanterns hung from a post. The men lived here, or at least spent some evenings here. He could smell some animal that had been cooked, and saw chicken feet scattered near the closest rubbish crate. The Finest had no time to study anything else, as the horses were racing out the broken door, trampling another man who'd tried to stop them.

It was dark outside, and with the press of horses and the mules, Gallant-Stallion saw only bands of black and gray. He made sure all four dogs were out, and he dipped his head when chickens and pigeons flew over him and out the door. Then Gallant-Stallion jumped across the body in the doorway and followed the fleeing herd.

Three men stood across from the building, all of them shouting for the horses to stop and waving their arms. None of them were foolish enough to rush at the horses and end up like their dead fellows.

"Find Raker!" one of the men bellowed. "Tell 'im the live-stock's loose."

"Shouldn't we try to catch them?"

Gallant-Stallion saw the first man shake his head. "We're not paid enough."

"Let's see if Josh had any coins."

Gallant-Stallion found them disgusting.

It was so late that no lights burned from the few residences sandwiched between businesses and rundown warehouses. Though the sky was clear and the stars provided some light, the shadows were too thick to make out many details. Gallant-Stallion couldn't tell where the herd was heading, even his keen eyesight couldn't see ahead of the charging horses. He couldn't even see Honest-Stormchaser, though he knew she was there. He heard her.

We are free, sisters and brothers! she called loudly in the horse tongue. She repeated so the dogs could understand. They howled in response, Stump baying especially long. The goat bleated in anger, complaining that he couldn't see where they were going and that the horses were stirring up the dust on the street, making it difficult to breathe.

Gallant-Stallion tried to thrust all the noise to the back of his mind and to listen for other sounds—the city guard, which if out in numbers might try to corral them and "Raker," who the men mentioned and who could have a force to thwart their flight. Too, he listened for other men who might be out this late, coming from taverns and oblivious to the rush of horses that might trample them. As intently as he listened, he heard none of those things.

But he did hear Stump.

Big punch, the dog growled. *I smell that stinky girl.*

Gallant-Stallion's legs locked in surprise. The dog stopped, too, watching the other dogs and the horses continue down the narrow street ahead of them.

Kalantha! Gallant-Stallion had been so distracted by the escape, he'd not thought about her being in this neighborhood. *Find her, Stump. Please, please find her!*

The dog barked and raised its lip in a sneer. *I told you, big punch, I will not help you. I helped you once and ended up in that very bad place. I will go home and be beaten. But I will be petted and fed.*

Gallant-Stallion reared back in distress and frustration. The small herd was more than a block ahead, and turning a corner south. *Then I will search for her myself, Stump.* He whirled and started down the street in the opposite direction.

She is not in that direction, big horse. You have a weak nose. Follow me, punch. There was a sigh in the dog's voice, as if he was appalled that the punch hadn't the ability to handle this task. The dog raised his front leg, as if pointing to game, then he ran south between two buildings, both abandoned and so close together that Gallant-Stallion scraped his sides following. The Finest hurdled broken crates he saw at the last moment and breathed deep when he pursued the dog onto a narrow, uneven street. The buildings were not so tall here, and so the starlight better illuminated it.

At one time it must have been a good neighborhood, as the street had been made of cobblestones. But the years had not been kind to it, or the buildings that stretched as far as Gallant-Stallion could see. Everything looked tired and worn and tattered, like discarded garments.

She needs a bath and a soaping, Stump said. Several yards ahead, the dog stood in the center of an intersection, holding his pointing stance. *She stinks as bad as that cage they had us in. Worse. Much worse than the interesting thing I rolled in.*

Gallant-Stallion charged past him, turning the corner and galloping toward a figure huddled on a wooden walkway.

"Rue?" Kalantha rose to her knees. Tears streamed down her dirt-streaked face. "Rue!" She awkwardly stood as he stopped in front of her, then leaned against the building behind her and took the weight off her sore leg. "Oh, Rue, I'm lame like you."

It was too dark for her to see that the Finest was no longer injured.

"Where were you, Rue? I went to the stables and couldn't find you."

Time for questions later, Kalantha. This is not a good place for you.

"You don't have to tell me that, Rue. I more than know it. I hate this city. It's filled with people you can't trust and who want to hurt you!" She hobbled forward and tried to climb on his back. She nearly fell, and Gallant-Stallion reached over her head and clamped his teeth down on her tunic. He pulled her up and tossed her on his back. She laced her fingers into his mane as he spun around and ran toward the dog. The Finest would have turned east toward the palace, but Stump bayed and took off to the west, running down the center of the street and howling ever louder.

Gallant-Stallion followed him, wanting to look after the dog who found Kalantha and get him back to the royal stables and his straw bed. He caught up in a few heartbeats and swung around the dog, thinking that would stop him.

The palace, and the stables, Gallant-Stallion began. *We should . . .*

We should follow all of those horses, Stump said, excitement in his words. *I want to go after those horses and dogs!* He dashed around the next corner in a great loping gate.

Ahead, the starlight showed the small herd of escaping horses.

Free! one of the cobs hollered.

Gallant-Stallion raced to catch up. Kalantha held tight and leaned close against his neck. "We have to find my brother, Rue. He will not end the war on his own."

19 · Bedside Manners

I persuaded the Finest Court to give me a charge, though Tadewi said I was not ready. I counted myself fortunate that the Court yielded to my frequent requests and listened to my promise that I would guide and guard one of the Fallen Favorites. Would that, instead, the Court had listened to Tadewi. I did not like Paard-Peran. The snow vexed me, and the constant chatter of the people hurt my ears. My Fallen Favorite was a good woman, and I returned to the Court lands requesting that Tadewi select a better Finest than I for a shepherd. I would never be ready for that place.

~Duncoat Splithoof

He thought about Eyeswide and the falcon Ninéon. The Bishop could do little else but think, especially when there was no one else in the room to tend him. He missed the owl. The creature had been easier to impress and manipulate than the falcon. Too, he considered the owl more intelligent and recalled many conversations they had shared at the High Keep Temple, and later here. The owl understood long-range plans and could envision Galmier and the neighboring countries years from now. In fact, he'd met the owl before he'd met Kalantha and Meven's parents . . . before he had nurtured the notion of becoming the power behind Galmier's throne.

Eyeswide helped him plan his eventual rise. They'd spent long hours in his study mulling one scenario's merits over another's. The owl could consider schemes that might take years to effect.

The falcon?

That bird had been the owl's one mistake.

The falcon had no desire for intricate plans that would weave themselves through the years. Ninéon, it seemed to the Bishop, wanted power now and was focused only on the moment. She was like a simple animal in that respect, he mused, thinking of today and finding the past and the future both too far away to worry over.

But she had an appetite that Eyeswide lacked. A corner of his pale mouth rose with that thought. She wanted to dominate those around her and gain more and more authority. In that respect, she and the Bishop were alike.

"But I am the wiser," DeNogaret said, frowning now at the sound of his voice. It still lacked the richness he liked to listen to and that he believed drew others to him. "Far wiser. Ah, I miss you, my old friend."

He closed his eyes and settled deep into the pillow, and he began to dream of a time, years ago, when he and Eyeswide had conspired long into the night. The pleasant memories eased the pain, and . . .

"Bishop DeNogaret, I've brought you some tea." A thin man a few years older than Meven and with hair of a similar color stood in the doorway, a silver tray held in front of him.

The Bishop opened his mouth to curse the man for interrupting his memories, but stopped when he noticed steam curling up from the teapot spout. So high in the tower room, and usually waited on by older servants, the tea was often cold by the time it reached him. But this young man must have taken the stairs quickly to keep the tea warm.

"Please," the Bishop said. It was a word he didn't speak often. "I would like some of that tea." He watched the young man move into the room, taking only four long steps to reach the stand next to the bed. "I've not seen you before. . . ."

"Dustin," he was quick to supply. He poured a cup and held it to the Bishop, careful not to release it until he knew the

Bishop had it held with both hands. "My name is Dustin Cald-well."

The Bishop raised an eyebrow and took a sip. "Pepper-mint."

"A little. Sara Anne says peppermint is good for all man-ner of ailments."

"Caldwell . . . the name is familiar."

Dustin smiled. "Yes, Bishop DeNogaret. My father and mother work here at the palace. My father is a groomsman, and my mother is . . ."

"A morning cook."

"Yes, Bishop DeNogaret."

"Still, I've not seen you before." Bishop DeNogaret took several more sips, then held out the cup.

Dustin refilled it, careful not to spill a drop. "I've not been here before, Bishop DeNogaret."

"Bishop is sufficient."

"Bishop."

"Go on. . . ."

"I was a soldier, Bishop. I'd been with a unit over the border of Nasim-Guri. We took three villages, and I came back to Galmier, bringing wounded. A few we brought all the way to the palace grounds. Places to the south, they couldn't take any more wounded."

The Bishop held the cup beneath his nose and inhaled. After a moment, he took a sip and held the tea in his mouth.

"I was set to return to Nasim-Guri, assigned to a unit under Commander Selren. I was looking forward to serving under him."

Another sip, then he tipped his head toward Dustin. "But . . ."

"King Meven declared an end to the war. Several of the knight commanders distribute his decrees. The units in the city have been released."

"And so you are here instead of fighting."

Dustin nodded, his lips pursed and brows drew together. "My mother found me work here, talked to King Meven himself. I saw the King before he left, from a distance. I'm very fortunate to have work within a day of . . ."

"Being released from the King's army."

"Yes, Bishop."

"Sit."

Dustin refilled the Bishop's cup before sitting in a straight-backed chair near the bed.

"What do you think of . . . Meven's peace?" The Bishop looked at his reflection on the surface of the tea. He thought he looked older than before, his wrinkles more pronounced. Perhaps it was merely tiredness, or because he hadn't yet recovered from the injuries inflicted by the horrid horse.

Dustin shifted in the chair, his look uneasy. "I . . . I lost too many friends in the war, and I grieve for them. But we were close to winning, Bishop. It was a matter of days, Commander Selren said. We'd taken all the northern villages of Nasim-Guri, some in the center. Plans were drawn to march into Duriam, and . . ."

"I am well aware of those plans, soldier. They were my plans."

"Bishop?"

"To take Duriam, soldier. Those plans were mine. Are mine. All of it, the war, was mine. Is mine."

Dustin stood so quickly he knocked the chair over.

"Galmier is mine, Nasim-Guri was to be mine, too. And it eventually will be."

Dustin stood the chair up and reached for the tray.

"Stop." A pause: "I'll have the rest of that tea, soldier."

Dustin seemed as immobile as a statue, but his eyes moved, shifting from the teapot to the Bishop, finally staying on the Bishop, caught by the old priest's unblinking, rheumy stare.

"You are not much older than Meven." The Bishop turned his head so he could more easily see Dustin. "Impressionable, like Meven. More respectful, though." He licked his lips and rested the cup against his chest. "You are respectful of me, aren't you, Dustin?"

The young man finally moved, nodded, not able to break away from those eyes. "Respectful, Bishop. Yes, I am respectful."

"DeNogaret."

"Bishop DeNogaret. Yes, respectful."

"I'll have more tea, Dustin."

The Bishop smiled faintly as the young man poured another cup, eyes still locked, fingers trembling slightly.

"Careful, Dustin."

He set the teapot back on the tray. "Yes, I'll be careful, Bishop DeNogaret."

"And respectful."

"Of you, Bishop DeNogaret."

The Bishop noticed flecks of gold in the young man's eyes. Eyeswide had had gold eyes. This young man was not the equal of the wise bird, but he would suffice as a pet. One more pet. A better pet than Ninéon had been to the owl.

"There are others in this palace who are respectful of me, soldier."

Keeping his eyes ever on the Bishop, Dustin managed to back up a step, finding the chair and sitting. "I am not a soldier any longer, Bishop DeNogaret."

The Bishop sipped at his tea for a few moments. It was cooling too quickly. He listened to Dustin's breath, coming fast because the young man was nervous. He heard the whinny of a horse on the grounds, and that made him think of the hateful punch that had put him in this bed, nearly killing him.

"You will be a soldier again, Dustin."

"But the war is over, Bishop DeNogaret."

"For the moment, perhaps." The Bishop's voice was a little stronger now, the peppermint tea helping. "When I am fit and up from this bed, things will change. As I said, I have friends in the palace. Carefully chosen friends who respect me. And I have friends . . . elsewhere."

20 · A Foul Flock

A problem is never what it seems, my Fallen Favorite taught me. A problem is merely a splendid opportunity presented in a challenging manner.

~*Faithful-Charger, Finest shepherd to Master Cooper Geoff Waveswept, head of the merchant houses of Rel-Suel and Suel*

The falcon rode the evening wind, circling the heart of the Old Forest and seeing something very far beyond the ancient oaks below her. As they stretched their dying limbs toward the stars she pictured a young woods filled with plump hare and ground squirrels, warm and juicy and waiting to fill her stomach. As she watched the dream scene, the animals turned into soldiers dressed in shades of yellow and green, King Silverwood of Nasim-Guri's colors. She imagined her flock stalking, then descending on the soldiers, she in the lead, striking at the men and slaying them, feasting, then flying again in search of more prey.

In the back of her mind she directed an army of crows and blackbirds to also swarm a force of King Meven's men, laying them low within minutes. She'd done just that only a few hours ago, and late the day before as well. While Ninéon intended King Meven to eventually win, she couldn't have him do so too

174 ~ JEAN RABE

soon, and so she had to kill some of his men to even the score a little and prolong the battle. When she did permit the war to end, several months from now, it would only be a brief cessation to the violence she'd become addicted to. She'd give the Fallen Favorites time to lick their wounds and embrace their wives, play with their children and think life was normal again. She'd let the young among them marry and start their own families—for the population would have to grow. More soldiers would be needed. Then Ninéon would have Bishop DeNogaret dominate Meven again. They would begin a war with another country, perhaps the one to the north called Uland. She intended this cycle to continue for a long while.

Ninéon did not risk dominating the young monarch herself. When she insinuated her thoughts into the mind of a Fallen Favorite she exerted too much control and too soon turned her puppet into an empty, drooling shell. She knew she could be subtler in her control if she tried, she just lacked the patience. And so she would use the Bishop to accomplish her ends as far as Meven was concerned. She took more pleasure in dominating and shaping her own kind.

Such power pulsed within her!

Ninéon knew she possessed a drive and intellect no other bird could match. She considered herself truly blessed that she had been chosen by Eyeswide, the owl who once served as Bishop DeNogaret's confidant. Eyeswide enhanced her at the Vision Pond. She awoke to her true potential when he made her drink the foul, stagnant water and when his mind bent her to his will. But the owl did not watch her closely enough, and soon her desire for power outmatched his. She slew him and took his place over the malicious flock, and she mourned his passing out of respect—he had made her, after all.

Made her superior to all the other creatures that crawled across the face of Paard-Peran.

She could sense the animals that moved through the canopy

and across the floor of the Old Forest below her. Only the birds she'd enhanced herself had purpose—all the others had meaningless lives and were of no value other than food. They cavorted in sad, insectlike swarms through the skies, singing, dipping down and drinking from streams, laying eggs, and starting the pathetic, worthless sequence again and again. But their rotting bodies fertilized the land, and their brief existence could be swept aside by a strong wind.

She raised her gaze to the stars, then closed her eyes and continued circling, relishing the chill air ruffling her feathers and soothing her agitated mind. So rarely did she relax that she forced herself to do so now, gliding and listening to the sounds filtering up from the ancient woods.

There was the faint rustle of branches stirred by the wind. But some branches were not clicking so rhythmically, and so she knew that some members of her flock were moving higher to catch a glimpse of her. In the distance a wolf called to its mate, and she opened her eyes when moments later a female answered the cry. So keen was her hearing, she even picked up the sound of her feathers fluttering.

The night was heady, and so she continued to circle, even though she knew her minions waited anxiously in the woods below. She picked up the scent of new growth and of a nearby tributary of the Sprawling River, the rich forest loam thick with layers of leaves from the fall. There was a hint of salt, from the Sea of Sulene.

When she grew tired of all the sounds and scents she tucked her wings in close and dropped through the uppermost canopy, angling her body so not a leaf or twig brushed her, and passing the most curious of her flock who'd perched high to see her.

No matter the time of day, the Old Forest gathered the shadows around it so the floor seemed as dark as a cave, and as dark as the falcon's soul. In most places the trees were so close together an animal of any reasonable size could not slip between the massive trunks. In no other place on Paard-Peran were the hardwoods so ancient and tall, some of them as wide around as silos and more than a thousand years old. Many of them stretched well more than three hundred feet, and they allowed few saplings to take root. The tight weave of branches permitted so little light to seep through there was nothing to nurture the seeds.

But there were infrequent gaps in the canopies, where some of the giants had succumbed to age or lightning or some other malady, and so their branches were skeletal. Here, sunlight and starlight could fight their way to the earth. This is where the only seedlings could be found.

Ninéon banked toward one of those clearings now, at the very center of the ancient woods, landing at the base of a half-dead stringybark tree. Save for a small swath of ground around the tree, the floor of the clearing was filled with more than a thousand birds, their dark bodies pressed so close together they resembled a pool of oil. Their eyes glimmered malevolently and fixed on Ninéon.

She savored the quiet adoration and strutted before them.

"The war goes well." She returned to her spot at the base of the tree to address them. "Because Arlee overheard Meven Montoll's plan to end the fighting, we reacted."

A large crow in the front row puffed out its chest and rose to its full height.

"Two commanders carrying declarations of peace have been stopped."

The resulting jubilant chatter from the birds, though soft, carried through the clearing like a swarm of cicadas. Ninéon skreed loudly to silence them.

"Two more commanders must be dealt with summarily, as well as Meven Montoll's superior entourage." Ninéon paused, wondering at her words. Was her vocabulary too sophisticated for her flock? At least for some of them? They possessed varying degrees of sentience, but none approached her level of reasoning.

"We fight for Ninéon!" Arlee called.

"Ninéon!"

Her name was a deafening chant taken up by her flock—crows, blackbirds, cowbirds, starlings, small kite hawks, black skimmers, grackles, herons, cranes the shade of slate, and more. She let them go on for several minutes, pleasantly drowning in the dissonance, then silenced them with another shrill skree.

"Arlee will lead some of you to find and slay the other commanders. You will know the men by the colors—blue, like a clear sky—and by the shiny buttons on their clothes and the shiny helmets decorated with long blue feathers."

"Ninéon!" The chant resumed softly.

"Kill no other troops. The numbers on both sides are dwindling."

"The war must continue!" This came from an eager young cowbird that Ninéon favored. "Kill no more men than necessary. We must not stop the war!"

Kill no more Fallen Favorites than necessary, Ninéon thought. She'd picked up the term from one in her flock, one she would meet with when this gathering was over.

"Ninéon! Ninéon!"

"More of you will follow Dukall." She referred to the cowbird. "You will search for Meven Montoll." Ninéon had given the flock a detailed description of the young monarch so that none would accidentally slay him. "Those who surround him should perish."

"Kill all but the King!" Dukall cawed.

Ninéon nodded. "Alone, he will not journey to Duriam. He will not bargain for peace."

"No peace!" a blackbird shrieked. "No peace!"

That became a chant that Ninéon quickly ended.

"The rest of you will patrol the border villages to make sure no declarations arrive from other sources." Ninéon explained about parchment, and that no piece should be tacked to fences and walls. Though she'd mastered the skill of reading, she knew her minions were not capable of it, and therefore were not able to distinguish a declaration of peace from a request for farmhands. "Every piece of parchment—shred it."

When she was certain her orders were understood, she fixed Arlee and Dukall with an intense stare that warned them they should be successful.

"Fly! Fly, all of you!" She watched the mass of black divide into three, one force led by the crow Arlee, another by the cowbird Dukall. A dark gray hawk led the third. The wind created by their buffeting wings stirred up dirt and dry leaves and small rocks that pelted the falcon. Ninéon slammed her eyes shut and held her breath until the air stilled. Then she glided to the center of the clearing, rotated her head to work a stiff spot out of her neck, and waited.

Minutes later, her second flock arrived.

It consisted of wholly different birds—sparrows and wrens and a few squawking jays, and it was considerably smaller.

Ninéon watched them form lines in front of her, though not with the precision of her dark army. Like her predecessor, Eyeswide, Ninéon favored the dark birds able to hide in the night and the shadows. These she schooled to fly in artful formations that often resembled men on horseback. The evening helped hide the details until the flock closed on its quarry and it was too late.

There were so many advantages to such minions, and she had more than Eyeswide had once boasted. The falcon had been busy, enhancing birds primarily from the Graywoods where she used to hunt, and from scattered light stretches of forest south of Rel-Suel and Suel and west of the Darkel Ruins and Resan's

Tower. She gifted only a few of them with an intelligence approaching a man's, and this so they could lead the divided flock and teach new additions the formations. None would be so wise as she, nor would drink as much from the Vision Pond. She could not afford to risk one usurping her power, as she had usurped the owl's. Eyeswide had been a fool to bless her with so much awareness.

The sparrows twittered nervously, some of them shifting their weight back and forth on their tiny feet. The wrens, practically hidden by the shadows of the larger birds, shivered in anticipation.

This flock numbered not quite one hundred. It was not formidable enough to strike at a military target, as she'd ordered her dark minions to dispatch. But in some respects this flock held more value.

"The wren and the sparrow are transparent," she'd recently told Arlee. "Small and commonplace, these little birds are everywhere . . . and are therefore invisible."

She strutted up to the front row and lowered her beak until it touched that of an aging sparrow. A red-brown crown of feathers began just above its eyes, and it had a black spot in the middle of its breast like a man had dipped his thumb in ink and set the print to the bird. It chirped in a loud, clear voice to Ninéon. This was the one who'd taught her the term "Fallen Favorite."

The sparrow had learned it on its voyage to the Finest Court.

"Invisible," Ninéon whispered. "Not even the mystical horses see you."

It chirped again, musically this time.

Ninéon had hung on each word the sparrow had given her about the Court and the horses gathered there. Eyeswide had mentioned the creatures, but the owl hadn't had a name for them, and didn't know a place like the Court existed. He knew, however, that the creatures had been birthed by the good powers of the world, just as he had been shaped by the dark ones.

"You please me," Ninéon told the flock, though she directed it to the red-crowned sparrow. "You bring me news of the war and of the villages."

"Of the Fallen Favorites," the sparrow chirped. It had a breathy voice, each word punched out as though the act of talking came hard to the diminutive creature.

"Yes, of the Fallen Favorites. A few in particular."

"Meven Montoll," the sparrow said.

Ninéon nodded.

"And the girl who rode a Finest horse."

Another nod. "Where is she?"

"Lost," the sparrow returned after a moment. "Lost in the city, and lost to me."

"And the Finest horse?"

"Caged once, but no longer. He broke free from a prison."

"Where did he go?"

The sparrow made a gesture similar to a man's shrug. "You summoned me, Ninéon. I came here instead of following him."

"But the girl is not with the horse?"

"No."

"I need to know more about the horse."

The sparrow twisted its head so far around that it appeared to look upside down. "Eyeswide would know more about the horse, and about the other special horses."

Ninéon made a hissing sound and fluffed her feathers. But the menacing gesture was lost on the sparrow. "Eyeswide is no more. I should be the one to know now."

The sparrow chirped and straightened its head. "They speak a language I do not understand. It sounds like the snorts of horses, but it is different. Their eyes are different, too, wide and wise. Some are larger than others, and it is the largest and most beautiful of them that rule in the magic pasture."

"The magic pasture?"

"The place I flew to when I followed the girl's horse. It is a place here and yet not here, far away and quick to reach."

"You speak in riddles."

The sparrow chirped loudly. "Because I do not yet understand it all, Ninéon. Only once did I travel there, and I came back with the girl's horse. I could not serve you if I became trapped in the pasture that is here and not here."

"I need to know more about the horse . . . and the other horses you mention."

"Many, many horses were in the magic pasture, Ninéon. But not as many horses as there are birds under your command."

"That you saw." Ninéon stretched out her neck and shifted her weight back and forth on her talons.

"No, not that I saw," the sparrow echoed in its whispery voice. It had earlier explained that the Finest horses were paired with Fallen Favorites. It didn't understand how it all worked, as it hadn't spent much time in the Court lands, not wanting to be trapped there. When the big punch returned to Paard-Peran, it had come with him, then promptly reported everything to Ninéon.

"But you will find this Finest horse later, the one paired with the girl."

The sparrow cocked its head.

"In case it returns to this Court you mention, I want you to go with it again. I want you to learn much, much more about the mystical horses."

The sparrow chirped in glee, obviously happy at the prospect of performing an important task.

"I want to know just how powerful they are," Ninéon

continued. "Because I will become more powerful when I more fully understand my enemy."

"Later," the sparrow chirped. "If I search later, what now? What am I to do now?"

Ninéon raised her gaze and looked to each bird in her invisible flock. It took her minutes, and in that time the wrens continued to shiver and most of the sparrows kept shifting from one foot to the other. The jays squawked softly.

"Fly across the front and into the villages. Fly to the palace and the royal stables and the tents where the men die. Unseen, you will see everything for me. And I will see through your eyes."

She dismissed them with a bob of her head, and again closed her eyes when they took flight, not wanting the grit to lodge in her eyes and irritate her. When she was finally alone in the clearing, she lowered her head and breathed deep, taking the decaying scents of the place deep into her lungs. Then she flew behind the half-dead tree to a smaller clearing, this one ringed by stringybarks. She favored the trees because of their rough, thick bark that had stringy fibers. Birds liked them for providing nesting materials and because the bark was easy to grip. The falcon liked them for their sorrowful appearance, the strings looking like wispy hairs on an old man's head. Small white flowers dotted the highest branches and lent an out-of-place sweet fragrance to a woods otherwise filled with the odors of damp wood and rotting vegetation. But the flowers would be gone before spring's end, leaving nothing to compete with the usual strong smell of this place.

The floor here, like throughout most of the ancient woods, felt thick and springy, covered with the husks of dead insects, moldy wood, fallen leaves, and the shattered bones of birds she and her predecessor had made examples of.

The Old Forest was the quietest here, as if the stringybarks acted at her behest to keep out all sounds. The only noise was what Ninéon created herself when she clicked her beak. A pond sprawled in the center of the clearing, stagnant and shimmering darkly in the starlight. Eyeswide had called it the Vision Pond, and Ninéon considered it an apt name.

As she stared at the water, the green film on it brightened until it looked like the surface of a smooth-cut emerald. She dipped her beak to stir it.

21 · Freedom's Peril

I am certain that all of the Fallen Favorites are born ready to face all the challenges the world presents them. However, not all of them come to realize their capabilities.

~Sorrel Wintermane, shepherd to Bernd Sameter,
first king of Nasim-Guri

We should go back to the palace, Kalantha. You need tending.

"I can't go back there, Rue." Kalantha's words spilled out so quickly she had to fight for breath and to be heard above the thundering hooves of the escaping horses. "Someone locked me in the cellar beneath the palace, then chased me." She twisted her fingers into his mane to hold on as he galloped down the street after the iomud. "They chased me across the grounds and into the city. I've no idea what I've done to make someone so angry."

Gallant-Stallion didn't reply. He focused on the horses around him, pressing tight and bumping against him and Kalantha's legs. The animals were jubilant, their neighs and whinnies translating into cheers at being free of the men and the building. Caught in their midst, the goat didn't have time to complain; he stayed busy keeping out from under the horses' hooves and away from the two mules that had raced past him, hind legs kicking dangerously in the air.

Behind them, chickens and pigeons raised a ruckus as they perched on buildings and cooed and clucked at each other, all wondering where they should go.

Not after the horses, Gallant-Stallion heard the capon squawk. *The horses and the dogs are tied to the ground.*

"I don't know who I can trust at the palace, Rue." She sucked in a breath when a cob rode even with them, its side bumping against her leg. Gallant-Stallion sped up to give Kalantha more room. "I don't know if I can trust any of them—Sara Anne in the kitchen, the guards. They can't all be bad. But we don't have the time to sort them all out. I'd like to know who wants to help me and my brother . . . but I don't have the time to deal with that now. We have to find Meven."

The small herd startled a few late-night revelers spilling out tavern doors. The iomud leapt over a man sprawled near a wooden sidewalk, and the rest of the horses tried to copy her, though the cracker horse ended up landing on the man's legs. Moments later the escaping horses turned a corner that led to a wider street where they could run faster and farther apart.

Kalantha leaned forward and wrapped her arms around Gallant-Stallion's neck.

"I've missed you, Rue."

It is good to be with you, Kalantha.

Of all the Fallen Favorites the Finest had encountered since coming to Paard-Peran, only she had been able to hear him. Each Finest had a gift, and Gallant-Stallion knew his was to communicate with his charge.

"Where are they going, all these horses?"

South of the city.

"How were you with them? Why weren't you in the stable?" Other questions followed, broken only by her gasps for breath. None were answered. Gallant-Stallion increased his pace and passed the mules and the cutting horses, catching up to the iomud and seeing that the dogs were in the lead.

Wearing the form of a riding horse, the Finest iomud could speed by them all. But she kept an easy tempo the others could match, even the goat.

I hear men behind us, Gallant-Stallion told her.

Honest-Stormchaser snorted. *The neighborhood wakes up because we make the sound of a storm with our hooves. None will catch us, as we catch them all by surprise. We have done good this night, Rue. We have kept these horses out of the bellies of men. We have given them freedom.*

Freedom for a time, at least.

They cleared the poor quarters and galloped down a row of merchant guildhalls and larger taverns, where gawkers peered out windows and doors to watch the herd run. It hadn't rained in some time, and so the horses sent a dust cloud in their wake, coloring the sky gray and causing Kalantha to cough so hard she nearly lost her grip.

Gallant-Stallion heard whistles blowing and through the din he picked out men and women calling for the city guards. Lights were coming on in the second and third floors of the tall buildings in the block ahead of them. The small herd entered a merchant district, and Gallant-Stallion picked up one of his favorite scents—bread baking. He spotted a bakery with oil lamps glowing in the front window; the people inside were busy baking for the coming morning. Then they were beyond that and the other businesses, so fast the Finest didn't register what the shops were. They veered around a large, open wagon a man was hitching a draft horse to. The horse spooked and fell in with the herd, the man shouting and waving behind them as he futilely tried to catch up.

Gallant-Stallion took the lead now, as this part of the city seemed familiar to him. Honest-Stormchaser fell back and whinnied encouragements to the horses.

Do not slow down! Freedom is close!

We are free, returned one of the cobs.

My legs burn! This came from the old cracker horse, who had dropped back next to the goat.

Gallant-Stallion slowed only a little to accommodate the trailing animals, then he turned another corner and galloped down the road that led south of the city. The sky was clear and the host of stars showed a scattering of farmhouses. Beyond them, at the very edge of the Finest's vision, were clusters of trees. That is where Honest-Stormchaser intended them to go.

"Kalantha Montoll! There she is!" The shout startled Gallant-Stallion, and when he paused suddenly to see where it came from, the iomud nearly ran into him. She snorted at him angrily and reared, called to the rest to follow her, and took off toward the farms.

Gallant-Stallion saw a man in uniform, sitting astride a warmblood and holding a lantern with one hand, the reins in the other.

"Kalantha!" he hollered. He was a block away, and kicked at the warmblood's sides to close the distance. "Everyone in the palace is looking for you!"

Gallant-Stallion paused only a moment, part of him wanting to hand Kalantha over so she could be tended. But the greater part trusted his charge—if she thought people at the palace were hunting her, they most definitely were. Perhaps not this man, as he might truly be interested in her well-being. But Gallant-Stallion wasn't going to take the chance.

"Rue, run!"

"Kalantha, wait!" The man dropped the lantern and grabbed the reins with both hands, leaned forward and kneed the horse faster.

"Rue!"

He didn't need Kalantha's urging. He sprang forward, hooves churning up the dirt and pebbles. He couldn't see the warmblood behind him; the dust kicked up from himself and the small herd was a haze that floated above the street and obscured even the buildings. Heartbeats later he'd caught up with the rest and passed them by, and for a moment he relished the sheer joy of running.

Their hoofbeats sounded muted against the earth, without the buildings to reverberate off. The air was clean here, not touched by the pleasant odor of baking bread, or by the foulness of ale, sweat, or dung. He lengthened his stride, knowing the horses, mules, and the goat could not keep up. The iomud would stay with him. He needed to get Kalantha away from the city.

Gallant-Stallion passed the first farmhouse. A candle glowed upstairs behind gauzy curtains, someone awoken by the noise of the small herd perhaps. He swung behind the barn and waited. A few minutes passed before all but the chickens and pigeons joined him. The fowl had been left behind in the city.

The iomud beamed at their success, prancing back and forth, head tipped up to soak in the starlight.

Two of us died. This came from the mule, still mourning the loss of his brother.

And at least two men, the cracker horse added.

Life for life, observed one of the cobs. *Though I count ours the greater loss.*

The goat wandered away from the barn and began munching on a tall patch of sweet clover. Kalantha, exhausted, slumped forward on the back of Gallant-Stallion's neck. Her fingers fluttered in his long mane.

"Thank you for saving me, Rue. You always save me."

He didn't tell her that saving her was part of his responsibility. Instead, he said: *Where is your brother, Kalantha? You said we must find him.*

She rubbed her cheek against his neck. "South. He said he was going to take one of the roads south. I was supposed to go with him." She quickly explained about how she asked that he stop the war, about the meeting he called with the knight commanders and the peace proclamations, about their planned meeting with Nasim-Guri's King Silverwood and seeking an end to the war. "I thought you were lame, Rue. I thought I'd have to ride another horse with Meven. Where were you?"

He didn't answer that. Instead, he directed his attention to Honest-Stormchaser. *We are free of the city. Now what do you plan?*

She bobbed her head toward the goat. *He will stay here, I think.*

And the others?

We will take them into the woods.

They conversed in hidden speak, none of the others understanding them.

There are dangers in the forest. Kalantha and I were chased by wolves. A companion of hers and his horse were killed.

A better chance than these creatures would have had in the city. Some of them would have been slaughtered this morning for meat.

The old cracker horse started plodding toward the south. She was tired, but she held her head high to show her determination.

They can forage in the woods, Honest-Stormchaser continued. *And if they stay together, they will find some measure of safety in numbers. Rue, do not worry for them, be happy their destiny is their own now.*

A door slammed, and the Finest heard the click of boot heels across a front porch. He wondered if the man in the uniform from the city had followed them down the road and would find them at this farm.

The iomud wuffled that it was time to move, and Gallant-Stallion agreed. Her tempo was relaxed this time, and she fell in behind the cracker.

The mule and one of the dogs—the oldest—stayed behind at the next farm they came to, finding the barn door cracked open and pushing it wide so they could go inside. The mule wished the others well, and said he would find this place comfortable. His voice was still filled with sadness, and Gallant-Stallion knew the mule would think about his brother for quite some time.

They reached the woods in the misty hour before dawn, and they gathered in a clearing where a creek gurgled merrily. The horses drank deep, while Gallant-Stallion hovered at the edge of the treeline, looking north and squinting to see if they were being pursued. Two of the remaining dogs wandered west, picking up the trail of something interesting. They thanked the iomud before they disappeared from view.

Stump remained, growling softly and scratching at his ear. *Big horse, I should be home, tied to the post, sleeping in the hay. Soft hay, a full belly. I hunger.* He scratched at a spot on the ground now, and a line of drool edged out of the corner of his mouth and dripped on a front paw.

Gallant-Stallion continued studying the northern horizon. *You could have stayed in the city, Stump. Your nose would have led you home. Nothing made you follow us.*

The dog scratched harder at the dirt.

You could go home now. You can see the lights of the city and the outline of the buildings. The palace is toward the Esi Sea, and you can smell the salt in the air when you near it. You can find your way back to the stables and to the post they tie you to.

The dog growled softly. *I tire of the post,* he finally admitted. Then he got up and went to the creek to drink.

Honest-Stormchaser talked to the horses, her words a series of wuffles and snorts to Kalantha's ears. She told them about foraging, about which berries were the sweetest and which kinds of grasses tasted the best. She mentioned the dangerous wolves and that large wild boars might pose a threat.

Your numbers will keep you safe, she said. *Together, you are a strong force.* She concluded by telling them about a large herd of mountain ponies to the west, and that they might find good fellowship there on the other side of the Sprawling River.

You will not go with them? Gallant-Stallion expected her to lead the band.

She shook her head, her mane sparkling with drops of dew and looking like tiny gems were caught in the hairs. *They do not need me any longer. The cracker will lead them well.*

To the Court then? To report on the death of your noble and to gain a new charge? Gallant-Stallion intended to ask her to report on him and Kalantha, but another shake of her head stopped him.

I will seek the Finest Court later, friend Rue. For the present, I will travel with you. I believe you could use some help keeping your charge safe, especially with the war punishing this land. I heard her speak of men chasing her and being unable to trust her fellow Fallen Favorites.

Gallant-Stallion only for a moment considered arguing with her. Kalantha's safety was important, and so he welcomed the iomud's help.

Where do you take her, Rue?

South. He flicked his head in the direction of a clump of young walnut trees. *She wants to find her brother. A village poised on stilts lies in this direction. We will stop there, or perhaps at a farmhouse a little farther away, so someone can tend her.*

Lead, then. The iomud nickered farewell to the horses who'd begun to graze by the creek.

Gallant-Stallion took off at a trot, careful not to trip over logs or spreading bushes. He had no desire to become lame again. The iomud kept at his shoulder, eyes flitting this way and that, ears pricked forward, listening for predators.

Stump followed several yards behind.

22 · The Vision Pond

Aspirations are like clouds. A Finest cannot meet them by rearing back and stretching. A Finest cannot touch them with his hooves no matter what mountain he stands upon. However, if a Finest is patient and trusting, he will achieve whatever aspirations are necessary to his life and the life of his Fallen Favorite. Grounded, those aspirations will be delivered to him, like the rain from the clouds comes to the earth.

~Blackeyes Longmane of the Finest Court

Ninéon stirred the emerald pond with a talon. Despite the cool spring and the chill evening, the water felt warm and relaxing. It invigorated her and made all her senses more acute. Eyeswide told her the Vision Pond had been formed by the dark gods Iniquis and Abandon, just as they changed him from a simple hatchling to a creature of great cunning and malevolence.

Ninéon had known nothing of divine beings before Eyeswide "touched" her. She'd thought only of simple things—food, shelter, and flying. Those days had been her Remorseful Time . . . until Eyeswide had awakened her. She'd been an apt pupil, listening attentively to his lectures about the gods. Iniquis and Abandon were named by Peran-Morab, sister to the eldest god, Paard Zhumd. Kazak, Toric, and Kladrub were the other gods—offspring of Peran-Morab's union with one of the first men.

Iniquis and Abandon were also offspring of that marriage, Eyeswide explained. That their hearts were dark was a blessing, the owl contended. Iniquis gave Eyeswide speech and intellect . . . so it translated to Ninéon that Iniquis so blessed her. Abandon gave Eyeswide fast flight, an almost endless endurance, and taught him how to enhance other creatures.

Hence Abandon gave those things to the falcon through her now-dead mentor.

Ninéon knew Eyeswide had respected only Abandon and Iniquis and considered the five other powers weak—even though they had created the race of mystical horses.

But Ninéon was learning more about those horses with each report of her invisible spies, and so they were becoming less and less a thing to be feared or to worry about. She knew far more about them than they knew about her. Ninéon intended to hold every advantage in the war in this world—and the war she hoped to someday bring to the land of the Finest Court.

Dominating those called the Fallen Favorites would be enough for now . . . but not for always.

She edged both talons into the pond and lowered her beak to drink. She drank from it nearly daily, and sometimes more than once on days she was depressed or thoughtful. She knew Eyeswide hadn't imbibed so often, and perhaps that was one of the reasons she was able to best him and take his place.

Each time she drank things became clearer and her mind could better focus.

She stared at the ripples that floated away from her beak. In the space between the ripples she caught glimpses of places—sometimes of lands she'd never seen. But she instinctively knew what those places were.

In the first whorl to move away from her she spied a marshy land that stretched away from her old home of the Graywoods and beyond the city of Dolour deep in the country of Vered. The marsh looked interesting, and Ninéon wanted to find a reason to fly there. Thin pools of stagnant water covered the ground in the low-lying places, and insects formed clouds everywhere. The spring was warmer there, helped by the wind coming from the coast. An abundance of animals to hunt made her salivate. She saw lizards skimming across ponds and skittering up the trunks of young cypress trees, turtles in the shallows, and small deer drinking from patches where the moss hadn't taken hold. She could smell the rich fetidness of the loam and feel the humid air ruffling her feathers.

Perhaps Meven Montoll should take the next war farther south to Vered, not Uland as Bishop DeNogaret had mentioned before. She would have this marsh as hers!

And what about the Bishop? Ninéon turned her thoughts to him, and in the next space between ripples she glimpsed the north tower of the Nadir palace.

A wispy layer of clouds obscured some of the stars, and so the palace took on a haunted, pleasing appearance to Ninéon. In the hour before dawn she could see lanterns lit on the lowest level—no doubt for the benefit of servants who were bustling about to prepare breakfast and to clean the halls.

But for the benefit of whom?

King Meven was not there, and neither was his meddlesome sister Kalantha. Were the servants like worker bees, scurrying about at the various tasks out of some instinct?

The falcon made a gesture that approximated a sneer; she was so much above all of them.

She looked higher, eyes locking on the topmost level of the north tower. There was light coming from a window, so faint she almost missed it at first. In the next ripple that spread away, she peered closer and looked inside the window. The nub of a candle burned on a plate; rivulets of wax spread away from it and across the top of a nightstand, marring its polished wood surface.

Ninéon saw Bishop DeNogaret, his face the color of the

pale candle wax, sleeping propped up in his bed, covers tucked in tight all around him to keep him from falling out and injuring himself further. He was breathing more regularly than when the falcon had seen him personally. The hint of color in his lips suggested he had improved, at least a little. On a tray sitting on a chair next to the bed was a half-full cup of tea and an empty soup bowl. Sitting on another chair, head bobbed forward and also sleeping, was a plump woman with an apron tied around her waist. Ninéon knew this to be one of Bishop DeNogaret's puppets.

The falcon had her own puppets in the palace, some more useful than others depending on the length of time they'd been serving her. The most recent acquisitions, including a stable hand and the man in charge of the kitchen, were the most useful. She hadn't yet turned their minds to the consistency of the Dolour marsh.

Ninéon decided she would leave for Nadir later this morning to visit with the Bishop again, to taunt and push and to make plans for this ongoing war and the one that would be waged next and next. She would visit some of her puppets, too, and make certain they were taking exceptional care of the Bishop. The falcon needed the old priest—at least for the time being. Perhaps she would have him teach her how to more subtly control others, and how to merely suggest things and not order the people about. The Bishop's puppets lasted so much longer than the falcon's. Maybe if she could learn his restraint she could send his spirit to meet Eyeswide's.

"No," she told herself. For some reason she was fond of the man. He worshiped Iniquis, the dark power she favored. It wouldn't do to dispatch too many of the dark power's children. "Would not do at all. At least not yet."

She closed her eyes and let the water warm all of her and lull her to sleep. When she awoke, it was well past dawn, and she still stood in the Vision Pond. She dipped her beak to take a drink and to stir the water again, turning it from the murky olive to the bright emerald.

She thought about her invisible flock, the wrens and sparrows and the few jays she'd included for a splash of color and a change in song. Then she thought about one bird in particular, one with a red-brown crown.

Valane, the falcon named her. It was the name of one of the early priestesses of Iniquis, in the days before men relegated the priesthood only for themselves and graciously allowed women to assume the role of acolytes.

"Valane," Ninéon called to the water. "What do you see?"

23 · Fighting for Peace

The good powers teach us that there will be a time when the best of the Fallen Favorites reach out with their hearts, not their hands. When they will grasp ideas and values, not coins and baubles. They will learn that selflessness, not selfishness, will lead to salvation.

~Dunlegs of the Misty Pasture, once shepherd to a Dolour King

Meven felt rested, despite having slept in a bed that was little better than a military cot. He was full, having eaten two helpings of stewed pigeon late last night. One of the village women cooked for all his men, roasting the pigeons on a hot fire and stuffing them with garlic and herbs. The garlic was still strong in his mouth and he wondered if there was any almond milk left to help ease the taste.

He also felt unclean, not having bathed since four days past. Some folks did not bathe more than once or twice a month, he knew, but when he lived at the High Keep Temple he bathed at least once a week—the priests and acolytes believed that cleanliness kept them closer to the gods. And in his palace he bathed every few days, often in the winter each evening, as the water was heated and felt too good to resist. He could ask for a bath here in one of their canvas tubs, and knew they would provide it—would be quick to provide it. But it was another two or three days to Duriam and he would wait and make himself more presentable right before his audience. He put a few drops of a musky oil on his neck and wrists to help cover any offensive smell, then replaced the vial in his pocket.

This morning he wore an avantail, at the request of the lieutenant. It was a mailed garment designed to protect his neck, suspended from a bacinet helmet and draping over his shoulders. Beneath that he wore a quilted tunic of dark forest green, embroidered with maple and fern leaves. He'd not worn anything in "his colors" since he'd confined Bishop DeNogaret to the north tower. In fact, he'd been considering changing his colors. He liked the maroon shade of his study drapes, and since neither of the neighboring countries used red, that would be acceptable.

The lieutenant gave him a buckler, a small round steel shield similar to the ones the soldiers carried. Meven knew how to use it, as he'd sparred often with the troops on the palace grounds for exercise. One held the shield by a wooden handle and kept it at arm's length to help deflect blows. Lieutenant Rendell had been overly protective of the King since they had discovered the remains of Javal and his men.

Meven thanked the villagers, making it a point to shake the hand or touch the arm of each man, woman, and child who arose before dawn to see him off. He accepted their gifts of food—a jug of caudell, wine thickened with chicken and duck eggs; several flat pieces of gruel bread, an unyeasted bread made from gruel, flour, oil, and salt; and two onion and cheese pies. Although it was not the fare he'd become used to, Meven was honestly grateful for it, as the villagers were giving him their best. He thanked them all and vowed to return to the village when peace was assured.

One of the farmers had groomed Meven's noriker, and though the man lacked some of the skills of a farrier, he had done his best to pick the bits of gravel out of the horse's hooves.

"They are kind to me even though they've lost brothers and sons in this cursed war I started."

"You're the King of Galmier," Lieutenant Renell returned. "They have to be kind to you."

No one spoke for the next hour, as the entourage wended its way south and over to the border between Galmier and Nasim-Guri. A branch of the Sprawling River marked most of the boundary, and Horcort found a place to cross where the water came up just short of the horses' bellies. There was a bridge far to the west, but it would add more than a day to the trip. The water splashed against Meven's legs and soaked through his trousers, but he did not become chilled. The spring was starting to warm, and he looked to the east, where a band of pink from the rising sun showed between the trees and above the horizon. Too often Meven missed the sun coming up. At the palace he tended to lounge in bed until breakfast was being put on the table.

On the other side they followed the branch west for a few miles before finding a merchant trail and taking it southwest. Lieutenant Rendell suspected it would lead to Duriam, the capital and largest city in Nasim-Guri.

"Signs of fighting here, Sire." Horcort had taken the lead, and now slipped from his horse's back, the entourage pausing while he knelt on the road and moved the dirt with his fingers. "Days ago, most likely, though no more than three or four. Some blood here and here." He stood and looked to the east, cupped his hand across his brow. "Our men, Sire."

Meven's gaze followed Horcort's pointing finger. A blue banner fluttered in the tall grass at the edge of a line of river birch. Something was holding it to the ground, and Meven guessed it to be a body since a crow flew off when Horcort hollered.

"Maybe neither side won," Meven mused.

"Maybe." Horcort pointed to parallel lines in the dirt, heading south. "A litter, I think, someone dragging wounded away."

"Or dead nobles to be buried at home." This came from one of the other soldiers. "Shall we bury him, Lieutenant Rendell, our man over there?" He nodded toward the body by the river birch. "And there might be more out there."

"No time," Meven said. "We stop the war, then we see to the dead. I don't think they'll mind."

A handful of miles later, the woods became thicker on either side of the road, and one of Meven's lead soldiers fell to an arrow that pierced his throat.

"We are attacked!" Horcort called out the obvious.

The soldiers reacted immediately, drawing their swords and dismounting, holding their bucklers up for protection as more arrows came from both sides of the road.

"Twenty or more of them!" Horcort said, judging by the number of arrows.

Meven didn't dismount fast enough, and one of the soldiers plucked him from his horse and pushed him off the road where the grass was tall and would provide cover. The horses galloped forward, stopping a dozen yards down the road, save Meven's noriker, which stayed near him. The enemy concentrated their arrow fire on the soldiers, leaving the horses alone.

Meven peered above the grass, holding the buckler near his face to escape the fate of his fallen soldier. He could see shapes moving in the trees, and caught a glimpse of yellow fabric, a tabard of a Nasim-Guri man.

"Stop, we yield!" Meven shouted. He waved his gloved hand, then pulled it back down as the fletching of an arrow brushed his fingertips. "We yield!"

"Die, dogs of Galmier!" came a shout from the trees to the west.

"Let your blood water our ground!" came another cry.

Meven heard the rustle of branches and saw more movement in the trees, the Nasim-Guri men finding a better position from which to volley. He glanced over his shoulder and saw that

Lieutenant Rendell and the others were crouched at the sides of the road, heads barely above the tall grass.

"We mean to make peace!" Meven tried. "I am . . ." Another rain of arrows cut off the rest of his words. Behind him, one of his soldiers fell to an arrow in his shoulder.

"Horcort!" Lieutenant Rendell was quick at his scout's side. "Don't pull the arrow out," he hushed. "Press on your wound. We'll tend to you when this is over."

"I am the King of Galmier!" Meven shouted. "We mean to make peace with King Hunter Silverwood of Nasim-Guri!"

Laughter came from the west side of the road.

"If you're a king, I'm a rich man with a thousand acres." Softer, though not so soft Meven couldn't hear: "Aim low where the grass meets the road." A pause: "Well, King of Galmier, prepare to meet the gods of Paard-Peran!"

Lieutenant Rendell jumped up and ran west, swinging his sword above his head and hollering. Three men copied him, darting left and right and moving so fast the archers could not draw a good bead.

Three more of Meven's soldiers ran to the east. Meven shuddered at the odds. If there were at least twenty Nasim-Guri men, ten to each side of the road, his soldiers could not survive this. He jumped up and ran with them to the east, drawing a thin-blade that was more ornamental than serviceable.

As he closed, Meven could tell there were only eight men on this side of the road. Perhaps they were not as outnumbered as they first believed. Not encumbered by the heavy chain mail armor the soldiers wore, Meven passed them by, nimbly clearing a fallen birch and racing through a creek. He held the thin-blade high, and it caught the early sun and flashed.

"Draw swords!" one of the Nasim-Guri soldiers ordered. In response, the eight men dropped their bows. The hiss of steel tugged from scabbards filled the air, and the men raced from the trees to face Meven's small force.

"Die, dogs of Galmier!"

"Die, you foul beasts!"

"We mean peace!" Meven yelled as loud as he could. Meven raised his sword high and brought it down on the arm of an advancing soldier. At the same time he kicked out with his foot, the heel of his boot striking soundly against the man's shield and knocking him off balance. The man teetered, and Meven followed through with another kick and another sword cut, slicing through the heavy jerkin and drawing blood. The man dropped his sword, hollering in pain. A third kick sent him sprawling on the ground. Meven raced over the top of him to parry the blow of an advancing soldier.

"We truly don't want to kill you!" Meven's voice was becoming hoarse, and he shouted in surprise when the Nasim-Guri man's sword came down hard on his thin-blade, shattering it.

"Funny, I want nothing more than to kill you," the man returned.

He drew the sword above his head, the pose of an executioner, bringing it down to cleave through Meven. But the King of Galmier was fast, spinning to his side and darting back to the soldier he'd knocked down. The soldier struggling to get up, lunged at Meven, who jammed a boot heel against his throat. Meven reached down and grabbed the fallen soldier's broadsword and brought it up just in time to parry the next blow.

The broadsword was much heavier than the thin-blade, and Meven didn't bother trying to lift it above his head. Instead, he dropped the buckler and gripped the pommel with both hands, swinging the sword at waist level and narrowly missing his opponent.

Out of the corner of his eye he saw that each of his soldiers on this side of the road faced two Nasim-Guri men. "I can't die," he whispered. "If I die, the Bishop gets the throne." The previous monarch had signed such a measure and Meven had endorsed a similar document days after he'd been crowned. Not having an heir or a brother, without such a document there would be a power struggle that could tear the country apart. He thought leaving the country to the Bishop was a good idea. Louder: "The Bishop cannot have the throne!"

The words revitalized him, and he fought with a passion his soldiers hadn't seen before. It spurred them on, too, and the man nearest Meven dropped one of his foes and wounded the next.

"We've no choice, Sire, but to kill these men!" the soldier called to Meven. "You want peace, but we want to live!"

"Aye!" shouted another Galmier soldier. "I've a wife and a babe at home!"

"Sire?" This came from one of the Nasim-Guri soldiers. He was young, no older than Meven, and he wore a leather jerkin instead of armor. His hair curled over his shoulders, no military cut, and his broadsword showed signs of rust and poor treatment.

"I told you I'm the King of Galmier!" Meven's voice cracked. He'd been shouting so much. He sucked down a deep breath and swung the borrowed sword faster, the metal whistling in the air. The blade knocked away his opponent's shield, and when he brought it back around and swung again, the tip sliced through the jerkin and drew a line of blood. "Yield! I want peace!"

His opponent sneered and lunged. Meven ducked beneath the sword and ran his own forward, skewering the man.

"By the gods!" Meven released the pommel, and the man dropped to his knees, then fell forward. Meven started shaking, staring at the body and unaware that the first man he'd dropped, the one he hadn't killed, was getting back on his feet. "I killed him."

"Yes, Sire!" one of his soldiers cheered. "Thank the gods you killed one. Six left over here."

"Killed one," he whispered. Fighting, being out here with his soldiers, this was all so very different from being in the palace. Not the locale, that wasn't the difference. This felt so real and intense. Things were muzzy back at the palace, especially when in the Bishop's company. Meven had been . . . detached . . . there. This was so very, very real.

Meven staggered backward, tripping over a rotting log and falling into the Nasim-Guri soldier who'd gotten up.

NONE OF THEM WERE LOOKING TO THE OTHER SIDE OF THE road, where Lieutenant Rendell and three men fought against a force of twelve. Outnumbered three to one, the Galmier soldiers were holding their own only because they were armored and were far more skilled than the Nasim-Guri farmers who'd been conscripted into the army. Their weapons were better, sharpened and polished, and Lieutenant Rendell directed his men with more authority and experience than the stoop-shouldered man leading the opposition. He brought down two of the Nasim-Guri farmers before one of them got in a lucky swing on a Galmier soldier.

"Lieutenant, Sandall is down! Dead!"

"No mercy!" Lieutenant Rendell shouted. "No peace for these louts! Kill them all."

Two more Nasim-Guri farmers went down, making the odds eight to three on the west side of the road. Lieutenant Rendell bettered the odds by one more when he sliced off the sword arm of their leader. He would have finished the man, but a shout from Meven stayed his hand.

EAST OF THE ROAD, FOUR NASIM-GURI MEN FACED THREE Galmier soldiers and Meven. All of their swords were held low to their sides, but none had sheathed the weapons.

"He called you 'sire.' "

Meven nodded to the Nasim-Guri soldier.

"I am King Meven Montoll of Galmier, and I do indeed mean to make peace with your country."

One of the Nasim-Guri men spat and rubbed the ball of his foot into the ground. However, the eldest of the lot stepped forward, eyes on Meven's royal ring.

"They say a boy leads Galmier and started this war," the older soldier said.

"I'm not a boy. Not anymore." Meven looked to the man he'd slain. "But I did start the war . . . and I was wrong."

The soldier who had spat tightened the grip on his pommel, his knuckles showing white. "You started the flow of blood!"

"Aye," Meven agreed. "And I aim to end it now." He called to Lieutenant Rendell to stop the fighting and to bring the declarations of peace.

The elder Nasim-Guri soldier noted the absence of their leader and shouted for his kinsmen to stand down.

It took several minutes for Lieutenant Rendell to comply, as he and his men cautiously backed away from their opponents, then gathered the horses. The declarations were in a deerhide pack he carried to Meven. The lieutenant did not sheathe his sword, though the other Galmier soldiers did at Meven's request.

"Lieutenant Rendell . . ." Meven gestured to the Nasim-Guri soldier he'd been speaking to. The lieutenant guardedly pulled one of the parchments out and handed it over.

"I am Officer Herran," the soldier said as an introduction. "Now in charge of this squad, as you've killed Lieutenant Lane."

"Herran." Meven bowed slightly and waited for him to read the declaration. But Herran passed it to another man for that task, and Meven realized the elder soldier could not read.

The Nasim-Guri men whispered among themselves for long

minutes while Meven and his soldiers stood silent and waited. Lieutenant Rendell still kept a grip on his sword and put himself between the enemy and his King.

"You might be the King of Galmier," Herran said after a time. "Or a messenger wearing his ring. And this . . ." He waved the parchment in the air and let the wind catch it and blow it into the lowest branches of a birch tree. "This is just parchment and ink. Forgive us, *Your Majesty,*" the last word said with a sneer, "if we don't believe you."

Meven puffed out his chest and took a step forward. Lieutenant Rendell moved in front of him.

"He is the King of Galmier, Officer Herran. And he does want peace. We've delivered declarations to villages along the merchant road. We've more to deliver here, and a treaty for your King Silverwood."

"And why should we believe you?" Herran continued. "Why would you want peace when you're winning?"

Lieutenant Rendell let out a deep sigh that sounded like leaves blowing across dry ground. He didn't have a good answer for that.

"Because the war was a mistake," Meven answered. "Please take me to King Hunter Silverwood of Nasim-Guri in the capital of Duriam. I don't need to convince you that I want peace. I need to convince him. Grant me the opportunity to stop this senseless war."

The Nasim-Guri men looked clearly skeptical.

"There was no warning for this war," Herran said. "No reason for it that the nobles saw. And I see no reason for an end. You are winning."

Meven shook his head. "There have been too many deaths on both sides for there to be a victor."

Herran let out a deep breath and straightened his jerkin. "All right, *King Meven Montoll,* I'll take you to my liege."

Meven brightened.

"But only if your men surrender all of their weapons."

Lieutenant Rendell protested.

"Now," Herran continued. His men gathered the swords and bucklers and tugged knives out of boot sheaths. When they were finished, Herran added: "And only if . . . *King Meven Montoll* . . . you agree to be taken to the capital as my prisoner."

Meven closed his eyes, clenched his hands, and sucked in a deep breath. He'd not considered surrender, it wasn't a "kingly" thing to do. A king commanded rather than yielded.

And yet his commands so far had brought about all this bloodshed.

He'd killed a man, moments ago.

Why wasn't someone here to advise him? Bishop DeNogaret . . . Kalantha . . . someone who could tell him what to do.

"I said . . . do you agree, King Meven Montoll?"

Meven nodded yes.

24 · Through Valane's Eyes

If you gallop after only worthy goals—with all the speed you can manage—you are certain to achieve much . . . even if you don't catch what you started after.

~*The Old Mare*

The sparrow loved cities, the larger the better, and she was headed toward one of the largest—if not the largest—in all of Paard-Peran.

Nadir, the people called it, a pleasant-sounding word for a marvelous place.

The sparrow loved that people in cities tended to be much dirtier than their counterparts in small villages. They discarded things with so little thought . . . scraps of food, bits of cloth . . . all of which the sparrow and her fellows found useful. It was easier to scavenge in cities than in villages and in the woods. And nests could be built in better-sheltered spots, such as in the rafters of stables and spots where tiled roofs overhung their buildings. The leavings of people were not as satisfying as carrion, but there was more than enough of that on the battlefields and beyond.

Too, the sparrow found cities more interesting than the

210 ~ JEAN RABE

woods. Much more color to take in, more sounds, hundreds of people to watch and try to comprehend.

Valane understood people better now. Ninéon had done something to her to make her smarter and cleverer. The water in the murky pond that the sparrow had initially railed against was the catalyst. And twice when Ninéon was elsewhere the sparrow drank from it again. Such a smart, resourceful bird!

Valane flew faster than in the Before Time, which is what she called her five years of life prior to Ninéon. Sparrows not touched by the murky water couldn't keep up with her, neither could many larger birds. She wondered how fast she could fly if she was able to drink more of the water . . . when the falcon wasn't around, of course. Ninéon seemed to guard the mystical pond closely. Faster still, the sparrow dreamed, and smarter so she could hatch intricate plans like her mentor did. Valane had no desire to take Ninéon's place, as she'd heard the tales of Ninéon slaying Eyeswide, an owl said to rule all the birds of the world. From the sparrow's observations, the ones in power were the ones facing the greatest risk—from enemies seen and from those not yet discovered.

No, Valane would be content to work from the shadows, but if only she could do so with more wiles and speed!

As she flew past the border between the two warring countries, she thought of the city and where she would visit first. A baker's just inside the merchant district was her favorite spot. In an alley behind the business rested all sorts of treats the baker deemed imperfect for the public. Valane didn't care what the treats looked like, just how they tasted. And they always tasted oh-so-good—better than the discarded sweets from other cookshops in this city or any other. In the Before Time she had to wait until the other birds finished feasting, and she could fly down in search of their crumbs. Now, however, she had first pickings, unless one of Ninéon's larger birds found the bakery first.

Then she had to wait.

Valane hated waiting.

The sparrow imagined what she might find—perfect imperfect sweet rolls with icing that tasted incredible and dough laced with cinnamon; still-warm bread that hadn't risen quite properly; pie crust that had broken. Such fine things could not be had in the woods.

The sparrow was grateful for Ninéon's assignment of traveling to Nadir. In truth, the sparrow would have suggested the notion to the falcon—a trip to look in on the mud-brown horse that travels to a place called the Finest Court. However, Ninéon had come up with the idea first, and Valane quickly volunteered for what she called an onerous, time-consuming task.

The sparrow was pleased that the falcon favored her.

The miles drifted by beneath the sparrow's beating wings.

She studied the land below as she went, finding the colors and smells more intense than in the Before Time. She savored everything and noted men in a field below her—some dressed as daffodils, in bright greens and yellows, more dressed in the shade of the sky just after sunset. The latter were winning; the ones in those colors usually did. They showed no mercy to their enemy. Ninéon would be pleased to learn of the fighting. Though as smart as the sparrow had become, she couldn't fathom why the falcon craved bloodshed.

A new thought occurred to her. Perhaps the presence of carrion was not a good thing after all.

Valane had come to abhor death. The fewer people on the land, the fewer tasty treats were left behind. The crows, particularly the ones bettered by Ninéon, enjoyed all the death and relished picking at the bodies. But Valane didn't care much for crows. And there were far better things to feast upon than corpses.

She listened to the wind playing with the leaves and the smallest of branches at the very tops of the trees. And she listened to the Sprawling River, which made little sound this morning. Its banks were flooded and it slowly washed against the trunks of oaks and maples long used to the rising water at this time of year. She heard the twitter of robins and focused on that, finding their song pleasing, though not so elegant as her own. Then she heard a voice and her heart sank. It was Ninéon, and the falcon was inside her head again.

The sparrow did not like the intrusion.

NINÉON STARED AT THE RIPPLE IN HER VISION POND, and with effort saw something far beyond the green water. She saw the Sprawling River winding beneath her, moving sluggish as it was fattened and lazily feeding off the land past its flooded banks.

She was seeing through Valane's eyes.

It was a function of the pond Eyeswide had never taught her, and she wondered now if the owl had even known he could use the water in this manner.

It felt like she had nested in the back of the sparrow's mind, comfortable and safe from the vagaries of the wind, like a man might look out the window of a tower from the comfort of a padded chair.

We have somewhere to go in the city, Ninéon told Valane.

There are always places to go in the beautiful city, Valane thought. She tried to concentrate on the countryside below her, not wanting Ninéon to probe deeper and discover her desire for the pond. She thought about the bakery and the beam in the stables where she'd made a nest of twigs and horsehair. She thought about the river.

To the palace, Ninéon said. *To the north tower.*

To look in on the old man.

Bishop DeNogaret.

The top of the tower, where there are biscuits to nibble and soup to drink.

Yes.

The sparrow had been there only once, but knew she wouldn't have trouble finding it again. Always a crow or two of Ninéon's perched there. More had perched there days ago, but archers had been shooting at clusters and had managed to kill several in Ninéon's flock. Now the dozen or so she relegated remained hidden in the shadows and against the eaves.

Valane wanted to go to the bakery first, as she was hungry.

Time for that later. Ninéon was reading her mind. *Fill your belly when I am done with the Bishop.* Ninéon had been perfecting another function of the pond and would demonstrate that today—she would talk through the sparrow to Bishop DeNogaret. That should unsettle the old priest and make him more respectful of her power.

After the Bishop, Valane agreed.

Ninéon continued to see through the sparrow's eyes. The falcon focused on the scattering of Galmier soldiers Valane flew over. Save for the one battle the sparrow witnessed, there were no confrontations. In fact, the largest group of soldiers had made a camp and did nothing. One held a piece of parchment in his hands, and Ninéon was certain it was one of foolish Meven's declarations of peace. She so reviled the notion of the war ending that her contempt transferred to the sparrow.

Valane's course took her over Fenland, a term people from the various villages in the heart of Galmier gave to the marshy land north of the Sprawling River. For as far as the sparrow—and thereby Ninéon—could see, water swirled high along the trunks of trees. Peering at the river's surface through the sparrow's eyes, Ninéon spotted bushes and ferns, drowned and rotted, and a few small animal carcasses.

In the distance, Ninéon made out homes perched atop tree trunks. From her puppets she knew the village ahead was called Stilton, short for Stilt Town. The falcon considered the people there more stupid than rabbits. Why they had built so close to a river that regularly flooded its banks perplexed her. Why not build elsewhere, farther from the river where they could safely farm? Too, wolves prowled Fenland, often hungry enough to swim in search of food. Ninéon decided when there was a pause between wars she would take a Stilton man as one of her puppets and pick through his brain to sate her curiosity. Maybe the people had found something special about the land, something valuable they wouldn't leave. Maybe something stretched beneath the floodwaters that deserved Ninéon's notice.

Suddenly her eyes snapped wide as she stared at the next ripple. The sparrow gained on the village, with a speed Ninéon gifted her.

Meat!

Ninéon smelled meat roasting. She smelled the rotting wood that floated on the surface of the engorged river. She smelled the people—the ones who poled from house to house on their pitiful rafts, the ones who milled about on porches that had become balconies overlooking the water, the ones she couldn't see who huddled in their stilt-homes.

Ninéon was using the sparrow's nose to smell. A moment more and she used the little bird's ears to hear the splashing of an oar, a child calling to a friend, the bark of a wolf.

Amazing! the falcon breathed.

She experimented then, extending her wings and seeing in her mind's eye that the sparrow had done the same. She imagined herself flying to the top of an old willow that shaded one of the stilt homes. In the ripple she watched the sparrow comply.

Valane, perch here, she ordered.

The sparrow did just that. Then it dove off the branch, as Ninéon imagined herself doing, dipping low and dangling her feet to brush the still river water, then angling up again and flying north to the edge of the soddened village.

Valane, this is truly amazing!

The sparrow did not answer, and it took a few minutes—during which the sparrow/falcon flew straight up, then came down to perch on a lofty branch of a pin oak—for Ninéon to realize the sparrow could not answer. She'd so assumed control of the little sparrow that it had lost all will and sense of itself. Valane was only a vessel for Ninéon's use. The sparrow was like the people the falcon had taken as puppets, though the sparrow was burning out much faster than men did.

No! She couldn't destroy this sparrow. Not yet.

Ninéon concentrated to shut out what the sparrow heard, then pulled back from the wind ruffling its small feathers. It took effort, but Ninéon managed to stop smelling the odors its tiny nostrils picked up.

Valane?

The sparrow chirped musically. *Yes, Ninéon?*

The falcon sighed and stepped to the shore of the pond, watching as the ripples became fainter.

Valane, I am going to visit Bishop DeNogaret myself.

I do not fly to the north tower of the palace?

No. You fly to the city this morning, Valane. After you visit the bakery, watch for the soldiers in the city, learn if they are ready for more fighting or if they are resigned to peace.

And come back to the Old Forest?

When you are done spying, Valane.

The sparrow cocked its head.

Three days, Valane. Dine well.

The sparrow chirped musically again, and disappeared when the pond's surface turned a flat, murky green.

Ninéon glided from the ring of stringybarks and to the center of the clearing where she called her flock. She was pleased with herself for discovering something new about the Vision

Pond, and she intended to take over another of her birds later. But not the little sparrow again—Valane had proven too valuable to be consumed and discarded. Not one of her invisible spies. An upstart crow perhaps, or an arrogant grackle. And not today.

She pushed off from the spongy floor of the Old Forest clearing and soon flew well above the highest canopy.

Ninéon would visit Bishop DeNogaret herself and see what tasty morsels the kitchen staff served him.

VALANE FELT DIZZY BUT DIDN'T UNDERSTAND WHY. AND SHE had a gap in her memory. She recalled flying toward the village on stilts, and seeing the southern edge of it. But now she was on the north side, above the last of the crude dwellings. She didn't remember landing in this tree, only that she was flying to the north tower in Nadir.

But Ninéon said she didn't have to go there, and so Valane again thought about the bakery shop and what delicious wonders she might find in the alley behind it. She hoped it would be something filled with cinnamon. She stretched her wings and looked to the northeast, then stopped herself just as she was ready to lift off from the branch. Shaded by a thick black walnut tree were a dog and two horses, one of them with legs that looked too short for its body and hide the color of mud.

The punch! Valane's tiny heart beat faster. The horse she'd followed to the place called the Finest Court! The sparrow glided across the swollen river branch and to the other side where the horses rested. She chose a branch low in the walnut tree so she could better see them.

But from her position she noticed something she hadn't before. There was a girl behind the tree, brushing at her clothes and combing her fingers through her red-brown hair.

Kalantha, the one who'd been separated from the mystical horse!

Valane's excitement grew.

Such news she would have to tell Ninéon.

The falcon would be upset, certainly, but pleased to learn the revelation. The sparrow chirped once more and reconsidered the notion. The falcon would be more than pleased if the matter was taken care of for her. Valane darted northeast, where she knew one of the falcon's crow sentries always perched. She relayed the information about the punch and the girl, then watched the crow fly south. There were other sentries along the line, and the word would be spread quickly.

Valane thought about the alley behind the bakery, then with a sad, low whistle, decided the delicious trip would wait for another day.

The horse and the girl were more important than cinnamon.

25 · The Pursuit

For more than one hundred years I shepherded Fallen Favorites, before assuming my role in the Finest Court. I discovered that those Fallen who were afraid to fail at a task achieved nothing significant in their lives . . . merely because they did not try. Those who failed in the trying—those were the ones I was proud of. The others, I cannot seem to remember their names.

~*Gray Hawthorn, Finest Court Patriarch*

Kalantha spent two nights in Stilton, and left the following midmorning despite the efforts of Becca and Trandal to get her to stay.

"Child, you are a wonderment." Becca stood on the porch of her house, looking down a rope ladder that dangled in front of a small boat. "Haven't seen you in . . . oh, what . . . more than a year? And when we saw you then, you had a fiery fever. What do you manage to get yourself into?"

"Trouble," Kalantha replied with a smile.

"And no parents."

"No." The previous stay in Stilton, Kalantha had told Becca and Trandal—and all of the village for that matter—that she was an orphan. She also told them her name was Kal Morgan, not mentioning then—or now—that royal blood flowed through her. "But I do well enough on my own."

Becca wrung her hands. "I suppose we'll see you again, Kal

Morgan, maybe in another year when some other malady befalls you."

Kalantha laughed. "I hope to see you again, Becca. But next time I hope I don't come in here limping." She hugged the big woman and slung a canvas sack over her back; it was filled with dried meat, bread, and cheese Becca and Trandal packed. Then she gingerly made her way down the rope ladder. Trandal was waiting in the boat below.

He rowed her to the other side of the swollen branch, and helped her out of the boat. He'd splinted her leg two nights past, after setting her ankle. He said he couldn't be certain, but he feared it was broken. "And splinting it just in case won't hurt." He wrapped her ankle tight with strips of cloth from one of his old shirts, then found a new pair of boots for her, ones made of soft deerhide that laced and would accommodate the splint. He'd gotten her another tunic and pair of leggings, bartering for them with a family who had a boy about Kalantha's size.

The bath had been the best part, Kalantha decided. She could tolerate herself now and figured Rue would appreciate her not smelling like something that had rolled around in the gutter.

"Thank you for everything, Trandal." She reached up and kissed him on the cheek, then walked carefully to Rue. The splint worked well; she didn't have to limp. But it was uncomfortable, and it prevented her from scratching her leg. "I will make this up to you and Becca. It might take a little while." She added to herself there was a war to stop first.

"Take care of yourself, Kal Morgan. We'll mend you again when you return."

The iomud and the hunting dog waited nearby.

Your charge looks much better, Rue, Honest-Stormchaser said. *The village was good to her. She could have been wholly healed, however, had we taken her into the mountains.*

Gallant-Stallion knew what the other Finest referred to. There was a Finest mountain pony in the Galmier range who could magically heal even serious wounds.

That curious pony was too far, Gallant-Stallion replied. *Kalantha would not have allowed such a journey. She is willful, and very intent on finding her brother.*

The King of Galmier?

Yes.

The one who started the war?

A nod and a sigh. Gallant-Stallion knew where this was going.

The war that led to the death of my charge.

"Rue!"

Gallant-Stallion was grateful that Kalantha's arrival stopped Honest-Stormchaser's sad banter. More than once while Kalantha was in the village he suggested that the Finest iomud return to the Court. And more than once she declined.

Kalantha awkwardly knelt next to Rue and reached inside the canvas sack, pulling out two dried strips of meat. These she offered to the dog, who was quick to gobble them down.

"I figured you were hungry, Stump." Kalantha had gleaned the dog's name from Gallant-Stallion. "Here, one more. But we have to save the rest." Then she grabbed Gallant-Stallion's mane and pulled herself up. "Sorry, Rue. Hope I didn't hurt you. I can't jump yet."

You did not hurt me, Kalantha. Are you certain you are well enough to travel?

She ran her fingers through his mane as an answer and scratched his neck. "Does your friend have a name? I forgot to ask before." She nodded to the iomud.

She is called . . .

Cornsilk, the iomud told Gallant-Stallion.

Cornsilk, Gallant-Stallion repeated, knowing Kalantha could not hear the other Finest. She was only able to hear Rue—and only when he wanted her to. *Cornsilk belonged to a noble from Nasim-Guri. He died, and she travels with us because she has no home, and seems not to want to find one in this village.*

The iomud snorted, but didn't argue.

"Cornsilk . . . sounds like a farmer's horse. But she doesn't look like a farmer's horse. Looks like she could race." Kalantha had watched a horse race once in the village near the High Keep Temple. Coins and livestock changed hands during wagers. She and Meven bet chores, and Meven won every wager, giving Kalantha a lot more work to do for the following few weeks.

"All right, Cornsilk, Stump . . . Rue is going to help me find my brother. I don't expect that you can understand me, but you're welcome to come along. My brother intends to end the war he started. And as much as I love him, I don't think he can do that alone." She nudged Rue in the sides to get him moving. "Can you talk to them, Rue? Can you tell them about my brother and the war and stopping it, and . . . can they understand you, Rue?"

Gallant-Stallion didn't answer her. He headed southwest, paralleling the Sprawling River branch, his hooves sinking deep into the mud. He'd picked up wolf spoor, though not terribly recent. Still, it concerned him and he wanted to be away from these woods. The iomud fell in at his shoulder, and the dog trailed behind a few yards, sniffing here and there and remarking how "interesting" these woods smelled and that there were interesting things he would like to roll in if they would only slow a bit.

Then you will stink, Gallant-Stallion told him.

Not like the girl did. Not ever so bad as the girl did, I think. Don't you understand, big punch? If you roll in something bad-smelling, no one can smell you. Stump added that he was pleased the girl no longer reeked like forgotten and ignored garbage.

Kalantha . . . there are several merchant trails to Nasim-Guri.

"Only a few are wide enough for big wagons, Rue, and Meven would've taken one of those. I know it. With the men and presents he'd have with him, he'd want a road more easy to travel." Much softer: "Meven usually takes the easy way."

The iomud nickered softly: *How is it that a Fallen Favorite can understand you?*

Gallant-Stallion replied only after Honest-Stormchaser repeated the question twice more. *Each Finest has a gift, and mine is to speak with my charge . . . when I desire that she understand me.*

Can she understand me?

No.

Does she know about we Finest, that we are not horses?

No. After a moment, Gallant-Stallion added: *But she calls me her magic horse.*

The Fallen Favorites are never to know about us, Rue.

He snorted loudly. *Do not lecture me, Honest-Stormchaser.*

Cornsilk. This is my name in the land of the Fallen Favorites. Please call me by that here.

As you wish.

Something interesting! Stump's clipped series of barks interrupted the conversation. *Something very interesting.*

The Finest paused while the dog darted to the side of the road and disappeared behind a shadberry bush. He came back a few moments later, head and tail down.

Nothing to roll in after all, big punch. Just a dead man rotting in the tall grass and feeding all the bugs. Been dead so long most of the best stink is gone.

Gallant-Stallion craned his neck, trying to see, and then deciding better of it. Probably a soldier, and it didn't matter what side of the war he fought on. The Finest thought he and Kalantha didn't need to see any more death.

It was well into the afternoon when the dog asked the horses to stop. The pads of his feet were sore and his legs ached from traveling for so long. The Finest could have continued well into the evening—throughout the night—as they were hardier than horses. But they stopped by a stream, and Kalantha seemed happy for the break. She struggled to get off Gallant-Stallion's back without falling, then walked to the bank and carefully sat at the edge of the water.

She is a determined soul, Honest-Stormchaser observed.

Gallant-Stallion watched his charge.

My noble was determined, too.

You should return to the Court for a new charge . . . Corn-silk.

I have free will, I say! She made a sputtering sound. *I will visit the Finest Court in my good time, Rue. You say that girl wants to help end the war, well that is what my noble sought. If I help you, I am honoring him. Perhaps his spirit will rest easier.*

Gallant-Stallion fully understood now why the iomud was with him—to help complete her dead charge's work. *You, too, are determined, Cornsilk.*

And the dog . . . he is determined to stay with us. I wonder why?

Gallant-Stallion snorted loudly, the equivalent of a laugh. *Because we are . . . interesting . . . Cornsilk. We are doing something, and he was bored where he lived. Though I suspect he will wish for that boredom the longer we travel. Though trained for hunting, he is not used to such long periods of being awake.*

Dogs do sleep a lot.

Stump sat in front of Gallant-Stallion and scratched his ear. He yawned wide and let his eyelids droop closed as he continued scratching. When the itch abated, he rose, stretched, turned around a few times and curled into a ball. He yawned again and fell instantly asleep.

Wake him up, Rue. He is your friend. We should be going.

Gallant-Stallion looked beyond the dog to the stream. Kalantha was stretched out under the feathery branches of a honey locust and was sleeping, too.

In a while, Gallant-Stallion said. *We will go in a while.*

The iomud let out a sigh.

THEY RESUMED THEIR TREK SHORTLY BEFORE SUNSET, Kalantha awake and chattering about all the things she had seen beneath the palace, lingering on the sack with the skull sculpture in it and on the names she could remember on the plaques in the family crypt.

"I wonder how long it will take us to catch up to Meven? Maybe we should stop in the next village and ask if he's been through. He hadn't been to Stilton, but then it wasn't really on the way." She put on an optimistic face. "We'll find him. We have to find him. More and more people will die if we don't."

26 · The Falcon's Perch

I used to try to understand a Fallen Favorite by examining everything he built and all that he accomplished. Then I understood my approach was flawed, and that I was learning nothing important. When I began to study what he planned to accomplish and how he aimed to go about it . . . then I gleaned much more. I was truly able to fathom his mind and heart.

~Roan Wanderer, shepherd to the warrior prince Doyle Neben

Bishop DeNogaret held the bowl of soup with both hands, the warmth seeping through the ceramic and settling nicely against his palms. He savored the sensation, becoming irritated when his visitor ruined the moment by talking.

"Good that you can eat that on your own."

"You mean good that you don't have to feed me." Bishop DeNogaret looked over the top of the bowl and to the foot of his bed, where Sara Anne sat.

"I wouldn't be doing that, Bishop. I left that task to Rachael and Bertrum and Mary."

"I guess you wouldn't." He sipped the broth, discovering it not so bland as what he'd been brought earlier. He stared at its oily surface. Shredded pieces of chicken or turkey floated in it, along with onion shavings and peas that had been dried. A little saffron, too, from the taste of it—an expensive spice. He suspected if he hadn't suggested to Mary, one of the palace cooks, that she use the saffron and fowl today, he would have continued to receive a bland, meatless broth.

The tray on the nightstand held the usual biscuit. But this time there were two, and there was a small pot with raspberry preserves and another with butter. Mary had taken all of his suggestions to heart. Tonight, he'd make additional suggestions for tomorrow's meals.

She had also brought two bouquets of spring flowers into his room. Their fragrance helped cut the odor of the balm Bertrum nightly rubbed on the Bishop's chest and legs. The old priest would have suggested that smelly practice stop, but it seemed to be doing some good. His broken ribs were paining him less, and they'd removed the wrap from his chest this morning. His legs still throbbed terribly, and no herbs that did less than render him nearly unconscious lessened the ache. He didn't allow them to use that potent of a medicine again—he needed to have all of his wits about him.

"My toes are cold, Sara Anne. Please put another blanket across them. My circulation has been less than perfect these past many months, a function of age, I'm sure. But the . . . accident . . . has worsened matters. Please, Sara Anne."

She let out a great sigh and eased herself off the bed. Retrieving a light wool blanket from the closet, she spread it across his feet and sat down again.

"If you would finish your meal, Bishop DeNogaret, I could return to the kitchen. I've things to do and—"

"Do you?" The Bishop held the bowl in one hand now and sat it on the tray, making a show of grimacing and moaning—the gestures lost on Sara Anne. "How can you have so much to do when the King is not on the palace grounds?"

Surprise showed in her eyes.

"Oh, I know where Meven went. Yours aren't the only eyes I have in this fusty place."

She drew back her shoulders and looked away from him.

"How was Meven doing before he left? Was he well?"

Sara Anne shook her head. "He looked well. Agitated, but well. He made it known to everyone he intends to stop this war." A pause: "Good for him. There's been enough killing. Boy like that shouldn't be warring with anyone. Should be spending his time learning about his own country."

"And Kalantha? Any word of her?"

Her shoulders shook and she got up from the bed again and started to pace.

"I said . . . is there any word on Kalantha Montoll?"

"I heard you, Bishop." Sara Anne stuck a fist on her waist and whirled on the old priest, her big white apron a cloud swirling around her. "Bad enough, Bishop, that I told Bertrum where that girl went . . . creeping around under the palace, exploring like a little mouse. He went looking for her, said you wanted to see her. But there was something in his eyes, Bishop, and that meant there was more to it, that you wanted to more than just see her. See her dead, I heard Bertrum whisper to that lackey of his. I should've told King Meven about it when I saw him. He was looking for her, and I should have told him she was in the crypt, and that Bertrum was down there prowling around after her."

"But you didn't."

She shook her head. "No, I didn't. I don't know why."

"You know why, Sara Anne. Yesterday I suggested you help Bertrum."

Both hands on her hips now, she let out a breath that sounded like a whistle. "I lied to King Meven, told him I hadn't seen his sister. By the good gods, why? I'd lied to that girl, too, and I tried to turn her over to Bertrum 'cause he was looking for her. Why and why again? Was I afraid of Bertrum?" She talked to herself now. "Bertrum is a mean one, he is. Tolerated him before, I did. But lately he's been unkind. Not one that should've been hired here. That's for certain."

"I hired him."

She made a clucking sound. "Oh, I see. You're a mean one, too."

"Now, Sara Anne . . . is that such a way to talk to a priest?" He mimicked her clucking sound.

"Are you finished with your soup? I've things to tend to in the kitchen."

He reached for the soup again and took another sip.

She tapped her foot, then paced at the end of his bed.

"You do not enjoy your time with me, Sara Anne?"

She didn't look at him. "King Meven warned people about you, Bishop. He told us in the kitchen. There's talk you're not a religious man at all, that you're just trying to steal the throne. King Meven told us to be careful. Only picked a few to come wait on you."

"Fortunate you were one of them, eh, Sara Anne?"

She shuffled to the window and pressed her face to the pane. Not all of the windows in the palace were glass, but Meven had ordered the ailing Bishop to be put in a room with a closing window to keep out a draft.

"King Meven cares for you, Bishop. But I think he's scared of you. More scared of you than I am of Bertrum."

"Sara Anne—"

She focused on a groom walking across the grounds.

"Sara Anne Whitsley."

The cook turned, slowly, eyes caught by the Bishop's stare.

"I am fortunate, Bishop DeNogaret, that King Meven selected me to be one of your caregivers." Her face relaxed and she unclenched her hands, let her arms hang limp at her sides.

The Bishop put on a benevolent expression. "No, I am the fortunate one, Sara Anne. I am blessed that you could take time out of your busy day to bring me this delicious soup." He took another sip, then tipped the bowl up and drained it. When he sat the empty bowl on the tray, he smiled to see that she still stared at him. "Blessed, Sara Anne."

"Blessed," she repeated.

Bishop DeNogaret was careful not to insinuate himself too deeply in the cook's mind. He preferred to hover near her thoughts without truly touching them, make a few suggestions now and then, nudge her but not push her.

"Blessed to be one of your caregivers. You are feeling better, aren't you, Bishop?"

"A little, Sara Anne. Because of your good care."

She smiled at him, eyes sparkling. "Bertrum says they'll have you walking with canes in a few weeks, get you out of that bed."

The Bishop shifted in the bed so he could better reach the tray and the biscuits. He broke one in half and lathered raspberry jam on it. He ate it in two bites and slathered the other half.

"Sara Anne . . . is there any word on Kalantha?"

She didn't hesitate to answer this time. "No, Bishop, not good word in any event. Bertrum saw her go beneath the palace. He told me, then he followed her."

"But he couldn't catch her. That's what you said."

"No, Bishop, he couldn't get close. She's fast, Bertrum said. Chased her across the grounds, and—"

"She didn't go to the stables, did she?" He brushed crumbs off the bed.

Sara Anne shook her head; thin gray hairs came loose from beneath her cap and looked like fragile web strands teased in a breeze. "I told you that three days ago, Bishop DeNogaret. She didn't get her horse. Bertrum said it wasn't there, it'd run off. She ran off, too, into the city. Just like I told you before, Bishop."

"I didn't ask about the horse before."

"No, I guess not. But you're feeling better. That's important."

"Any sign of Kalantha in the city?"

She shook her head. "Every day Bertrum sends one of the kitchen help to the guard's barracks. No word yet. Bertrum thinks she's fled Nadir."

The Bishop reached for the second biscuit and buttered this one before spreading the rest of the raspberry jam on it. "But not with the horse."

"The horse should be slaughtered, Bishop, after what it did to you. Nearly killed you!" She turned from him and unlatched the window and opened it wide. "Not chilly today. Spring's finally warming up."

She walked around his bed and picked up the tray.

"You're very good to me, Sara Anne."

The cook continued to smile. "I'm pleased to be of service to the High Prelate of Nadir. Blessed, I am."

She smoothed his blanket, then picked up the tray. "I will make certain you have something more substantial for dinner, Bishop."

"I would like roast goose, I think, Sara Anne."

"I'll see to it." She balanced the tray on one hand and opened the door. "I'll return at dinner, Bishop . . . and not before." A hint of her defiance returned. "I'm not so young, and all these stairs set my legs to aching."

A corner of the Bishop's mouth tugged up in a grin. "Of course, Sara Anne. You rest your legs. And I'll rest mine."

She gave a clipped laugh and closed the door behind her.

Several minutes later the Bishop had another visitor. Nineon flew in through the open window and perched on the nightstand.

27 · Ruminations

The dog took the lead, moving slowly at first, from one side of the road to the other. He put his nose to the ground and made loud sniffling noises, then he seemed to catch the scent of something and took off at a run.

The Finest had no trouble keeping up.

My senses are keen, Rue, yet I smell nothing but dirt, the river, and the hint of rain coming. The iomud grudgingly admired the dog.

Gallant-Stallion's nostrils flared and he picked up the trace of water in the air. It would rain during the night.

While I want you to succeed, Honest-Stormchaser continued, *I believe what your charge is trying to do—find her brother—is near impossible. Finding one boy—warlord—in an entire country, and with a dog that does not have the boy's scent . . .*

Gallant-Stallion watched Stump. The dog's ears were long

and dragged on the road, and the Finest realized the ears helped the dog smell, in effect scooping up the scents and fluttering them in front of his nose.

Stump wagged his tail and ran faster.

"Rue! The dog's found something! He's tracking Meven!"

He cannot smell the warlord, Honest-Stormchaser insisted.

No, but he can smell horses, and that is what he's tracking.

Honest-Stormchaser tipped her ears forward in question.

For the most part common folk do not own horses, Gallant-Stallion explained. *Stilton had only a few, and that was for the entire village.*

So he smells the horses of the soldiers and the warlord.

Gallant-Stallion didn't need to reply.

Stump followed the trail past two villages, where they took a different road and where farmers told Kalantha the King of Galmier and his men had passed by not quite two days ago. She told them who she was and somehow they believed her, giving her bread and two chawettys, small tarts stuffed with spiced pork and dates, since she said there wasn't time to eat a meal with them.

"We're catching up, Rue!" There was genuine hope in Kalantha's voice, and her expression was the brightest the Finest had seen in quite some time. "You're faster than my brother's horse, Rue, I know it! And so's your friend Cornsilk."

They stopped rarely, and this only to give Stump a chance to rest his feet and eat some of the bread, and give Kalantha an opportunity to walk and stretch. She napped occasionally on Rue's back, and they slowed a little then, Gallant-Stallion being cautious and not wanting her to slip off.

They'd encountered few people on the road—a farmer and his boy, and a merchant with a cart full of rugs. The latter told Kalantha it wasn't safe traveling by herself, given the war. He'd heard a rumor that it was ending, and expected he'd learn more traveling north. She refused to go with him, but thanked him for the information and wished him well.

Near sunset Gallant-Stallion paid more attention to the countryside, wanting to find a place to pass the evening. He'd not been on this merchant road before and didn't know if there was a village or farmhouse nearby.

People, Stump, do you smell people?

The girl on your back, the dog was quick to answer. *I smell her. I smell you. I smell horses that went this way a time ago. Men were with them. But you smell . . . not like the other horses. Tired,* he added after a moment. He'd stopped in the middle of the merchant road and pointed his snout to the sky. *I am sore and tired and it is time to sleep. Perhaps it is time to leave you, big horse. Time to go somewhere and sleep a long, long, long time. This is not so interesting as it was before. I am more tired than it is interesting.*

Please. There was desperation in Gallant-Stallion's voice.

The dog cocked his head and laid his ears back, and regarded Gallant-Stallion for a moment. *I have done nothing important before,* Stump said.

This is important, Gallant-Stallion returned.

Very important, Honest-Stormchaser added. *We want to stop the war.*

The dog drew his features forward in consternation, not understanding.

The war, Gallant-Stallion tried. *An end to the men killing men.*

The dog barked and scratched at his ear. *You will never stop men from doing that. But I will help you in this very important work.* He scratched harder. *If we stop and eat and sleep now.*

Then help us find a place to do that, Gallant-Stallion answered.

The dog did just that a mile later, leading them off the road to the remains of a stone farmhouse. Fire had taken the barn;

only charred planks rested amid a tangle of weeds and wild-flowers. It had taken the fields, too, and part of the house. Only a few strips of blackened wood showed where shutters and the door had been. The slate roof was mostly intact, but the inside walls and furniture were ruined. It still smelled of ashes and smoke, but not so strongly as to keep them out.

Kalantha slipped from Rue's back and wrinkled her nose at the burned smell of the place. She pulled a thin cloak out of the sack Becca had given her, then she broke a small branch off a bunchberry bush. Just inside the entrance, Kalantha brushed at the floor, clearing a spot of ashes and dust. Spreading out the cloak, intending to sleep on it, Kalantha looked out the door-way and to Rue.

"This isn't a very nice place to stay," she said. "But I know outside might not be safe." She stared at the Finest a moment, then yawned. "We shouldn't stop at all. We should keep going after Meven." She yawned again. "Maybe an hour or so of sleep wouldn't hurt though."

Stump stretched and walked past her, looked at the cloak, then went to one end of it and started pawing at it to put some proper folds in it. He turned around a few times and curled down. Before Kalantha joined him, curling too because there wasn't enough room now to lie straight, he was asleep, aching paws twitching in a dream.

You should have found better for her, Rue, Honest-Stormchaser lectured. *This place is ruined, not fit for a charge.*

Gallant-Stallion dug at the ground, leaving a line in a mix of wood ash and dirt. *The dog and she need rest, and I would not mind a little sleep. This is a temporary place, Cornsilk, and it will do.*

Her head tipped up, a gesture he considered aloof. Her charge had been a noble, used to fine things. And while Kalantha was of royal blood, there'd been little finery in her life. It had been one of hardship and living with a herd of ponies in the

Galmier Mountains, running from assassin-birds, and accepting the kindness of strangers like the merchant Bartholomew, the priests at the Vershan Monastery, and the villagers in Stilton.

This will do, he repeated.

I suppose, but I am not tired, Rue, Cornsilk stated, nostrils flaring and ears pricked forward. *I want to help stop the war.*

That is not for us, Gallant-Stallion said. *We guide and guard, advise on occasion. It is up to Kalantha to assist her brother.*

I have free will. A moment more: *And still I am not tired.*

Then watch over them for me, if you would. He added: *Please, Cornsilk.*

She tossed her head. *While you sleep, too? Or while you journey to the Finest Court in search of counsel?*

No, he was quick to return. *While I investigate. Something feels very wrong, and has felt wrong for well more than a mile.*

28 · The North Tower Roost

Evil is the prickly dandelion infesting the garden of Paard-Peran. I pray to the good powers that I have the strength and wisdom to guide my Fallen Favorite as she weeds the bed of flowers that is her troubled world.

~Gallant-Stallion, Finest shepherd

B ishop DeNogaret watched the falcon. It perched on a post at the end of the bed, talons digging in and purposely scratching the oiled wood.

The bird had held the position for nearly an hour, regarding the old priest, closing its eyes and resting, opening them again and staring before resting again. Occasionally it cocked its head, listening to sounds outside and beneath this room in the tower. No one came up the steps.

The Bishop rested, too, waking to find the falcon gone, then seeing it return before sunset.

"I have been surveying the palace and the grounds," Ninéon announced. "And I find things that displease me."

Bishop DeNogaret raised an eyebrow.

"There are tents for the wounded, and I see the pile of dead men between them."

"And this displeases you?"

The falcon shook her head. "Everything eventually dies."

"Then what, friend Ninéon?"

The falcon's eyes narrowed. "There are soldiers on the ground, and they do not practice this day. There are archers watching the palace roof and shooting at members of my flock. One dared to shoot an arrow at me."

The Bishop propped himself up so he was practically sitting in the bed. "Meven is trying to end the war. But you know that, Ninéon."

"I will not allow him to succeed."

The Bishop watched the falcon fly to the nightstand and grip the edge, again marring the wood.

"You have not done your part, DeNogaret. Your puppets . . ."

"Are well insinuated in this palace. And while they could not stop Meven or catch Kalantha, they are in position for when either young Montoll returns." The old priest worked a sore spot out of his neck. "I thought your flock was going to stop Meven from spreading his declarations."

The falcon leaned forward until her beak was inches from the Bishop's ear. "My flock stopped his fool commanders and shredded his precious parchments."

"But you did not stop Meven."

Ninéon flew back to the post on the bed. "Not yet."

The Bishop smugly smiled. "Do not worry, my friend. If the war ends, we'll just start another one."

The falcon pushed off the post and flew out the window, spreading its wings as wide as possible and catching the wind. "I will start another one, DeNogaret. It will be my war, and when I am finished with you, old man, you will be one of its casualties."

29 · Shifting Shadows

I like the night the best on Paard-Peran. It is a blanket that covers the ugliness. It hides the buildings the worst of the Fallen Favorites have burned, shadows the graves of the men killed in the war, softens the squalor of the poorest quarters of the cities, and it welcomes the stars.

~The Old Mare

Something was amiss, but Gallant-Stallion couldn't put a name to what bothered him. There was little wolf spoor, and so that wasn't the concern. The war? Certainly. The danger of enemy soldiers finding his charge worried him. But Honest-Stormchaser stood watch. The weather? He thought perhaps a storm was coming, as the scent of rain in the air was stronger now than when he first noticed it late in the morning. The clouds built over the day, and were thick and gray now in the dying light of the setting sun. The cottage's tile roof had holes in it, and so Kalantha could well get drenched and her sleep interrupted.

Something more, he said. *Something more than all of that festers at me. What?*

He spiraled outward from the ruined cottage, discovering more signs of fire—a shed, the posts and roof of a well, a charred split-rail fence. There were bones here and there, from cattle and goats, slivers of bones that were likely from geese or ducks; Gallant-Stallion decided not to look closer. The bones were unimportant. Weeds had taken over what used to be a pea field. A few pea plants had survived from dropped pods and were starting to gain some height. He wondered if the farm had burned during the early part of the war. It had been set on fire purposely, he knew. An accidental fire would not have burned all the structures, nor would a lightning strike. He wondered if the people managed to flee in time, and knew that if he looked through the cottage he would have that answer.

Gallant-Stallion put down his curiosity and resolved not to find out.

He liked the scent of the air before a rain, and allowed himself to enjoy it as he quickened his patrol. It had a sweetness to it, somehow enhancing the odor of the tall grass and wildflowers and cutting the tang of the burned buildings and the stench of a rotting fox he spotted beneath a leaf-curled maple.

The sky darkened abruptly, the last light gone and the clouds covering whatever stars might be out. He'd ranged a few miles from the cottage, into a lightly wooded area that had been a well-tended orchard at one time but had been abandoned at least a decade ago. Now large scraggly apple trees overshadowed maple and oak seedlings and the myriad weeds growing between the rows.

He started back toward the cabin, reversing his spiral and relaxing a little. He saw a flicker of lightning and heard the soft boom of thunder. He felt fat drops of rain against his back, but then nothing after a few moments. Lightning continued to play, and he wondered if it might be a dry storm. The thunder continued soft and distant, like someone tapping on a kettle drum. Then he heard the snort of a horse, and he cursed that his Finest sister had followed him.

Honest-Stormchaser . . . Cornsilk . . . you said you would stay with Kalantha!

The iomud didn't answer.

Is your promise worth nothing? Kalantha must be guarded.

The snort sounded again, closer, but he couldn't tell from what direction it came.

Cornsilk? Gallant-Stallion peered down a row of apple trees. *Cornsilk!* anger showed in his voice. Had something happened at the cottage, and the iomud came to get him? Had she brought Kalantha with her? Was she playing some game?

Kalantha! He called to his charge now. *Kalantha, are you here?*

Another snort, and this time he could tell where the sound was coming from—behind him. He whirled, scraping his neck on a scraggly branch, and looked into the thinnest section of the old orchard, where most of the apple trees were dead or dying.

A horse galloped down an aisle, away from Gallant-Stallion. Lean and fast, it certainly could have been the Finest iomud, mane and tail flying.

Honest-Stormchaser! Cornsilk! Stop!

The horse turned behind a dead apple tree and raced out of sight.

No games, Cornsilk! I will play no games with you! Not here and now!

He thought he heard the iomud reply *This is no game,* but he could have imagined the words in the wind. Though his hearing was acute, the angry, worried beating of his heart made things indistinct. He concentrated and shut out his own sounds. He picked up a softer snort now, followed by a wuffling. There were no words in the noise, just simple sounds like a man might make—snorting or sneezing.

Who is there?

Indeed, it might not be Honest-Stormchaser, Gallant-Stallion considered. The Finest iomud had been helpful to this point. It could be a wild horse, frightened by the growing storm.

Again a snort came from somewhere in front of him, answered a heartbeat later by a snort behind him. So there were two horses in the orchard! One of them Honest-Stormchaser, and one unknown. He thought the snorting and nickering that came behind him had a familiar tone, and so he guessed this was the iomud. Perhaps she'd just joined him in the orchard.

A piercing whinny came from behind, and this time when he spun, he saw a larger horse, one with the build of a jutland or a heavy draft. Not the iomud after all. This one moved as fast as the light horse he'd spotted moments ago, but it was not as graceful. He watched it almost clumsily turn past a tree, heading deeper into the orchard, its hooves hitting the ground like muted thunder.

Who are you? he called out now in the tongue of all Paard-Peran horses. *Why run from me?* He wanted to talk to them. Perhaps what had spooked them was not the storm, but the same unknown thing that made him uneasy—this orchard, this night. He galloped after the jutland, knowing he could more easily catch up to the heavy horse. He spied it trotting now, the aisle here narrow and the branches brushing against its sides. *Stop. Please speak to me!*

The jutland didn't stop, but it wuffled to Gallant-Stallion; the sound echoed off to his right, where the lithe horse ran parallel down an aisle several yards away. There were no words in its wuffling. Just sound.

More sound came from his right and was growing louder. Another set of hooves hitting the earth. In a moment, Gallant-Stallion could see both horses, muzzle to muzzle, though he could not see them well because of the clouds and the trees. Everything indistinct, Gallant-Stallion focused on the jutland and galloped faster.

Speak to me! Gallant-Stallion called again. *I mean no harm.*

"Who means no harm?" Gallant-Stallion was certain he heard words now, though they weren't in the language of horses. "Do we mean no harm?"

Who are you?

"Who are we?" the voice parroted.

Then suddenly the jutland was free of the orchard and running across a swampy meadow and toward a rise. The slighter horse was gone, as if it had simply vanished. Gallant-Stallion took off in pursuit of the jutland, not wanting to waste time looking for the other horse. Neither was Honest-Stormchaser.

A part of him thought he should return to the old house and Kalantha, that trying to talk to wild horses would yield nothing of consequence and would only swallow time. But his curiosity won out, and he desired to catch up to one of them so he could learn about this place and ask them about any unusually smart birds in the area. Too, he wanted to know why the wild horses were so frightened and continued to run from him. Were there predators in the overgrown orchard that had made them skittish?

He could see better here, beyond the thick rows of trees, and he thundered down the aisle clearing the last of the orchard. Out of the corner of his eye, he spotted the second horse. It cleared the trees, too, several aisles to his right, and it opened its stride. Clearly he could see it wasn't the iomud, the neck was not long enough, and the tail was too bushy and short.

What are you running from? Gallant-Stallion's high-pitched whinny sliced through the rumble of high thunder. *Let me help you! Speak with me!*

"Speak to me! Speak to us!" The words came from the direction of the jutland, but again they were in the tongue of the Fallen Favorites.

What are you? Gallant-Stallion demanded in the language of horses.

The jutland churned up the rise and reared when it reached the top, hooves flailing at the air. It whinnied, once more making noise without words. The smaller horse galloped up the rise, too, then cast its head back and looked over its shoulder at Gallant-Stallion, who had paused halfway up the rise.

"What are you?" Gallant-Stallion repeated in as loud a voice as he could manage. This time he spoke in the Fallen Favorites' tongue.

"We are your bane," the lithe horse said in an eerie, feminine voice, as it continued to run. "Chase us, Finest."

"Chase us. Chase us. Chase us," the jutland replied, hooves still flailing.

The smaller horse reached the top and stared down the rise. "Finest. Finest. Finest."

How could horses speak in the tongue of the Fallen Favorites? Gallant-Stallion could, but he was a Finest. And he sensed these horses were not his brothers or sisters. They smelled different, and looked different. And, more, Gallant-Stallion wondered, heart pounding, mind racing—if they are not Finest, how could they know about the Finest?

"Chase us, Finest," they called in unison.

He intended to find out how they knew.

And he did make a discovery, though not what he'd expected—just before he reached the top of the rise.

The jutland burst apart, black shards flying into a dark gray sky. The smaller horse shattered, too, becoming a flock of ravens, grackles, and cowbirds streaking down the rise toward Gallant-Stallion.

No! Gallant-Stallion shouted. *I am a fool!*

So concerned about the war, he'd forgotten about the assassin-birds. When they first struck against a wedding party he traveled with, they'd flown in the formations of cloaked men on horses and slew almost everyone. Later they used the shapes again to attack him, Meven, and Kalantha in the Galmier Mountains. The young Montolls heard word that dark men on dark horses had laid waste to two villages, and Gallant-Stallion knew it wasn't men or horses at all. It was the birds slaying people in their path as they searched for Kalantha and Meven.

Had the birds who flew at him now purposely led him away from Kalantha?

He hesitated for a heartbeat, stomping in anger and intending to race back through the orchard and to the ruined cottage where he'd left her. But perhaps that is also what they wanted—for him to lead them to her.

He reared and lashed out at the first wave of birds to reach him, stretched his neck up and clamped down with his teeth on a large raven, breaking its neck. The bird dropped, and he snapped and grabbed another and killed it, too.

Fool! Fool! He continued to berate himself as he fought the birds, hooves bludgeoning them. A dozen lay broken in the grass around him. He felt needlelike talons rake his sides and neck, and he felt beaks stab him. Individually, one of the birds could cause him little suffering, the beaks and talons small. But there were so very, very many birds that the pain became intense and threatened to overwhelm him. He faltered, legs starting to buckle. Dozens of birds perched on his back, driving their beaks into him.

No! I won't fall! The words were directed at himself and the assassin-birds and seemed to buouy him just enough. He planted his weight on his front hooves and kicked out with the back. The birds were so light, it felt as if he batted away at a curtain. But he felt himself connecting, again and again, and so he continued on this tack until there no more birds flew behind him.

They concentrated on his sides now, and he started spinning, like a wild horse would when someone tried to saddle it. Alternately kicking with his back hooves and rearing up to flail with his front, he spun and bit and used his head like a club.

The pain still severe, he could ignore just enough of it to keep up his deadly gyrations. He didn't want to force all the pain away, as that could be dangerous. Instead, he used the pain now to inspire him. He fought his way through the birds, still kicking out with his back legs and continuing to grab birds with his mouth and clamp down until they were dead. He reared once more and pivoted, pointing down the rise now and galloping as fast as his legs could carry him.

Three times a fool, I am! I should have known all along the birds masqueraded as horses. The clues were there, I was just blind to them! In the back of his mind he realized that the "jutland" he'd chased through the orchard hadn't churned up the earth anywhere, and when it raced across the marshy pasture, water hadn't sprayed up from its hooves. *I deserved to be snared by their trap. I deserve this pain! But Kalantha does not deserve to be left alone in this world.*

He instantly thought about Honest-Stormchaser, finding some measure of relief that a Finest would remain with Kalantha if he fell. The girl was worthy of being protected.

Gallant-Stallion shot across the pasture now, hooves sinking in the water-soaked earth. The mud pulled at him, slowing him momentarily and allowing the birds to catch up. He heard their caws and squawks, the flapping of their wings—all of it terribly cacophonous and hurtful.

"You will not win!" He forced himself to run faster still, the birds keeping up with him, hundreds of them, he guessed, their wings beating furiously and sounding increasingly deafening, like a herd of horses thundering. It was the same sound when the birds attacked the wedding party, and later attacked him, Kalantha, and Meven in the mountains. That the birds could talk still puzzled him, and that they were smart enough to mimic the wuffles and snorts of horses infuriated him.

That they knew what a Finest was frightened him.

I will not let you win! Who controlled them? He'd killed a bird that called itself Fala, many long months ago on the palace grounds. That bird had seemed to order the others around, but he saw no larger bird amid this flock, and he heard no orders being issued. "You will fail, as you've failed before!"

"You will fail, Finest," a crow returned.

"Finest. Finest. Finest," the flock echoed.

Suddenly Gallant-Stallion couldn't see, as if an inky curtain had been pulled over his head. It was the birds, their bodies pressed close in front of his face, the musty scent of their feathers strong and choking him and blotting out what scant light he'd had to see by.

They started clawing at his head now, the larger birds cutting gouges into his blaze. The blood was warm and grimly competed with the malodorous scent of the birds and made him gag. The Finest felt blood run into his eyes, stinging and causing him to blink. He hurt so much all over! Once more, he felt his legs start to buckle.

"He falls!"

"The Finest falls. Falls. Falls!"

"Never!" Gallant-Stallion answered, finding strength in the victory cries of the birds. "I will not fall to you!"

He charged forward blindly, trusting to his memory, feeling the marshy ground beneath his hooves pulling at him, and then feeling firmer ground.

"Slay the Finest. For Ninéon!"

So they did have a leader, this one called Ninéon. Was Ninéon with them? Gallant-Stallion tossed his head this way and that, snapping madly and bludgeoning birds that flew too close. He managed to bat enough of them away that he could see through a gap in their bodies, finding bands of gray that represented the rows of apple trees in the overgrown orchard. Angling himself toward one of the aisles, he plodded on, as the cloud of black descended again.

"For Ninéon. Ninéon. Ninéon."

The name was musical and pleasant, and Gallant-Stallion

prayed the leader was indeed with this flock and that he could kill this Ninéon—even if he had to fall, too.

"Stop the horse. Stop the Finest."

Gallant-Stallion continued to churn forward, only fighting the birds with his head and teeth now, as his legs were tasked with carrying him forward. Finally he was rewarded when he felt branches scratch against his sides and felt the air cool around him—some of the birds had been forced back by the small spidery branches of the orchard.

Gallant-Stallion barely heard snapping and cracking sounds, and realized some of the flock had been caught in the thin branches. Faintly, he heard a few small bodies drop and scented blood other than his. Perhaps the birds had been speared by the thornlike branches of the dead trees.

"Bad horse!" one of the birds screeched. "Bad. Bad. Bad horse."

"Kill the horse!" another cried. "For Valane and Ninéon!"

"Hurry!" This was a small, thin voice. "Hurry and kill the Finest."

"Finest. Finest. Finest."

For birds to recognize a Finest . . . not possible, Gallant-Stallion thought. Not even the normal horses of this world, not even the most astute of the Fallen Favorites knew about the Finest.

A bird could not know.

None of the Fallen Favorites knew.

Steadfast! Steadfast, hear me! Gallant-Stallion fought harder, and he shouted again and again for the spirit of his mentor. He stumbled over an exposed root and bumped into the trunk of a tall apple tree. He scraped his side on the bark, adding to his pain, but slamming a handful of birds between him and the trunk in the process. He felt their small bodies break. *Steadfast, come to me!* He knew his mentor's spirit could not help him, but he wanted to tell someone that the birds knew about the Finest.

He scraped against another trunk, and then another, crying out when he opened a gash along his withers. The air lightened a little when he went deeper into the trees, and the pressure eased around him. The trees were closer together here, the branches tighter and closer to the ground. With all these branches, the birds couldn't so easily swarm him. They had to come at him in twos and threes, giving him the edge now. And the largest of them could no longer easily reach him. He clamped down on one after another, rearing and bucking, branches raking his neck as he slew dozens of them. More flew down to take their place, and Gallant-Stallion edged deeper still into the orchard, nearly stumbling over the mound of bird bodies in front of him.

His neck and head stung horribly from all the scratches, and his right side felt on fire where the largest birds had concentrated. He couldn't remember feeling this much pain ever before, not even when the assassin flock struck the wedding party. Fortunate for him, he decided, these birds did not attack with quite the same precision this time.

Perhaps this Ninéon they mentioned, or Valane . . . a name uttered once . . . were not present to direct them. Thank the good powers, he thought.

Gallant-Stallion fought them for many long minutes more, suffering additional wounds, but inflicting far worse on the birds. By the time he made it to the heart of the old orchard, they retreated.

A few dozen perched at the tops of the trees around him, the rest flying away, all of them angrily squawking at the horse. Their cries were hushed by the thunder, louder now.

"Bad horse. Kill the bad horse."

"Hurt the horse."

"Hurt the Finest," a tiny voice corrected. "For Ninéon and us, we must hurt him."

Gallant-Stallion couldn't see the speaker, had a difficult enough time seeing any of the birds amid the clumps of leaves and all the shadows. The wind blowing now made things worse, the dead branches clacking and the leaves and wings fluttering—bands of gray and black competing for his attention.

The patter of rain came next, sounding and feeling comforting. The rain cut some of the heat of his wounds, and he leaned his neck back and let the fat drops fall into his eyes and along his bleeding blaze. He crept forward, hearing some of the birds following in the trees overhead, and hearing more of them fly away.

"We fly to Ninéon," a crow cawed. "We tell Ninéon about the bad horse."

"Ninéon," the small voice agreed. "Ninéon will know what to do. And Ninéon must know that we hurt the horse. Ninéon will be pleased and angry."

"Happy we hurt the horse."

"Angry the horse killed so many of our flock," the small voice added.

The Finest could not see that it was a diminutive sparrow chattering, the same one that once nested on a beam in the royal stables, the same one that had followed him through the portal to the Finest Court.

There was a great flash of lightning, thick and jagged and followed by clap of thunder so loud the ground shook. The rain came even harder now.

Another great flash, another loud boom, and the remaining birds shrieked in anger. It sounded like they all flew off then, but Gallant-Stallion stayed in the orchard for the rest of the night, listening and peering through a steady, pounding rain that eventually turned gentle.

The birds had made no mention of Kalantha, and so he was determined not to show them where she was by going to her now.

He prayed they hadn't spotted Honest-Stormchaser and that the Finest iomud had stayed watch over Kalantha. When the sky began to lighten, and when he couldn't see a single bird in the apple trees, he headed across the field toward the ruins of the farm, moving slow and watching over his shoulder with every few steps.

It was dawn before Gallant-Stallion reached the cottage.

Kalantha stood in the doorway, hand cupped over her eyes, searching. When she saw him, she called out, and Stump barked excitedly. Even Honest-Stormchaser seemed pleased to see him. But their joy plummeted when they saw the scratches that covered his hide. The welts were thick and ropy, and blood still glistened on the most severe of the cuts.

"The birds," Kalantha said, rushing toward him, dragging her splinted leg, looking nervously at the sky. "Oh, Rue, those horrid birds are back."

And the birds, Gallant-Stallion said in the Finest tongue. *Those birds, Honest-Stormchaser, know about us.*

30 · Unsettling News

I believe the Fallen Favorites are like the leaves of a willow oak. Small, blunt, thick, and with smooth edges. They have no teeth like an elm tree's leaves, and so individually they have no bite against nature and large forces. But when the Fallen Favorites band together, they are capable of great goodness or extreme cruelties. They are like clumps of willow oak leaves, so numerous they block out the beautiful sunlight, or so thick they provide shelter from a storm.

~Stoutspirit, seventeenth Finest

Gallant-Stallion was exhausted, and his hide throbbed from hundreds of scratches and gouges that were trying to heal. None of them was deep, but the sheer number of them took a heavy toll. There were scratches around his eyes, and he counted himself fortunate that he hadn't been blinded. Kalantha rode on Honest-Stormchaser's back, constantly looking at him and occasionally leaning and stretching out a hand to touch his neck.

"Poor Rue."

You should return to the Finest Court, Rue, heal and return to the road farther south. You will find us again.

No.

"When we find Meven, one of his grooms will help you. I know you must hurt, but we can't turn back now, understand? We're too close, and this is too important."

I will take care of your charge, Rue, and guide her while she searches for her brother. I want the war to end, my brother, and I will defend her with my life. I give you my word.

Gallant-Stallion snorted. *You have not seen the birds . . . Cornsilk . . . you cannot know the danger they pose.*

And you told me before that you do not know why the birds pursue you. Your ignorance is a danger, too.

Gallant-Stallion looked to both sides of the merchant road. Wildflowers grew in profusion to the west—brilliant blue flowers the size of buttons, yellow ones that challenged the brightness of the sun. Beyond them stretched a meadow, much drier than the one he'd ran through last night, shot through here and there with more patches of wildflowers. To the south the road went on as far as he could see, gently turning around a chunk of granite the size of a cabin.

The birds want Kalantha dead, and me because I stand in their way. Gallant-Stallion snorted for emphasis. *The birds know about the Finest. They called me a Finest. That is a dangerous thing, to be discovered. We live in the shadows, hidden among the creatures of Paard-Peran. The Court must know of this. The force behind the birds wants to end the Montoll bloodline, I am certain of it. And if the birds work against her, they work against her brother. I believe an old priest is behind this all.*

Because a bird could not divine this plan on its own?

Because a bird, any creature, could not be so vile as to plot something like this. A Fallen, Fallen Favorite is behind all of this, Cornsilk. But I aim to keep Kalantha safe, and the only way I can do that is by staying with her.

Your presence guarantees nothing, Rue.

Gallant-Stallion shook his head. *You are wrong, Cornsilk. It guarantees that I am trying my best.*

Stump was more eager this morning, having slept a long while the night before. Nose to the merchant road, he hurried along, only glancing back at the horses once in a while and offering a sympathetic expression to Gallant-Stallion. He didn't ask what had happened to the horse during the evening. His knowing or not knowing would not ease the horse's pain.

They stopped once in the morning, Stump deciding he needed to roll in a bed of clover and wade into a stream. Shortly after resuming their trek, they stopped again. To the east of the road, they saw four Galmier soldiers and twice that many horses. The men tamped down earth over a grave and stabbed a sword into the ground for a headstone. They bowed their heads, either oblivious to the presence of Kalantha and the horses, or resolute in finishing their task.

"Cornsilk, stop!" Kalantha eased down from the riding horse's back and waited for the men to finish the prayer. Then she waved and walked toward them, still stiff-legged because of the splint. "Have you seen Meven?" She addressed this to the one with more shiny buttons and braids than the rest.

He turned away from the grave. There were a dozen mounds stretched along a row of poplars, the trees shading them. It was different than the mass graves she'd passed closer to the border. Four of the graves had helmets placed near the swords and pressed into the earth. Blue tabards fluttered from the cross-pieces. The other eight also had swords, but no helmets and nothing to mark their nationality.

"You are King Meven's sister." It had taken a moment for Lieutenant Rendell to recognize Kalantha. "Good, Lady Kalantha, that you were not riding with us. Good, that we are not burying you."

She dropped to her knees and gasped, threw her hands over her mouth. "Meven!" came the muffled cry. "By all that's holy Meven is—"

"Not dead, Lady Kalantha." Lieutenant Rendell helped her to her feet. "The King of Galmier is alive."

"Then—" She stared at the graves.

"My men. Four of them. Half my unit. The other graves belong to Nasim-Guri men."

"Meven . . . where's Meven?" The worry was thick in her voice, and she was doing her best not to cry. "He was with you, wasn't he? We've been looking for him." She gestured to the horses. "Rue and me, we've been looking. We were supposed to—"

"Go with him. I remember. We waited, but the Meven said you were lost in the palace and—"

"Where is he?"

While Kalantha talked to the soldiers, Gallant-Stallion talked to their horses.

Big punch and pretty horse, there was fighting. This came from the noriker ridden by Lieutenant Rendell. It spoke with more authority than its fellows. *It was not long fighting, not as long as others we have watched. We were not hurt in this fight.*

Obvious, Cornsilk observed.

Not hurt like you, the noriker continued. *Not in a great battle like you. Did your soldier die?*

Gallant-Stallion ignored the question. *A young soldier with you, they would have addressed him as King Meven.*

The noriker snorted. *I understand what a king is, punch. King Meven rode with us. Then he fought and lost. Unhurt, he rode away.*

Gallant-Stallion pricked his ears forward and nickered.

Rode with other soldiers wearing the colors of spring. King Meven's soldiers stayed here to bury the dead and the stink.

Twelve dead, Gallant-Stallion thought. He noticed that unlike the other graves they'd passed, this area was cleared, as if it was a small cemetery. Trees had been cut down, and the wood stacked behind the row of poplars. Weeds had been pulled around the mounds, and clearly more care had been taken around the four graves belonging to the Galmier soldiers. He listened to Lieutenant Rendell now.

"Lady Kalantha, your brother bade us to erect this cemetery in the name of Paard-Zhumd, son of the creator god. And to honor men from our country and the enemy land."

"We are in the enemy land." Kalantha stared at the graves, uncertainty on her face. "You promise me that my brother is not here." She pointed at the four graves with blue tabards fluttering. "You promise me!"

"Aye, Lady Kalantha. I am not a man who is friends with deceit. Your brother is alive. He's on his way to Duriam." Lieutenant Rendell took off his helmet and wiped the sweat off his brow. His face was dirty and the backs of his hands were sunburned. "It was nearly three days past we were ambushed by Nasim-Guri men. Your brother was not hurt. Took us this long to clear the land and bury all these men properly. And we worked hard and fast."

"Farmers, really, the men who attacked us." This came from a soldier little older than Meven. "We're certain they were conscripted into the army. They didn't fight well." He knelt and smoothed a spot on the grave they'd just finished.

"But they had numbers," Lieutenant Rendell added. He nodded to the graves. "Numbers and more than enough arrows. The only solace we have is that more of them died than us."

Kalantha noticed that one of Rendell's soldiers was wounded, a bandage wrapped around his chest. "You tended him?"

A nod from the lieutenant.

"Could you help my friend Rue?" After a moment and noting his puzzled expression, she pointed to Gallant-Stallion. "Rue. Please."

Lieutenant Rendell grabbed a pack off one of the norikers and approached Gallant-Stallion. "Looks like he's been through quite the fight. What happened to him? Were you ambushed, too?"

"Rue was." She stayed between the graves and the road,

watching the lieutenant sift through the pack and produce a clay jar. "The birds got him." She noted a surprised reaction. "Have you seen lots of dark birds around here?"

He shook his head. "Easy, boy, this might sting a little bit. Hmm. No bridle on you, nothing to grab on to."

"He won't run." Kalantha finally joined him, though she cast a glance over her shoulder at the poplar trees, searching for birds and finding only a few jays. "He knows you're going to help him. Rue's awfully smart."

Lieutenant Rendell smoothed the ointment on the longest scratches. "I can see that birds could have done this. Must've run into some angry flock for this to happen." After he finished, he handed Kalantha the jar. "You can put some more on him later." Then he pointed to one of the soldiers. "I'll have Roddick take you back to the palace. He is heading to Nadir anyway, with news of your brother. The rest of us are staying here, waiting."

It was her turn to shake her head. "I'm going after Meven. I told him I'd help him stop the war. He's a good man, my brother. But I think he needs me."

The lieutenant smiled sadly. "Lady Kalantha, I didn't lie to you. I said your brother went to Duriam . . . but he went as a prisoner of the Nasim-Guri men. He stopped this fight." Another gesture to the graves. "Then he surrendered himself. He believes he can make peace with the enemy King this way."

"No." She leaned against Rue, feeling the strength drain out of her. "Surrendered to them? He wouldn't do that."

"It ended this fight."

"We would have prevailed, Lady Kalantha." The soldier named Roddick strode toward them. "But we would have a larger cemetery here. Your brother saved lives."

Perhaps at the expense of his own, Honest-Stormchaser said.

"You should be proud of him." Lieutenant Rendell gave her a genuine smile then. "A most honorable man, your brother and my King. Not the same man who started this war."

Kalantha looked numb. "Surrendered. Will they kill him?"

"No." The lieutenant answered her almost too quickly. "They wouldn't dare kill the King of Galmier." He stroked his chin, as if deciding how much more he should say.

"What would he do, the enemy King?" She repeated the question, clearing her throat and speaking louder. "What would King Silverwood do? Tell me."

Lieutenant Rendell glanced at Roddick, then looked back to Kalantha. He bent until he was eye-level with her. "I don't know for certain."

"What would he do to Meven?" Her eyes were daggers aimed at him.

"I'm not lying, Lady Kalantha. I truly don't know. My words are only conjecture. King Silverwood might do nothing untoward. He might listen to your brother and gratefully and graciously accept peace. Nasim-Guri is nearly beaten. He could well send your brother back home with an honor guard."

"Or?"

"Or he might lock your brother away and make demands on Galmier. Ransom him to Bishop DeNogaret and try to exact a heavy price for all his casualties."

"To the Bishop? Why the Bishop?"

"If King Silverwood does lock your brother away, it will be up to Bishop DeNogaret to respond . . . to meet the ransom, or to continue the bloody war and crush Nasim-Guri, winning your brother back that way."

"Up to Bishop DeNogaret." Kalantha paled. "Oh, no." She reached a hand up and wrapped her fingers around a hunk of Gallant-Stallion's mane. "Power cannot fall to the Bishop."

"He's a wise man, Lady Kalantha. And I'm sure he's mending and can handle the task."

"A bad man," she hissed. "King Silverwood must make peace with Meven. I've got to help." She stepped to Cornsilk, grabbing her mane now and jumping, pulling herself up onto the iomud's back. She smoothed the mane and apologized. "I follow this road?"

"You can't let her go, Lieutenant. She's a girl, King Meven's sister. It isn't done, letting a girl run loose in the countryside, let alone a royal one. You can't . . ."

Lieutenant Rendell held up a hand to silence the soldier. "She came out here on her own."

"You can't force me to do anything." There was only a hint of defiance in Kalantha's voice. She watched their eyes, learning she was right—they couldn't stop her. She was of royal blood, and even though women held no real power in this world, she did not answer to them.

"No, I can't force sense into you." The lieutenant let out a deep breath. "But it would be sorrowful news if you *and* your brother were taken by King Silverwood."

"What would it matter? I'm of no real consequence. The throne doesn't fall to me. It falls to Bishop DeNogaret . . . at my brother's decree." A whisper: "According to the Bishop's design, no doubt. I wish Meven had read that book."

"Pardon, Lady Kalantha?"

"I ask you again. Do I take this road to Duriam?"

The lieutenant nodded. "You could take one of these horses, since you insist on this course. It has tack, and—"

"I would think a horse finds all of that stuff uncomfortable. Bad enough they carry the weight of someone on their back. I've done well without. This road?"

"There's a village a few miles down, and another road branches from it, wider, if I remember correctly, and heading straight west. You follow that one. And you be very careful, Lady Kalantha. Very, very careful."

"I may have nothing to worry about, good sir. Meven may be a welcome guest, and this war could well be history."

"Be careful nonetheless."

"And you be careful, too." She looked again to the poplar

trees, then to the trees across from the small cemetery. They were predominantly blackgums, tall and with smooth, shiny leaves. Sprinkled among them were slippery elms, with hairy twigs she knew were good for relieving throat ailments; her old gardener friend taught her that. So fully leafed out, it was difficult for her to find birds perched in them. She spotted only a few—sparrows and wrens, tiny birds that posed no threat.

Gallant-Stallion explained to Stump what the conversations were about, and the dog seemed to understand most of it.

Those were the horses I tracked, Stump said. *The ones I smell. More horses go down that road. I can follow them.*

Gallant-Stallion considered asking the hunting dog to stay with the soldiers. If the lieutenant's directions were good, they could find Duriam and King Silverwood's palace with little effort.

I will follow the other horse smells now, the dog continued. *This is very important work.*

Very important. Thank you, Stump.

You are welcome, big punch. It is good to do something important.

"I should have asked them for something to eat." Kalantha frowned. Last night she'd eaten the last of the food Becca had given her. "They would have had maislin or pandemayn breads. Maybe a bag of filberts to share." She combed her fingers through Cornsilk's mane. "No, I did right not asking them. They're waiting for Meven, word of Meven. They need whatever they have. We'll find something to eat on the way."

Find something? The iomud looked to Gallant-Stallion.

I told you that we lived with the ponies in the Galmier Mountains for a time. She knows how to fend for herself. There was pride in his eyes. *She's resourceful.*

For a child.

Resourceful. And she is no longer a child, Cornsilk. Fate took her childhood and replaced it with challenges and hardships.

It has given you hardships, too. And challenges, this jour-ney being one of them. You can hardly stay awake.

Gallant-Stallion snorted, a sound with no words in it.

The Finest iomud said nothing else as they continued down the road at a pace Gallant-Stallion could manage.

They passed the village a few hours later, avoided two small patrols, and stopped near a thicket of wild dewberries. Kalantha ate her fill, then gathered as many ripe ones as she could find and put them in the sack Becca had given her. She gathered handfuls more and fed them to the iomud and Gallant-Stallion. The iomud gobbled them down, never having tasted such sweet spring berries before.

Resourceful, Gallant-Stallion repeated.

Stump disappeared during this time, and the Finest thought the dog gone for good. But he returned shortly before they continued their journey, licking his lips and tail wagging.

Follow me, he told Gallant-Stallion. *The scent of those horses is stronger here. Hurry.* The dog took off at a loping run, and the Finest stayed back several yards.

"King Silverwood has to be treating Meven well," Kalantha said. "Bishop DeNogaret cannot have Galmier. He just cannot." She talked about this fervently, keeping her mind focused and her hopes strong. "He is behind the birds, Rue. We both know it. Meven and me should have let you kill Bishop DeNogaret."

It was the first time she had spoken so venomously, and it sent a shiver down Gallant-Stallion's back.

Resourceful and vengeful, Cornsilk observed. *An interesting combination, Rue.*

They listened to her fume well into the afternoon, when the walled city of Duriam came into view. The city was perched on a swell of land, defensible and impressive-looking. They waited in a shallow valley filled with blue beech, crack willows, and catalpa trees in full flower. Stump was anxious, pawing at the ground and pacing, pointing to the road that led to the main gate.

The horses I smelled are in there. So the man you want is in there. We should be in there finding him, punch. We should be in there now.

Kalantha lay in the tall grass, watching the road.

Stump, remember the barn in the city, where they caged us?

The dog growled at the memory.

We will wait here for the dark to come.

Men grabbed us in the dark, big punch, Stump said.

Honest-Stormchaser cut in. *I do not believe it will be any safer then. But this is the Fallen Favorite's choice. They do not know her here, and so have no reason to detain her. Light or dark, it should make no difference when we enter the city.*

But she wants to go to the palace, Rue said.

Then it will be safer for your resourceful, vengeful charge to cling to the shadows.

If there is such a thing as safe for her, Gallant-Stallion added. He recalled a conversation he had shared with Steadfast's spirit:

"Steadfast, I am to guide her on the path to perfection, but I do not know where that path lies. Danger surrounds this girl."

"Danger and the future of Galmier," Steadfast's spirit replied. "The future rides with you."

When it neared sunset, Kalantha took the splint off her leg and tested it, finding her ankle still sore, but probably not broken. She motioned to Gallant-Stallion and started up the low hill, circling the walled city as she went, careful that she didn't step in any depressions or trip. A quarter of the way around, she found a smaller gate, and she headed toward it. The guards here gave her curious looks, but did not stop her.

Duriam was an open city, and she appeared to pose no threat to anyone.

"I'm going to see my brother," she told them. "He's visiting in the city."

"You'll have to stable those farm animals," one returned.

Honest-Stormchaser snorted at the affront, but without tack or saddles, the Finest could have been mistaken for such.

The guard gave her directions and assumed she had the coin to pay for the stable. Inside, they followed the wall, passing by a merchant district and a quarter with stone houses with gaily painted shutters and window boxes. It was darker in the city than out, the high walls cutting the last of the sunlight. Guards were numerous, perhaps on alert because of the war, or perhaps because of the time of day. She avoided them, and she ignored the curious looks of people on the street who pointed at her and the animal entourage.

Candles and lanterns appeared in windows by the time they headed toward the center of the city. The streets sloped upward steeply, leading toward what looked more like a manor house than a palace. There was a wall separating it from the rest of the city, with open gates that Kalantha eyed. Guards were not posted at these gates, but rather patrolled the grounds. When she had their dull and predictable routine memorized, she slipped inside.

"Rue, you stay . . ." She meant to tell him to stay outside. But two horses and a dog, unattended, would draw attention. They'd either be shooed out of the city or caught and penned. "Hurry, Rue." She darted to the closest building, large and low, with a tightly thatched roof. It had the look of a stable.

Moments later, they hid in the shadows outside it. She peered in a crack, but couldn't make out any details. There was no lantern burning. She worked her way around to a wide door, standing flat against the wall when two guards came by. Then she opened the door. The starlight spilling in showed several empty stalls.

"Stay here, Rue. Cornsilk, Stump. You stay here, too."

The dog snuffled and pawed at something in the dirt. *Important work?*

Important to stay here, Gallant-Stallion said.

The dog went inside the stables, Cornsilk following.

Be very careful, Kalantha.

"I might have nothing to worry about, Rue." Her words were not convincing. "But I don't know what else to do. Maybe I should've asked that lieutenant to come with me." A moment later, and after two more guards passed nearby: "But he was told to wait there by the graves." She stepped away from the stable, and watched Gallant-Stallion go inside. "I will be careful, Rue."

Then she hurried to the manor house, pausing to hide behind trees, watching the guard, then running again.

She will be careful, Honest-Stormchaser said. *She is resourceful, as you say. But she may not stay safe.* The iomud selected the empty stall closest to the door. Gallant-Stallion found one nearby.

I pray to the good powers my charge finds what she seeks.

My charge is in the manor, too. He seeks peace for this world. The speaker was a fine-looking noriker in the stall across from Gallant-Stallion. *My charge is the King of Galmier.*

31 · Mouse in the Manor House

I love the Finest Court, the Shimmering Paddocks, Wistful Lake, and
the Scattered Woods. The Court lands are perfect. But I love the imperfect land of Paard-Peran more. I embrace the storms that uproot
trees and scar the land, the heat of the summer sun that scorches corn-
fields. It is far more . . . interesting . . . to live where it is not perfect.
And I have far more important work to do here. May the Court and
the good powers forever give me charges to guide and guard.

~Shatterhooves, elder Finest pony

Kalantha expected that King Silverwood would have a palace
to rival Meven's, but it was probably less than a third of the
size. There was only one stable, though it was longer than any
in Nadir. Four small stone buildings, plain but sturdy-looking,
were likely the chapel, brewhouse, bakehouse, and residence
for the elite servants. The manor house itself was only three lev-
els high and blocky, but with ornate stonework on the corners
and along the roof. There was only one tower, this also square,
and it rose to only four or five storeys, with two sentries
perched on top.

A sentry stood at the front entrance, near tall doors of
ebony wood carved with whorls and lions. From her hiding
spot at the base of a white oak, she could see the detail in the
wood because of twin large lanterns that hung from posts on
either side of the door. More lights shone from windows, and
only a few of the windows were dark or had curtains drawn.

She could stroll right up to the front entrance, give the sentry her name, and ask to see Meven. But she had seen no celebration in town, no banners flying anywhere to herald the end of the war. And so she worried that Meven might not be considered an honored guest. In fact, the more she thought about it, the more she was certain Meven was not a guest at all. If she were the King of Nasim-Guri, and the enemy who started the war turned up, she certainly wouldn't be civil—too many people had died to exchange civilities.

"Better I be careful. I told Rue I'd be careful."

When the sentry's attention was drawn by someone walking out of what she thought might be the chapel, Kalantha darted toward a row of hedges against the manor. Pain pulsed up her leg with each step, and she wondered if she should have left the splint on. She wished she had on something more presentable. She certainly didn't look like royalty. She looked like a peasant, and if she got caught by a sentry, he'd likely brand her a thief and not bother to listen to any explanation.

She followed the hedge around the corner of the building, passing by a window where several candles burned in an elaborate display. She stopped and stared at the pane itself. Not glass, but crystal, she guessed, beveled at the edges and catching the light and sparkling pale green and blue. A glance at the other windows showed they were made the same, all beveled along the margins, and some with faint, etched patterns in the center. An opened rose in this one, a lily in another. She pressed her face to the window, happy to discover that no one was in the room beyond.

Kalantha guessed it would be called a sitting room, as comfortable-looking high-backed chairs were against the wall, and two cushioned couches sat opposite each other in the middle. A smaller couch was on a dais between two urns. The walls were painted a deep red, and they were decorated with mirrors and pictures, the frames of which were shiny silver. The pictures she could make out were of beautiful countrysides— not a single stern-faced man, like in Meven's palace. When she tilted her head, she could see the floor—the same ebony wood as the front door. Thick rugs of red, black, and white were scattered across it, some shot through with metallic thread that glimmered in the candlelight. Were all the rooms so orna- mented?

She knew that powerful and wealthy people prided them- selves on their households. The appearance of a home was a direct reflection on the owner, and the more ostentatious, the better the owner appeared. She stretched her arm through a gap in the hedges and ran her fingers along the stone. Marble, polished, and very costly. Marble was quarried at the far nor- thern end of the island-continent, and therefore it had cost quite a bit to bring it this far south, carve and smooth it.

How long ago had the manor been built? Meven's palace was generations old, though parts of it were more recent, as it had been added to. This building was older, she decided. It looked older and felt older. She saw someone walk into the room and she pulled back from the window, not taking time to see what the person looked like. Kalantha took a few deep breaths to steady herself, rubbed at her sore leg, then followed the hedge around to the side, then the back. She passed a few more win- dows, where lights burned, but she hunkered below these, dart- ing into the scratchy hedge once when more sentries came by.

Let Meven be alive, she prayed, as she extricated herself when she was certain they were out of sight. Let him not be rotting in some dungeon. She'd help him escape if need be. With each step she was more and more certain he was a prisoner of King Sil- verwood. She certainly would not have been civil to her brother.

How to find out where Meven is? She passed another tall ebony wood door, and ducked into the hedges again when she heard the sentries return. *The kitchen!* She practically shouted the words in her excitement. She'd go to the kitchen. If the cooks here were anything like the cooks and kitchen help at the Nadir palace, she'd learn about Meven. The cooks in Nadir were gossips—she'd learned that after only a few days at Meven's palace. They knew more what was going on than Meven's advisors, and they were quick to spread the news and share their opinions. Further, with so many servants working in the larder, pantry, kitchen, and the buttery, she'd likely go unnoticed . . . one new young helper for the palatial estate.

Kalantha saw that the hedge ended and a stretch of flat stone tiles began. Benches and chairs were arranged on it, and large pots of colorful flowers were placed between them. She scurried from one pot to the next, imagining herself a mouse running from one clump of hay to another in a stable to avoid being seen and stepped on. She prayed to stay as unnoticed as a little mouse. She heard things as she went: a pair of sentries talking out of sight, their voices muffled by the distance; the cry of some night bird, which sent a shiver down her back; the laughter of a woman, coming out of an open window from a floor or two above. Soft music was coming from the same room—a harp, she guessed, the player expert. Were she here under other circumstances, she might pause to listen longer.

At the edge of the stone tiles there was another door, this wider and not as tall, and made of a common wood. There were stone steps leading up to it, and crates sitting to one side. The entrance to the kitchen.

She listened at the door, hearing footsteps and pans clinking. At Meven's palace, someone was always in the kitchen—no matter the hour. Sentries patrolled throughout the night, and so someone had to feed them when they were finished. Cooks were always baking breads and desserts and preserving fruits and vegetables. There would be no perfect time to enter the kitchen, save at mealtime when she might get lost in the sheer number of servants bustling around. Kalantha looked into the crates, thinking perhaps she could find something in there to bring into the kitchen—an excuse for being there. The crates were empty, and so after a quick prayer to the good gods of Paard-Peran, she opened the door and stepped inside.

Two women were kneading balls of bread dough on a floured countertop. On another counter three large bowls were covered with cloths—more bread. The room was warm from the fire in the oven, and it smelled buttery and delightful to Kalantha.

"Hello," she said when the women paused to look at her.

"Hello to you," the taller woman answered. The other returned to pushing her fists into the mound of dough. "Haven't seen you here before."

Kalantha looked around the kitchen—it was roughly the same size as the one in Meven's palace. "I'm supposed to clean for you," she lied. She tried to keep her voice convincing and didn't meet the women's eyes. "Where should I start?"

"The floor, girl. There's rags in the closet, and buckets. Some water's boiling over the fire. Use that. And don't get in our way."

Kalantha did as she was told, and moments later was working on her hands and knees, rubbing at the tile floor and listening to the women talk, pleased that her ruse had worked. It was uninteresting prattle: deprecatory comments about cooks who worked during the afternoon hours, a dinner party next week that would require people brought in from the town to help, how many loaves they would bake tonight before going upstairs to sleep, and the handsome head groom newly hired from a noble house in Vered. Kalantha planned on finishing this floor—she was nearly done by the time the cooks had run out of things to talk about—then going elsewhere in the manor to snoop. It should be late enough then that most of the servants would be sleeping.

The last of the loaves were in the oven baking, scenting the air and making her think of Rue. She knew the horse loved the smell of bread baking, even though he would never eat it. Rue would be proud of her, sneaking into the manor and . . .

"Isn't it your turn to feed the King's guest, Agatha?" This the taller cook directed to her companion. The word "guest" hissed out of the cook's mouth. "There's soup left from dinner. I set aside a bowl of it over there." She gestured back with her head. "Cold, I suppose you could set it in the oven for a bit."

"He's not worth heating it. And it isn't my turn. Off you go." Agatha fluttered her fingers toward a door that a willowy man with a long nose and a narrow face stepped through. Finely dressed and young-looking, Kalantha guessed him to be a butler or a pantler, someone in a position of authority. She looked away and scrubbed harder on the floor.

"You, girl."

Kalantha ignored the man and kept working, hoping he was talking to one of the cooks. *Be an unnoticed little mouse,* she thought.

"I said, girl, look at me."

She turned her head toward him, her hair partially obscuring her face. "Sir?"

"I've not seen you here before."

"She's a new hire, like the head groom," Agatha supplied. "Certainly you know her." She had the bowl of soup in her hands and nodded to the man as she left the room.

He harumphed and tiptoed toward Kalantha, trying to avoid stepping on the wet floor. He leaned over and grabbed a fistful of the back of her tunic.

"I've never seen you before, I say. You'll come with me, girl."

32 · A Greater Force

The good powers, I have not met one or seen one, or in my dreams heard one. But I know they exist because I exist. The good powers created me to be a bane to the badness of the world and to redeem, if I am strong and worthy, a Fallen Favorite or two. When my work is done and my bones turn to dust in the Shimmering Paddocks, I think I will see the good powers—if I am strong and worthy.

~Pureheart, from the Finest Court Canon

Ninéon stirred a talon in the Vision Pond, chasing away the drab olive film. The bright emerald green water reflected her stern expression. She thought of the Galmier Mountains, the southern curl that crossed the Nasim-Guri border to the far western point. The peaks were dusted with snow, and down from them tiny blue wildflowers grew in crevices where dirt had settled. Farther down, past a village of goatherders, men fought on a twisting trail. Some wore the green and yellow tabards of Nasim-Guri, but those with them were obviously from the village, wielding pitchforks and other farm implements against a group of Galmier soldiers.

It pleased the falcon that word had not reached all the Galmier soldiers that Meven wanted the war to end.

She watched the uneven fight. Though the Nasim-Guri men outnumbered the Galmier men two to one, the latter were more skilled and had better weapons. Only three of the Nasim-Guri men had armor, this being boiled leather breastplates and grieves. It was heady, the exhibition, and Ninéon imagined that she was one of the Galmier soldiers, the one with broad shoulders who deftly sliced through his opponents. There was a greater viciousness about him, and she reveled in it, getting as drunk as a man swigging down one ale after another.

The trail was slick with blood, and the Nasim-Guri men fell. A few of the Galmier soldiers fell, too, and Ninéon cheered the lanky goatherder with a scythe, who battled ferociously like a rabid dog. She was sorry to see him die, even though it was at the hand of her broad-shouldered champion. She watched the battle until the end, Galmier the victor. She listened to the soldiers congratulate each other, and offer succor to their only seriously wounded comrade. They gathered near him, seemingly oblivious to the bodies strewn around them. Ninéon leaned so close to the pond her beak touched the water, sending out a faint ripple and distorting the scene. She cried shrilly when she missed the man's last breath, and she turned away when his fellows chose a spot to bury him.

She stirred the pond again, searching along the border for more soldiers and finding none, looking deeper into Nasim-Guri, past burned villages where Galmier tabards hung like flags, past mounds where she knew those who died in the war were buried. There were scattered individual mounds with swords or markers, and she saw several bodies that hadn't been buried and were providing a feast for the crows. For hours she played with her Vision Pond, finding scattered melees and watching each one until its conclusion. When she found no more fights, and when she heard a fluttering in a nearby clearing, she withdrew from the pond and watched the brightness fade.

Ninéon pushed off a floor covered by fallen leaves and bone shards. She glided from the ring of stringybarks and into the shadow cast by one of the oldest trees in the ancient forest. Predominantly sparrows and wrens were in the clearing, and several jays and cowbirds. She nodded to each, a courtesy she could not extend when her massive flocks were present.

Valane was in the front, chirping to get the falcon's attention. She'd told Ninéon earlier about the flock she'd gathered to attack the Finest punch, after spying the horse and the girl in Galmier.

"We hurt the horse, Ninéon." The sparrow talked quickly, wings twitching, as it shifted back and forth on its tiny feet.

"But did not kill the horse." Ninéon lowered her beak until it was even with Valane's.

"Ninéon, you bade me follow the horse to the place called the Finest Court. So we sought to hurt it and force it to return there."

"Commendable," Ninéon purred. The falcon touched her beak to the red-brown crest on the sparrow's head. "And its success?"

The sparrow stopped twitching and hung its head. "We hurt the horse, Ninéon. He hurt us, killed us. Killed many, many of us. But he would not leave for the Finest Court."

"He protects the girl."

"Yes, Ninéon. He protects her fiercely."

The falcon paced away to the trunk of the oldest tree, then returned, again standing in front of the sparrow.

"The girl is not so important any longer, I have decided."

"She travels to Duriam on the Finest horse. She thinks the war will end, plans to help it end."

Ninéon extended her neck. "The girl and the Finest horse are already in Duriam, and were entering the heart of the city when I spied on them last."

"The horse . . ."

"Valane, I want you to find this Finest Court again. But we will have time for that, a long, long time. Now the war goes on here, and that holds my attention."

A cowbird ruffled its feathers and squawked.

Ninéon turned away from the sparrow. She stared at the cowbird, so dark brown it looked black, nothing elegant about it, clumsy-looking compared to the other dark birds. She'd named it, but could not recall the name now . . . too many other things to think about.

"Ninéon. Sweet, sweet Ninéon," the cowbird began in a voice that sounded at the same time harsh and yet tiny. "I am tired, sweet, sweet Ninéon. I flew far and fast to get here to you. So very fast, Ninéon."

The falcon cocked her head, inviting the droll cowbird to continue.

"I saw the one called King Meven, the one who started the beautiful war."

"Puppet of the Bishop," a jay cut in. "The puppet, you saw him."

"Watched him with the daffodil men," the cowbird continued.

"The Nasim-Guri soldiers," Ninéon corrected.

The cowbird squawked. "Sol . . . sol . . . soldiers. Soldiers." When it had the word correct, it went on. "Taken as if in a cage, wings tied, sweet, sweet Ninéon. Carried to Duriam. Caged."

"Captured," the jay helped. "Caught. A prisoner. King Meven is a prisoner of his enemy."

"Of the daffodil soldiers." The cowbird stretched to its full height. "Put in a stone box."

"King's castle." This from the jay again.

"Castle. Castle. Soldiers. Soldiers. Meven caged inside it. I saw that. I saw. I saw!"

Ninéon made a sound like a dove cooing, and the small flock breathed easy that she was pleased. "Captured, the war will go on."

"Until all the men are gone," Valane said.

"They will make more," the jay spoke smugly. "There will always be more men."

"If there are not enough men to fight here, there will be elsewhere," Ninéon finished. Her eyes were large and shiny, unblinking and staring at something beyond this time and this clearing. "We will make wars go on for a very long, long time." Her voice was musical and hushed, and the flock was held by it. "There will be suffering for years, and the blood will soak into the ground. The crows will gorge themselves, and eventually the number of men will dwindle. The land will be ours. And the pain will be our gift to the twin dark gods."

"The dark powers of Paard-Peran will accept our gifts," Valane said.

"And reward us," Ninéon said.

With a flick of her beak, she dismissed them.

33 · A Finest's Choice

My first charge was a baker, and I thought the Finest Court meant to punish me by assigning me such an unimportant man. I pulled his wagon as he went from home to home, delivering breads and pies, cakes and strawberry cookies. It was the same each day. The same streets, the same people. Only the fare changed, the breads darker or lighter, the pies of different fruits, the cookies dusted with sugar and raisins. Then I learned about coins. And then I discovered my Fallen Favorite did not gain them from the people we delivered to. His coins came from the wealthy who ordered cakes made like castles and pies the size of tabletops. The wealthy let him feed the poor. And the baker taught me generosity and how to be humble. The Finest Court gave me a delicious assignment.

~Brookwader, Finest shepherd of Dunbar Cookson

Gallant-Stallion stepped out of the stall so he could better see the noriker. It was a beautiful horse, and had it not conversed with him in hidden speak, he would have thought it simply one of King Meven's prized stock.

You are a Finest? He hadn't meant it as a question, though it came out that way.

Shimmermane, a veteran of the Court Lands, named after the Shimmering Paddocks where I was born, called Noble-born by my charge.

Gallant-Stallion regarded the noriker's sleek form with a touch of envy. Even though there were no lights in the stables, there were two high windows, and the stars shone through. Gallant-Stallion didn't know all the Finest, especially the ones who had been on Paard-Peran for a length of time. He mused that he'd met several simply by being in the right stable at the right time.

And your charge is King Meven Montoll?

Shimmermane snorted yes.

He already told you that, Rue, Honest-Stormchaser said. *Cannot you hear?*

He hears well enough, the noriker cut back. *He has trouble believing that I have the Fallen Favorite intended for him.*

Honest-Stormchaser whinnied in surprise. *Rue . . . Gallant-Stallion by his Finest name . . . has a charge. She is of royal blood.*

Oblivious to the conversation, Stump stretched his paws forward and raised his rump. He yawned wide then stood, stretched again, and turned around four times before lying down in a ball at the front of the iomud's stall.

Impossible. Meven intended for me? Gallant-Stallion's mind raced back to his arrival on Paard-Peran. His mentor, Steadfast, was at his side, and they were part of Prince Edan's wedding party. The Prince was cousin to Meven and Kalantha, and Bishop DeNogaret decreed the children could attend the Prince's marriage to Princess Silverwood of Nasim-Guri. Gallant-Stallion pestered Steadfast about who his charge was to be . . . Prince Edan?

"Patience," Steadfast had told him.

I was too patient, Gallant-Stallion decided now. The wedding party was attacked by a band of assassin-birds, swooping in looking like dark men on horseback against a black, stormy sky.

Steadfast never told Gallant-Stallion who his charge was. The veteran Finest fell to the evil flock. All he managed to his apprentice was: "Get the cousins to safety. Get your charge to safety."

So Gallant-Stallion watched over both of them for a time, while they lived with the ponies in the Galmier Mountains, and then when they returned to the High Keep Temple. He thought during all that time Meven was indeed his charge, as with Edan dead the young man was the Prince of Galmier. And when Gallant-Stallion went to Nadir and learned that the King was dying and Meven would inherit the throne, he was certain he was to shepherd the boy and that Meven was destined for something great.

But unusal events swirled around them. Bishop DeNogaret wanted Kalantha sent to Dea Fortress . . . away from the palace and locked into a religious life. Meven agreed, but Kalantha didn't. She escaped from her escorts, eventually returning to the palace grounds and finding Gallant-Stallion in the stables.

She understood him, even though Fallen Favorites were not capable of hearing the Finest—or so Gallant-Stallion had been told. Each Finest possessed a gift, and his apparently was the ability to converse with his charge. In that moment he knew he should be shepherding Kalantha—that he'd been wrong about Meven.

But I wasn't wrong then, Gallant-Stallion said. *It was Meven all along. Why not tell me, Steadfast?*

He recalled again the words Steadfast's spirit spoke:

"Danger and the future of Galmier surround this very important girl. Guide and guard her well. The hope of Paard-Peran rides with you, Gallant-Stallion."

Why not tell me the name of my charge when I asked you in the wedding party? That Meven was my ward? Why not tell me later when your spirit came to ground? Why? He practically screamed the last word, and it took the iomud and noriker by surprise.

He half-expected Steadfast's spirit to arrive, but there was no chill in the air, and his breath did not feather away from his nostrils.

Steadfast is dead, Gallant-Stallion. Shimmermane spoke with authority. *The dead do not speak to us.*

But he has spoken to me, Gallant-Stallion thought. Perhaps

my gift is to be heard by those I desperately want to hear me. Aloud in the hidden speak, he said: *I have been to the Court several times since I began to shepherd Kalantha. They did not say I erred.*

They would not, Honest-Stormchaser said. *Finest have chosen their own charges before. Mara claims the whole village of Bitternut. You claiming a different charge is not without precedent.*

Gallant-Stallion remained stunned. Honest-Stormchaser continued to talk, but he didn't hear her. He shut out all the words, instead hearing Stump whimper in a dream, the horses wuffling, the wind outside blowing at a loose shutter.

Meven was to be my charge, he hushed.

Yes, I say again, Shimmermane snorted. *Good that you did not keep him, Gallant-Stallion. Good that I was given the opportunity to guide and guard this conflicted soul.*

How long . . .

I have guided and guarded Meven Montoll for only days, since he left his palace to come here.

Gallant-Stallion's chest was tight and he fought for breath. *Meven was to be mine. I erred. But Kalantha is worthy! She is determined and courageous. She has more heart and drive than her brother. She wants to help others. Meven . . . why didn't the Court tell me? Or Steadfast tell me?*

Honest-Stormchaser whinnied to interrupt. *Why did it take so long for the Court to name a shepherd for Meven Montoll? Rue has shepherded Kalantha for a few years. Meven was left without a guardian during that time. Why was there a delay?*

Shimmermane didn't have an answer for that, and so the Finest trio lapsed into silence.

Gallant-Stallion's mind churned. He recalled his most recent journey to the Finest Court that Tadewi stared into his eyes and mentioned his "chosen charge." If he'd shepherded

Meven, like the Court had intended, perhaps there would have been no war. Perhaps he could have guided the boy down a righteous path and kept him away from Bishop DeNogaret. All the people dead. Could he have prevented it? His head throbbed and he pictured mound after mound along the merchant road, recalled the moans of the wounded from the tents on the palace grounds. Could he have saved lives if he'd shepherded Meven like he was supposed to? He was to be with Meven? Not Kalantha? No! Kalantha could hear him! Kalantha called him her magic horse, while Meven called him ugly, rueful-looking. Kalantha looked beyond herself, while Meven was selfish.

Was selfish.

The air turned chill around Gallant-Stallion.

Steadfast! Why didn't you tell me I was to shepherd Meven Montoll?

Because the Court is not infallible, my friend.

Steadfast, I—

Chose well, Gallant-Stallion.

He thought he saw the misty outline of his mentor in the aisle between his and Shimmermane's stalls. The other Finest did not seem to notice the spirit.

The war—

You could not have stopped it. Meven was not strong enough to prevent it.

But the Court, why did they wait so long to name a shepherd for Meven?

Because you chose well, Gallant-Stallion. Because Meven was not the worthy one until the day he said he would stop all of the fighting. And it was your charge who convinced him to do just that. Your charge.

I chose—

Well.

Kalantha—

I meant what I said when I told you that danger and the future of Galmier surround this very important girl. Guide and guard her well. The hope of Paard-Peran rides with you, Gallant-Stallion.

The air grew suddenly warm around Gallant-Stallion.

34 · Kings

People in my village do not often decorate themselves. But in cities, the people are like crows, gathering shiny bits and holding them close. Putting things that glimmer around their necks and wrists, letting shiny bits dangle from their ears to catch the sunlight. I enjoy my village and its people without all the decorations. The decorations, no matter how they sparkle, do not change how a crow struts.

~Mara, guardian of Bitternut

Please don't throw me out!" Kalantha stood on a stone stoop outside the kitchen. The long-faced young man still had a fistful of her tunic in his clenched fist. "And don't call the guards. They'll only arrest me and—"

He raised his arm, as if to get the attention of a passing sentry, then dropped it. He still held tight to the back of her tunic, but he didn't look at her. He cast his gaze to the sky and studied the constellation of Peran-Morab. "And why shouldn't you be thrown in some cell, girl? Trespassing in House Silverwood is a great offense. You'll have gray in your hair before—"

"You can't. I'm not a trespasser."

"No?" He continued to stare at the stars, focusing on a different constellation now. "Then what are you?"

"Desperate," she said after a moment. "I'm very desperate. And hopeful."

He lowered his gaze and turned her around, still holding

tight to her tunic, so that he could look at her face. "Give me a good reason why I shouldn't call the manor guards and alert the steward."

She quivered, looking at a stern face that was not quite so young as she first thought. His skin was smooth, and his hands and fingers lacked calluses. His hair was precisely trimmed close to his shoulders and curled at the ends. She'd initially thought him perhaps twenty years old, but his eyes, and the faint lines around them, suggested that he could be twice that. He held her with a strong grip.

"I want to see my brother, King Meven Montoll, he—"

He released her tunic and brushed the palms of his hands against his trousers. "Is a guest . . . of sorts . . . of King Silverwood."

"I know, Meven came here to stop the war."

The man looked again to the sky, brow furrowed and lips working.

"I'm not a trespasser, sir. I just . . . well, I just didn't think I'd get in if I went to the front gate."

He held his face farther back so he was staring at the stars directly overhead.

"I want to help my brother. I want the war to stop. I want . . ."

"You're quite willful for one of your few years and sex." He looked at yet another constellation.

"You believe me? That Meven's my brother and that he wants peace and—"

"Aye, girl. The stars tell me to trust you—whoever you are."

"Kalantha," she was quick to supply. "I'm Kalantha Montoll."

"Well, desperate and hopeful Kalantha Montoll, I am desperately hungry Lathan Hollow." His gaze followed a shooting star that arced to the northern horizon. "Fortunate for you I went to the kitchen for something to eat. A guard would have tossed you over the city wall, or in some slimy cell. You're very fortunate this night, Kalantha."

She looked up to the sky, too, trying to find what was holding his attention. She guessed he was looking at the constellation of the Three Sisters; it was one of the few she could recognize. "I want to see my brother, and then we need to see King Silverwood. The King has to know that—"

"Oh, he's well aware the King of Galmier is his houseguest. And in his good time he'll talk to your brother, but—"

Kalantha tugged firmly on Lathan's sleeve. "Now is King Silverwood's good time, Sir Hollow. Now, before any more soldiers die."

Lathan gave her a cryptic look. "I'm still desperately hungry, Kalantha. Would you join me for something to eat out here in the yard? The stars are too lovely to leave to themselves this evening."

"My brother—"

"Is not so hungry as I and is not going anywhere. Join me?"

"I am hungry, too," she admitted. "Desperately."

They dined on cold chicken with blueberry sauce, and drank warm cinnamon tea. The plates were decorated with tiny hearts and roses, and each had a pale rose in the center that shone ghostlike under the stars. Dessert was circlettes, round almond and cardamom finger cakes with currants. They were topped with raspberry preserves.

"My brother—"

Lathan let out a great sigh. "You are indeed a fortunate girl, Kalantha Montoll, that I believe you." He wagged a finger at her. "Not just any man would believe a wild tale from a raggedy-looking girl pretending to clean the kitchen floor."

"He's a prisoner, isn't he, my brother? He's not a guest."

Lathan nodded.

"I knew that when there was no music in the city."

He raised an eyebrow.

"People would be celebrating with the war over."

"War is adult business, Kalantha. A child your age should be concerned with other things."

She shook her head, her eyes flashing angrily. "I'm not a child, Sir Lathan. I never had time for it."

Lathan smiled faintly and collected the dishes. "Well, desperate and hopeful Kalantha Montoll, let's go visit with your brother."

They stopped in the kitchen, where Lathan set the dishes near the sink. Only one cook remained, and she wrinkled her nose at the prospect of working later to clean up after the pair. They walked slowly, as Kalantha's ankle had started to burn, and she limped. Lathan noted the injury, but said nothing and did not offer to help her. They passed the larder and pantry, and Kalantha inhaled deep all the wonderful scents. Neither room was as large as its counterpart at the Nadir palace, but she suspected there were fewer people to feed in this household. There couldn't be near as many servants as Meven had.

She marveled at the inside of the manor house. The woodwork was birch and oak, light and friendly and not dark and rich-looking like in Meven's palace. The walls were either paneled with more birch or painted light greens and yellows. The only exception seemed to be the fancy sitting room she had spied from a front window. There were paintings everywhere, an equal mix of landscapes and portraits. Among the latter were large paintings of women in fancy dresses. She couldn't recall a single portrait of a woman at the Nadir palace.

Lathan led her up a tight spiral staircase, then down a narrow hall. They passed a few workers as they went; one woman cleaned picture frames with a feather duster, another scrubbed the floor of the music room; three men arranged books in the library. She lingered outside the door of the last room, smelling the leather bindings and wondering what treasures King Silverwood had in there.

They stopped at the end of the hall, outside a heavy oak door where a guard stood at attention.

"Lathan," the guard said with a nod.

"The King of Galmier has a visitor. Step aside."

The guard paused a moment.

"King Silverwood will not mind. Consider her another prisoner if you'd like."

The guard opened the door and Kalantha hurried in. Meven had been sitting in a straightbacked chair by the window, but he jumped up when he saw her and met her with a fierce hug.

"How did you get here? Who came with you? Did they hurt you?" More questions tumbled out, a rapid buzz that Kalantha didn't have a chance to answer.

Lathan stood in the doorway and watched them. "I guess you were indeed telling the truth, desperate and hopeful Kalantha." He looked past them and out the window, where another shooting star arced toward the horizon. He cleared his throat to get their attention. "Make yourselves presentable. I'll arrange an audience with King Silverwood."

He left the door open, the guard standing in the frame, hand on the pommel of his sword.

"An audience with King Silverwood, Kalantha. Just how did you manage that? I've been here three days, a prisoner really. The King would not agree to see me."

She glanced around the room. It was simply furnished but pleasant, with a large bed and a table with another straight-backed chair pushed against it. A tray in the center of the table was filled with slices of spring cabbage and strawberries, and there was a crystal pitcher filled with water. A thick candle in a glass globe warmly lit the room. It wasn't an ugly prison.

"I came to see the King, Kal, and offer peace. I thought—"

"You're in no position to offer anything, Meven. This wasn't the right approach. He has you, and he can sue for peace on his terms now. This might have seemed like a good idea. I thought it was a good idea. But this wasn't right. You should have sent a messenger, not yourself."

Meven hugged her again, then released her and tugged her to sit on the bed. He didn't notice that she limped. He was so relived to see her.

"I should have waited for you, Kal. I figured you were lost, and—"

She interrupted him by thrusting her hand against his mouth. "I was lost, Meven." Then she told him about the crypt and the secret stairs, neither of which he knew about. She talked about the men who chased her, about not trusting even Sara Anne. Then she pulled the folded pages from her pocket. "Read this, Meven. You wouldn't read the book I brought from the Vershan Monastery, and you should have. Read this now. When you're done we'll worry about getting out of here."

He started to argue, but her flashing eyes stopped him. He took the pages over to the table, spread them out, and leaned over them. "I'm two years older than you, Kal. I'm the King of Galmier. Why haven't I the sense the gods gave you?"

She didn't reply. She propped her leg up on the bed, leaned back, and started to pray.

Meven read aloud:

DAY FIFTY-ONE OF THE YEAR OF WELLSPRING
I talked to the King again today. It is the final time I tried to convince him that the deaths of Kelka and Patrice Montoll were no accident. He will not listen, so caught up in the words of the high cleric DeNogaret. The Montolls were killed to limit the bloodline, I am certain, the stars scream that to me. And yet, no one listens. Astrologers are out of fashion and growing increasingly unpopular. I suspect I will be leaving his employ soon, as he is angry I cast aspersions on DeNogaret.

DAY FIFTY-EIGHT OF THE YEAR OF THE WELLSPRING

I leave for the isle of Farmeadow this evening, on a trade galleon bound for the island chains. The stars will be brighter there, and I will have things to better occupy my mind than politics and manipulations. I pity Kelka's children, now entrusted to DeNogaret, who has been named Bishop of the High Keep Temple. DeNogaret told the King he will watch over the younglings and see to a good, religious education for them. He persuaded the King that the children should not live here and that he had enough concerns raising his own son, Edan. The stars tell me terrible things have been set in motion. I leave this journal in the event the King rises from his grief and opens himself to another's words.

Meven reread the entries, including the earlier ones. Then he pulled out the chair and sat heavily in it.

"Bishop DeNogaret has been a father to me, Kal."

"A bad one," she returned.

"He loves me."

"Probably, in his way. But he loves you more for the power you've handed him. He has Galmier, Meven. With you here, he leads the country. I think that's why the birds tried to kill us . . . so the Bishop would have the country. And with the war, he'd have this country, too."

Meven cradled his head in his arms, his words muffled. "And I was as blind as that King, listening to the Bishop when I should have been listening to you. He has the country, and—"

Lathan cleared his throat again, announcing his return. "King Hunter Silverwood of House Silverwood will see you now. You are to follow me."

35 · Declarations

Do not lead them, but guide them. Do not force or coerce, but suggest. Be their shadow and their protector. Through you, they can be redeemed. Through them, you will find purpose.

~Gray Hawthorn, Finest Court patriarch

I *should visit the Court, tell them about the birds.* Gallant-Stallion pawed through the thin layer of straw in his stall, his hoof drawing a line in the dirt floor.

Birds? There are birds everywhere, though not in this stable tonight, Shimmermane said. *Birds are beautiful creatures, Gallant-Stallion. But I take care not to stand directly under where one is perched.*

Honest-Stormchaser nickered to draw Shimmermane's attention. *Rue means the dark, evil birds. The ones that know about we Finest.* She was quick to explain about the assassin-birds, snorting that Rue should be the one doing the talking. But Gallant-Stallion was lost in his own thoughts, and so Honest-Stormchaser went on at length.

Shimmermane was clearly interested in the story. *I recall Meven being ever watchful for birds, and I heard him talking to the soldiers about flocks that could swarm men. I think you should indeed journey to the Finest Court, Gallant-Stallion, and . . .*

I have told them about the birds. Patience and the Court are well aware of the vile flock and want to know more about them.

Then go, brother! Honest-Stormchaser and . . .

Cornsilk, she corrected.

Cornsilk and I will stay vigilant here.

Shimmermane, we are both apart from our charges. Myself from Kalantha, you from Meven. I know that I cannot always be at her side, such is not practical. Yet . . . I feel I should be with her now. My feelings usually are not wrong. I will report to the Finest Court later.

Shimmermane tossed his head, the strands of his mane floating in the still air. *We cannot be in the homes of men, brother. You are right, it is not practical. Nor is it comfortable. I have looked through the windows of countless homes throughout Paard-Peran. It does not matter whether they are castles or hovels, they are all the same, crates for the Fallen Favorites to hide in and sleep in and to keep away the stars and the blessed wind.*

Gallant-Stallion edged out of his stall and stood in the wide aisle that ran down the center of the stable. *My feelings usually are not wrong,* he repeated.

LATHAN USHERED THE MONTOLLS INTO THE RED SITTING room Kalantha had viewed from the front window. The room was prettier from the inside, and the air was scented with exotic incense Kalantha guessed came from the southern islands.

King Silverwood sat on a divan on the dais, his legs propped up on a stool. He wore brocade robes she thought might be fancy bedclothes. His eyes were puffy, as if he'd been recently awakened. He was an older man, though not what she would call old or elderly. His face was wrinkled and tanned from the sun, and his eyes were so dark brown they looked black. His hair was brown, too, streaked with gray at the temples, and his short beard was shot through with white and gray. He leaned forward, resting his chin on a hand, then looked to Lathan.

There were four other men in the room, all with thin-blades hanging from tooled leather belts, all dressed in the same dark green tabards and tunics. Two of them were broad shouldered, and all of them had angular faces and muscular arms. One carried a scroll, and with a nod from King Silverwood, he opened it and began reading.

"Byron Welther, Joshua Hart, Elden Hart, Tendrick Hart, Crelb the Just, Varian-Barbirick, Deaver Pack, Sabad Samstag, Samual White, Eric White, Lothar Whiten, John Markson, all of Grent's Crossing. Daniel Middleton, Ellard Slade, Harold Johnstone, James Wardston, Bruce Helliard, Bryce Campstone, Marick Greensward, Thomas Darkmoor, all of Millerville. Anaston . . ."

"That's enough." King Silverwood steepled his fingers and kept them beneath his chin. "We've recorded all the names of the dead, Meven Montoll." He did not give Meven the honor of addressing him as a king. "All the dead we've found so far. The list is very long. I will make sure you hear it later."

Meven stood speechless. He'd recited several times what he'd intended to say to the King of House Silverwood, but the words stuck in his throat.

"My brother came here to stop the war," Kalantha said. She carefully approached the King, stopping when she saw a sentry place his hand on the pommel of his sword. "He didn't send a messenger or a soldier, he came himself, so important is this task."

The King studied her, his eyes traveling from her worn, laced boots, noticing she favored one leg, up her soiled leggings and tunic, and stopping at her face.

"He's been here three days, my brother, and during that time I bet more people have died. The dying should stop. This war should stop."

King Silverwood kicked the stool away and stood, fists clenched and one of them raised, face turning red. Kalantha stood her ground, though she shivered to see him so mad.

"Of course more people have died! Too many people!" His words came fast and loud, spittle flying from his lips. "Too many of my people are under the ground because a boy-king was greedy for more land . . . when he's already got more land than he can manage. No warning for this! You gave us no hint, and we'd done nothing to provoke you. We were at peace. Blessed peace! My people, your people, they were happy and healthy, prosperous, the land fertile." He gasped for air before continuing his tirade. "Prosperity? Now we have more cemeteries than farms. Soon we will have more grave markers than homes. We have widows and orphans and burned cities. You were within a hair's breadth of crushing us utterly, and now you dare to say you want peace? What I want is your head on a post in front of our city gate."

He sank back in the chair and wiped his forehead. "But more than your head, boy-king, I do want peace."

Kalantha let out a breath she'd been holding and she released her own clenched fists. She looked to Lathan, who'd soundlessly moved from behind her to beside King Silverwood.

"I could demand all of Galmier, you realize, boy-king? I've messengers ready to send to Bishop DeNogaret, acting regent in your country. I could demand all of your riches. I could demand everything for your life. But I doubt the good Bishop would cave to my requests. I suspect your good Bishop is ready to marshal the rest of your forces and sweep down and take precious Nasim-Guri from me."

"N-n-no," Meven stammered. "I don't think he . . ."

"Or, I could demand peace in exchange for your life. Nothing more, no coin, no land, just an end to this awful bloody battle you started."

"But Bishop DeNogaret would not cave to that either." Kalantha had found her voice again. "Bishop DeNogaret wanted the war. It was his plans, not my brother Meven's. My brother just got rolled up in things and went along for a while."

Meven nodded behind her. "Please," he risked, his voice cracking. "Can't we just end this? Stick my head on your post if you want to, I certainly deserve it. But let's end this first. Let's stop this war."

King Silverwood leaned back on the divan, resting his head and looking up at a ceiling decorated with pale stone chips. When he spoke, the words were whispered, and everyone in the room had to strain to catch them all.

"My astrologer says I should listen to you . . . Kalantha. He says the stars tell him that and that they find you worthy."

Lathan nodded.

"Then perhaps I should see these stars myself, see if they'll tell me the same thing." He rose and let out a deep breath, rubbed his temples and gestured to the guards. A moment more and he walked past Meven and Kalantha, not meeting their nervous glances. "Lathan, bring the boy-king and his sister, will you? Let us all see what the stars say about these two."

The King's course took him by a surprised cook, who was scrubbing the counters in the kitchen. He offered her a weary smile, then went through the door and stepped outside. Through wispy clouds he gazed at the scattering of stars, brow furrowed as if he was reading them like he might read a book.

"The stars, Lathan, are beautiful tonight." He walked farther out into the yard. "So beautiful."

"Aye, my liege. The clouds can't keep their shine from coming down."

"If I could interpret them as easily as you, perhaps I would have seen the war coming. Perhaps I could have done something to save some of my soldiers and farmers."

Lathan didn't answer, but he ushered Kalantha and Meven away from the back of the manor and onto the stone patio. He pointed to a bench, and then nudged them when they didn't move. "Sit," he hushed.

Kalantha sat so her left shoulder touched her brother. She glanced up only briefly, then directed her attention to the King.

"Years past, Lathan, many people could look to the stars and find hidden meanings and hints of the future. Astrologers were welcome everywhere then."

"A long time ago, my liege."

"Too long." The King let out another sigh and folded his hands in front of him. He took a few steps toward Meven and Kalantha, then looked down at the tips of his shoes. "Perhaps I should have spoken to you, Meven Montoll, three days past when you were brought to me. But I could not see beyond my rage. It clouds my vision still, like these clouds mask some of the stars. But Lathan insists that the stars favor you and your sister, and that I should listen to the girl. Listen to . . ."

"Kalantha," Lathan supplied.

"Yes, Kalantha. A pretty name for a pretty girl. Beneath all that dirt, you are pretty."

Kalantha raised her hand to her neck, where a ropy scar ran for several inches.

"Perhaps I should listen to her, Lathan, this girl. Or perhaps I should just lock them both away and wait for the Bishop to send the rest of his forces. Perhaps . . ."

The King tipped his head up again, searching the sky. He took another step forward and craned his neck to see through the branches of a willow tree. "What is that? Lathan, would you . . ."

"Birds!" Kalantha cried. She spied what the King was looking at, a darker cloud that cut across the sky and dropped toward them. "The assassin-birds! They've come. Run!" She jumped up from the bench, stumbling on her injured leg, but tugging Meven up with her. "Inside, we have to—"

Her warning came too late. Before any of them could take another step, the black cloud wrapped around them.

"Death comes!" a large crow shrieked. It led with its talons, slashing the face of King Silverwood and cackling as it swooped around to slash at Lathan. "Death comes to the Kings!"

36 · Warring Kings

The Fallen Favorites break easily, their bodies and their minds fragile compared to us Finest. Yet they are precious and worthy of our protection, brothers and sisters. They have so few years upon the earth, compared to us. Life is . . . perhaps . . . more precious to them. We were created to give them hope. I find they give us hope in return.

~Patience, Finest Court matriarch

Death comes! Death comes!" The chant was immediately repeated by all the members of the vile flock. The swirl of words became so loud it drowned out the thunder of their beating wings.

"The stars!" Lathan shouted. "They've stolen the stars."

"Steal your lives," a young cowbird taunted. "But slowly." He jabbed his beak into the astrologer's cheek then lit upon his head, driving his beak into Lathan's scalp and digging at the man's flesh with his small claws. "Slow, to enjoy your screams."

The astrologer did scream then, as several blackbirds dove at his back, knocking him to the ground. They swarmed him and began plucking at the flesh on his hands. The King's guards rushed forward, grabbing at the birds with one hand and drawing their weapons with the other.

"See to Lathan!" the King shouted. He swung his fists at the birds flying at him, striking a crow, but leaving his side open for a haze of blackbirds and cowbirds to rush in. The birds tore at his royal garments and jabbed at the flesh beneath. "And the children! See to them!" The King continued to struggle, pulling an ornamental dagger free from his waist and slashing with it.

Meven became overwhelmed by the birds, as the flock concentrated on him and the other men.

"Kill the Kings!" This cry was shrill and clear and came from overhead. "I demand the death of the warring Kings!"

Kalantha looked up and saw nothing but the mass of black. She batted at the birds between herself and Meven, keeping her face pointed up, searching and still finding only blackness.

"Spill the blood of the Kings!"

There! When more of the birds dove on the Kings, Kalantha spied a falcon through the gaps in the wings. It was shades lighter than the other birds and seemed to hover above them.

"Taste the sweet, royal blood!" the falcon shouted. "For me, you will do this!"

Kalantha remembered a dark hawk that had been called Fala. It orchestrated at least one of the attacks on Meven and her, and Rue had killed it. But now the assassin flock had another leader, one equally vicious as far as she was concerned.

"Meven! I see the one that leads them." She started waving frantically, trying to attract the attention of the guards. "Have you arrows? Can you shoot it? The falcon? It's a gray bird!"

But the guards didn't see Kalantha. They were too busy pulling birds off Lathan and Meven and their King. One of the guards had a broadsword and was swinging it in a wild arc. The edge sharp, he sliced through the large crow that had been crying "Death comes, death comes," then batted down a pair of grackles.

"So many birds!" Kalantha shouted. "Never so many before!" But in truth she realized there weren't as many as the first time she'd spied them—when they flew so tightly together they looked like men on horses, when they attacked her and Meven and their cousin all bound for Nasim-Guri for a wedding. But there were more here than when they'd attacked her and Meven on the palace grounds. More than when they attacked her in the woods when she traveled with a priest and friend from the Vershan Monastery. "Too many to fight!"

The birds had killed so many people and animals—Prince Edan and the wedding party, all of the fine horses they rode, townsfolk in their path, the priest, her friend.

She screamed in rage and rushed toward Meven, her fists like hammers pounding at the birds that plucked at his clothes and skin. She could barely see him through all the black bodies. But she faintly heard him hollering and cursing, and finally calling out to her. Vaguely, she also heard a door slam open.

"What's going on here?" It was a woman's voice.

Kalantha couldn't hear the speaker, but she guessed it was the cook who'd been scrubbing in the kitchen. She wanted to call to her, tell her to shut the door and call for soldiers and guards. But the birds were battering at Kalantha now. They clawed at her and poked her with their sharp beaks, bringing back all the memories of the previous attacks and sending shiver after shiver through her slight frame.

The ropy scar that ran down her neck and drew stares from people she passed—that had been caused by the bird called Fala. Scars that had healed, and some small ones she would carry forever, all caused by the horrid, spiteful birds.

"Why?" Kalantha shouted. "Why all of this?"

She didn't expect an answer from the birds, but she got one.

"For the war!" It was the falcon, and it hovered above Meven and her. "My flock slays you for the war!"

"For Ninéon! We slay you all for Ninéon!"

"Ninéon, Ninéon, Ninéon!" became the new chant.

298 ~ JEAN RABE

More birds descended, a second flock coming from the northeast. When Kalantha saw them through a gap in the black curtain her throat went tight. The statement she'd made earlier was true now. Never had she seen so many birds in one place. There were more here than attacked the wedding party.

"Oh, Rue." All she could see was a sheet of blackest black. Never would she see her magical horse again, or see anything, she was certain. Kalantha wondered if death would hurt. She prayed it wouldn't hurt much more than what she was feeling now. "Meven! More birds!"

Her brother couldn't see the new flock, as so many birds flew around him and took turns darting in to pluck at him.

Despite the numbers, Kalantha still wouldn't give up. She pressed in close to him, protecting his back and opening herself up to more attacks. She grabbed at them with her hands, catching one and hurling it to the ground, then stomping and feeling it crush. She choked on the smell of them, the scent of their musty feathers filling her nose and mouth and making her gag.

"Kal, I'm sorry!" Meven shouted the words, but they sounded no more than a whisper. He shouted something else, but the added noise from the second flock became a wall of squawks and caws and shrill trills that was deafening.

The dissonance became as much of a weapon as the birds' claws and beaks, and it made Kalantha dizzy. She grabbed onto Meven to keep from falling, and the birds jabbed at her exposed hands.

I KNEW YOU SPOKE THE TRUTH ABOUT THE BIRDS, GALLANT-Stallion. But your words pale to this! Shimmermane raced behind Gallant-Stallion, out of the stables and toward the back of the manor, where still more birds descended.

Honest-Stormchaser followed them, urging the other horses

to hurry. As she had in the run-down building in Nadir, she encouraged the animals to run and help. *We must fight the birds! We must win!*

They whinnied in fear and excitement, kicking up clumps of dirt and grass in their wake. Stump followed, barking and leaping and taking care not to get trampled.

"Death comes!" a blackbird cried above the swarms.

Your death comes, Gallant-Stallion returned. *Your death, not Kalantha's.*

Then Gallant-Stallion joined the fray, just as guards spilled out the back door of the manor, all armed with swords and shouting orders that could not be heard above the rush of wings.

Lights were being lit in the back rooms of the manor, and attendants peered out of the windows, trying to get a look at the menacing flock. Objects were hurled from some of the windows, mostly ineffectual against the birds, but a few things striking them.

Your death comes! Gallant-Stallion shouted. *Your death comes now!*

Gallant-Stallion had felt anger before, but never so much absolute rage as that which coursed through him now. He felt on fire as he reached the edge of the swarm, his hooves bright flames that licked at the vicious blackbirds and cowbirds and sent them spiraling to the earth where he trampled their small bodies. So great was his anger, Gallant-Stallion pictured his whole body a fire, burning and spreading and consuming the malevolent birds.

Honest-Stormchaser and Shimmermane picked up his fever, tearing into the mass of black and forcing many of the birds to scatter. The horses that had joined them paused only a moment before copying the Finest Creations and biting and stomping the birds.

The sound of everything grew impossibly louder—the cries of the birds, the shouts of the people, and the harsh whinnies and snorts of the horses and the Finest. The sound reached out into the city proper, where lights were being lit and men and women were coming out of their homes toting brooms and axes, anything that might serve as weapons. Like a wave, the growing crowd surged, curious and uncertain, flowing toward the manor house and the source of the racket.

"Kal!" Meven spun to face his sister now, drawing her head against his chest and setting his mouth to her ear. "There's no hope, Kal. I'm so sorry."

She shook her head and pushed away. "Rue!" She hollered the name with as much force as she could summon. "Rue is here! I feel it." Then she pushed farther away and started flailing at the birds with her arms again. Her sleeves were practically shredded, and cuts crisscrossed her arms and face. The pain was terrible.

Meven drew inspiration from her, pummeling the birds and gulping in air when the darkness wasn't quite so dark. The birds had thinned around him, and he could smell fresh air. He blinked furiously, all the while swinging at any piece of black that darted in front of him. At the same time, he took one step and then another toward the King of Nasim-Guri.

King Silverwood had the greatest concentration of birds around him. The guards who'd tried to reach him had their own flock to contend with. Meven fought his way to the monarch and managed to swat away enough of the birds so he could put his back to Silverwood's.

The King shouted something to Meven, but it was lost in the clatter of beaks and the cries of "Death comes to the Kings!"

Meven didn't know how long he struggled. It seemed like forever. His arms felt as heavy as sodden logs and he gritted his teeth and forced himself to raise and lower them, to keep pounding at the birds. His legs ached from where the birds had sliced through his trousers, and he felt a bird that had grabbed hold of his boot drive its beak into his knee. Meven was certain he'd die here, and the only thing that kept him from dropping and letting the birds finish him quickly was thoughts of Kal.

She continued to fight the birds, Meven knew; he could see her through breaks in the swarm. She was faring better than himself, her eyes slammed shut and her lips curled up in a snarl. He'd never seen her look so angry and ugly. He tried calling to her, to again apologize for everything and to tell her he loved her. But the birds were making too much noise.

Through the wall of sound, other noises eventually intruded. Meven vaguely heard the whinny of a horse, then another and another. He heard the shouts of guards, though he couldn't tell what they were saying. Finally, he heard King Silverwood.

"Together, boy-king. We'll fight them together. Then we will end the war."

This was war, Meven knew, and it was terrible. He'd done a terrible, horrible thing making war on Nasim-Guri. "Together!" he called back.

Time dragged on, and the monarchs leaned against each other to stay on their feet. Their hands were slick with blood, and blood from cuts on their face trickled into their eyes and mouths. Four guards forced their way through the feathery mass and were slicing at the birds swirling around Meven and King Silverwood. One of those guards fell, but the remaining three doubled their efforts.

"King Silverwood!" One of the guards tugged on his monarch's arm. "We must get you inside."

"You must get me that man's sword." Silverwood pointed to the downed guard. "And get the boy-king a sword, too."

The bloody fight continued, with the Kings and guards cutting through so many birds that the ground was carpeted by the black forms. Kalantha was at Lathan's back. She'd taken a thin-blade from a downed guard and was skewering birds on it.

"Rue's here!" She hollered to the astrologer. "My horse! He'll stop them!"

The astrologer didn't reply. He alternated between batting at the birds and covering his face.

At the edge of the swarm, the horses and the Finest fought even harder. Hundreds of birds were on the ground now, and the animals' hooves thundered over them.

Kalantha! Gallant-Stallion called to her in hidden speak, willing her to hear him. *Kalantha!*

"I'm all right, Rue!" Her voice belied the words, though. "There's so many birds!" But she knew there were fewer now.

And heartbeats later there were fewer still.

Blackbirds, crows, starlings, cowbirds, and hawks continued to dive in and strike at the people. But the attacks were farther apart, and more of the birds were taking to the sky after a strike and not returning.

"We fly!" It was a thin, piercing cry. "We fly, Ninéon commands. We live and fly!"

"We live!"

A hawk shrieked inches from Kalantha's face, then banked away and up. "We flee!" it cried. "We flee and live!"

Other cries cut through the air, these coming from the townsfolk who'd made it onto the manor grounds. The people struck at the birds without pause, calling to each other and calling to King Silverwood. Questions whirled in the air about the King and the birds, and someone speculated it was part of the war Galmier had brought to them.

Kalantha! Gallant-Stallion pressed through the thinning cloud of birds and bolted past guards and townsfolk. *Kalantha!*

"Oh, Rue!" She saw him and rushed away from Lathan. She threw her arms around the Finest's neck. "Never so horrible!

Nothing ever so horrible!" She sobbed against him. "I thought we would all die."

Not this day, Kalantha, Gallant-Stallion wuffled to her. *I will keep you safe. Nothing ever so horrible will happen again.*

37 · Resolutions

I have heard that some Finest select their own charges. How can that be? The Court does the picking. They picked each of my charges. Still, I think it would have been a good thing to have found my own Fallen Favorite to shepherd. I would have chosen a young girl, I think, one full of hope and uncertainty. We could have explored Paard-Peran together.

~*Prudent-Flehmen, shepherd to Bartholomew the Bold and Sir Scuddles*

Certain conditions must be met, Meven Montoll."

"Anything," Meven replied. "I will agree to anything. And then you can put—"

"If I put your head on a post it will only draw crows and flies. And I've seen more than enough crows for the rest of my life." King Silverwood pushed himself out of his thronelike chair. His arms and legs were covered with bandages, and his face was smeared with ointment. Three days he'd been in bed, tended by his aides.

Meven and Kalantha, too, had been bedridden, as had several guards and townsfolk.

King Silverwood leaned on a cane as he stepped around a stool and stopped directly in front of Kalantha. He stared at her, not Meven. "I want land—some of Galmier, but not much. I want enough to make our countries equal in size. I will take in the southern villages and farms, which will help in the recovery of the villages and farms burned in my northern territory. Meven will sign a truce to surrender the land I want. It is a symbolic gesture, mostly, but a necessary one if you want your lives and truly want peace."

Meven swallowed hard and mouthed *yes*, the gestures not noticed by King Silverwood.

"Then Meven will abdicate the Galmier throne."

"What!" Though Meven was ready to give his life, this request startled him. "By blood, I—"

"Blood, by blood, yes. Too much blood has been spilled," King Silverwood cut back. "You will abdicate the throne in favor of your sister here."

Meven sputtered. "I can't. She's . . . she's a girl. Women have no political or royal power in Galmier. They can't inherit something like—"

"You can arrange it," King Silverwood continued. "Draw up whatever decrees are necessary to end your male-dominated monarchy. Lathan, here, will mentor her, making sure peace is continued with Duriam and that Duriam's interests in Paard-Peran are looked after."

"Women have no power," Meven feebly said.

"Then give them power in Galmier," King Silverwood snapped. "When I die, my throne goes to my daughter, Saedell. She was to marry Prince Edan, you'll recall. And the Bishop made overtures to me that she marry you."

Meven looked only mildly surprised at this.

"Oh, my daughter will marry. But not you. And whoever he is, he'll be her advisor. He won't be the King of Duriam. That's all well in writing and announced to my people." King Silverwood touched Kalantha's scar with his thumb. "Boy-king, I'll write the decrees for you, if necessary. All you will have to do is sign them in the presence of your advisors, notarize them, and tack them up on every wall in your fabled city. It will be humbling."

"I can write them myself."

"Men, women, we're all the same really . . . so my daughter has taught me through the years. And your sister—" He traced Kalantha's scar again and stood back from her, a sad look in his eyes now. "Had she inherited the throne to begin with, I suspect there'd have been no fighting."

King Silverwood finally properly addressed Meven, locking him in place with his glare. "Your sister is young, perhaps too young. But she is wise, and Lathan, my astrologer, puts great faith in her. Lathan will help her rule."

Meven knelt and bowed his head. "I accept all of your terms, King Hunter Silverwood of House Silverwood."

"Then I accept your proposal for peace."

38 · Loose Ends

We must study the birds of Paard-Peran and find the ones possessing keen intelligence, like us. We must find the ones full of hate, so unlike us. Forces that created us could not have created these birds. But something is responsible for them. And that something, and the birds themselves, has drawn the full attention of the Finest Court.

~*Gray Hawthorn, Finest Court patriarch*

Ninéon perched on the end of Bishop DeNogaret's bed. The Bishop sat all the way up this evening, and in the light of the lantern that burned on the stand, the falcon could tell the man was mending.

The Bishop's eyes were brighter, and color had crept into his cheeks. His chest rose and fell with no effort, and he could reach for the biscuits and broth on the stand without help.

"Soon," the Bishop told Ninéon. "Soon I will be up from this soft prison and walking around my palace. I was up this morning, briefly, using canes."

The falcon cocked her head.

"I walked from this bed to the water basin. I do not mind being pampered, my friend, but I do not like others to wash me." The Bishop turned from the falcon to take a piece of biscuit and smear it with honey. "I would offer you some, Ninéon, but I am hungry this night. And the food will help give me strength."

The falcon fluttered to the back of a chair that sat near the bed. She stretched her wings and preened a few feathers while the Bishop ate.

"The war," the Bishop prompted after a few minutes. "Is it truly over, or have you found a way to prolong the fighting?"

"It is ended," Ninéon said. "This war."

The Bishop nodded. "But there will be another. I've already been thinking about how to stir up the men again."

"There will be another," Ninéon agreed. "I have been thinking, too."

The Bishop's eyebrows rose, and his expression asked the falcon to continue.

Instead, she let out a sharp skree.

The flutter of wings reached through the window.

"I have been thinking that you know too much, Bishop DeNogaret. You know about me, about my flock."

The Bishop frowned and brushed at a crumb on his chin. "Of course I know."

"No one . . . no person . . . should know. My flock and I should live in the shadows." Ninéon skreed again, and a cloud of black swept in through the window. "I've not many left, Bishop DeNogaret. The horses and the Kings, the girl, they cut our numbers."

The Bishop sputtered and waved a hand, trying to dismiss the small flock. "Enough. Disperse, I command you. I've heard enough."

"But I have enough for this task," Ninéon continued, disregarding the Bishop. "And I will gain more. It will just take time."

"Enough? Such insolence! Enough for what, Ninéon?" The Bishop's eyes were wide with anger and a touch of fear.

"Enough to slay you, Bishop DeNogaret. You know too much."

The flock descended on the bed, pulling the covers back and finding the Bishop's form beneath. They fell upon him, beaks and talons slashing.

Ninéon flew to the window and perched on the sill, watching her minions perform their grisly deed. "I have enough for this. And I will have more."

39 · The Homecoming

It took nearly three weeks to return to Nadir, as they stopped in every village along the way and at many of the farmhouses to spread news of the war's end. Lieutenant Rendell and his three soldiers looked to the villages along the Sprawling River's eastern branches and the ones around Lowe's Lake. Other messengers were named in Stilton and Cobston to take the word west and over the Galmier Mountains.

Kalantha spoke as little as possible during the trip, save to Rue. Often she tried to trail behind the entourage—which consisted of her, Meven, Lathan, who'd been riding the iomud, and nearly four dozen armed guards and sentries from House Silverwood. Kalantha speculated that King Silverwood had left Duriam practically defenseless. But she knew the monarch could not afford to have Meven go back on his word, and so sent all of these men.

Once, when she'd managed to slip away to a pond east of

the village Hathi, she rolled up her leggings and dangled her feet in the water, giggling when tiny bluegills and sunfish darted close to see if her toes were edible. The cool water felt good on her mending ankle.

It is good you enjoy yourself, Gallant-Stallion said. The Finest punch clomped up behind her and nibbled from the clover at the pond's edge. *I've not seen you enjoy yourself in quite some time, Kalantha.*

"Peace, Rue. I wasn't sure it would happen." She wriggled her toes and laughed softly when the fish swam away. "And Meven's all right, mind and body. I think a part of me worried that King Silverwood might cut off his head and display it outside Duriam. I don't think I could've lived with myself if that had happened."

You saved your brother, Kal. And it was you who brought about the peace.

She shook her head. "It was a lot of things. All the death, the people tired of it, King Silverwood so terribly tired of it, Meven wanting it to end. I only helped."

Gallant-Stallion raised his head to the late-morning sun, not minding that the brightness hurt his eyes. He was proud of his charge, and he knew in his heart that he hadn't made a mistake when he chose to shepherd Kalantha. It might not have been what the Finest Court had originally intended, but it was the right thing.

"I've sent word ahead, Rue, to the palace. There's some housekeeping I want done before we get back. Sara Anne, Bertrum, and some other folks, they'll be gone by the time we get there. I don't trust them, and there are too many servants at the palace anyway. No one needs that many servants. No one needs such a big place to live in either. A waste of coins and space." She leaned forward and dangled her fingers in the water, circles spreading away from her and distorting her reflection. "All the coins could be better spent."

Gallant-Stallion came closer to take a drink, then stepped back, startled. He looked different, his head more elegantly shaped, his ears longer, his mane silkier than before. Another step forward and he could see that his broad chest wasn't quite as broad as before, and his legs were longer. He was a punch . . . but certainly not a rueful-looking one.

"What's the matter, Rue?" She caught him staring at his reflection. "Don't you think you look handsome this morning?"

Kalantha, I look different.

Again she shook her head. "Maybe to you, Rue. To me, you've always been my handsome, magical horse. Maybe you just never saw yourself in the correct light." Then she was on her feet and drying off in the tall grass, pulling her leggings down and getting on his back. "Maybe you just lacked some confidence before and never realized your potential."

You are too wise for your young age, Kalantha.

"I'm fourteen, you know." He couldn't see her broad grin. "No one can call me a child anymore. I'm fourteen. Maybe we'll have a party, Rue. I would like a cake with strawberries. A very sweet cake. I'd share it with you."

When they returned to the entourage—Lathan was relieved to discover Kalantha hadn't escaped to somewhere—her expression turned serious and her thoughts turned away from the pond and the fish and back to Galmier. Meven rode behind her, lost in a cavalcade of thoughts and worrying at a thread in his tunic.

"I would like to read that book, Kal, the one you brought from the Vershan Monastery," Meven said when the gates of Nadir came into view. "It's the first thing I'll do." He paused and looked to Lathan. "After I write those decrees. I will have them posted everywhere, Kal, like I promised King Silverwood. Then I will read that book, and make certain it is returned to the monastery. And then I will talk to you, Kal. I've something important to say."

"Important? Tell me now, Meven."

"After the decrees and the book, after I speak to Bishop DeNogaret. After, Kal. I'll tell you after."

KALANTHA WOULDN'T ACCEPT "AFTER." "I'VE SOME THINGS to tell you, too, and to tell Lathan Hollow."

The three were seated in the palace's largest dining room, at a table spread with bowls of stew, plates of spring fruit, and thick slices of cheese. Kalantha couldn't eat anything, but she encouraged Lathan and Meven to—and the three Duriam sentries and three Nadir guards who stood nearby.

"Lathan, Meven . . ." She paused, searching for the words. She'd discussed all of this with Gallant-Stallion the previous night, practicing on him what she intended to say. The words sounded fancy and important last night. Now she was having trouble explaining it all. "I've decided I will not be Galmier's Queen." She ignored their gasps. "Meven, you can write whatever decree you want, but I won't accept a crown."

Meven's mouth dropped open, and Lathan slammed his fist on the table.

"It was agreed," the astrologer said. "Meven would abdicate and—"

"Meven will abdicate," Kalantha said. Air hissed out between her teeth. "Galmier doesn't need a queen, or a king for that matter." She gestured at the fine paintings and the fancy furniture. "This country doesn't need someone to take their people's coins and spend them on a house too big to live in and on servants that wash floors that won't be walked on for days or weeks because the palace is simply too large to use all the rooms." She took a deep breath. "Oh, I'm not saying there shouldn't be a ruler. But it doesn't have to be just one person. Meven, you've a half dozen advisors, and some of them haven't been tainted by Bishop DeNogaret. They—the good ones—could lead Galmier. Lathan, too. And I'll be happy to help. I'll even head up this counsel for a while, make sure everything is going along properly. There's a lot of work to do, and a lot of things to change around here."

Meven and Lathan stared at her, both at a loss on what to say.

"I'm good at helping," she continued. "And that's what I want to do—help lead Galmier. And help solve a lot of its problems." She leaned across the table and met Meven's stare. "You can write a decree to say all of that, can't you, Meven? King Silverwood, I don't think he'd object to that. Do you think he would object, Lathan Hollow?"

The astrologer blinked and glanced at the ceiling, as if he could look through it and the floors above and seek counsel from the stars. "No, Kalantha. I do not think he would object. In fact, I think he would fancy the idea."

"Good. Now, Meven, what did you want to tell me?"

He shook his head, as if he didn't believe she just turned down the throne of Galmier. "I . . . I'm leaving Galmier, Kal. I'm going to Uland, to Dea Fortress."

It was her turn to be surprised.

"I've given this a lot of thought, Kal. I want a religious life. I don't know if I'll ever be anything other than an acolyte. But I was happiest when I was at the High Keep Temple. I want to be truly happy again."

"When will you—"

"I'd like to leave as soon as possible. After the decrees, of course." He smiled warmly. "And after I read that book and have a piece of your strawberry cake."

MEVEN WENT ALONE TO THE NORTH TOWER TO VISIT BISHOP DeNogaret. Kalantha wanted him to take Lathan or a few guards along, but Meven firmly declined.

"I can stand up to him, Kal, this time. But I need to do it alone. I want to ask the Bishop about our parents and some other things."

He stood at the door, fingers on the knob, trembling slightly. Taking several deep breaths, he held his shoulders back and head high, then he turned the knob and entered.

"By the good gods!" Meven stared at the Bishop's prone form. His shout startled the crows picking at the body.

"For Ninéon," one of them whispered as they flew out the window.

Epilogue

As a Finest, I will live a long life. I hope to shepherd many Fallen Favorites during the time I am granted on Paard-Peran. I know that each will be special, and that each is worthy of redemption. But I do not believe any will be so special as my first charge. The future of Galmier is in her very good hands.

~Gallant-Stallion, Finest shepherd to Kalantha Montoll,
principal advisor to Galmier

Ninéon and Valane flew south, leading a huge flock of predominantly black birds. There were several jays among them, and sparrows and wrens—but these birds were unseen amid all the black feathery bodies.

The falcon explained to the flock that Bishop DeNogaret's death was necessary. The priest-puppet had outlived his usefulness, and she didn't want any of her secrets spilled from his old, pale lips.

From Valane's reports, Ninéon knew there were too many Finest Creations in Uland, Galmier, Nasim-Guri, and Vered to the south. And while she didn't yet understand all of their divine strengths and capabilities, she knew them capable of thwarting her.

"South," she told Valane. "We fly to the islands in the far south, where horses are a rare thing. The islands will be easier for us."

"Easier," Valane said. "Safer."

"We will grow powerful there, and venerate the dark gods," Ninéon continued. "And when we are powerful enough, all of us will visit the place called the Finest Court."

"The Finest Court," Valane chirped. "Not now. Later. We will wait, and our time will come."